Rebel

S. MASSERY

INTRODUCTION & WARNING

Dear reader,

Thank you for joining me! If you are unfamiliar with my
work, fair warning: my stories run dark (violence, explicit
content, etc.). Sterling Falls is no different.
Reader discretion is advised.

xoxo,

Sara

Prequel: THRILL
#1: THIEF
#2: FIGHTER
#3: REBEL
#4: QUEEN

WOLFE

Parker Warton leans against the wall outside the holding cell. He seems particularly smug; his hands are in his pockets, and an idiotic smirk curves his lips. Besides that, I take note of the rest of him: a muscular build, sandy-brown hair gelled into place, boring blue eyes. When he'd locked the cuffs around my wrists at our house, having burst in with the sheriff and deputies and waving guns around, he'd made a comment in my ear about Kora. And then I knew that *he* was the monster she had been running from when I met her.

The thought of him and Kora together in any capacity—but especially *that* way—sets my teeth on edge. I hope it drives him crazy. To know that three men are willing to bow down to her, when he isn't worth enough to even kiss her shoe.

"A confession would go a long way." He doesn't so much as shift. He's been there almost as long as I've been in this damn cell. Watching. Waiting.

"Toward your impending promotion?" I raise my eyebrow. "Right."

He shrugs. "We can do this the hard way."

I step up to the bars. "Oh, yeah? Fucking try me."

Parker's smile widens. "Are you threatening me?"

"I wouldn't threaten you, Parker. That's pointless. But sooner or later, your past is going to catch up to you."

He inches closer, curiosity flashing across his features. "Do you mean Kora?"

I lunge forward and manage to grab his tie. A tricky thing with handcuffs on. Both hands have to go together, moving through the same space between the bars. I yank at the tie, wrapping the fabric around my hand, and pull it into the cell. He falls against the bars, and suddenly we're face-to-face.

He snarls at me.

In a low voice, one that won't get picked up by the audio recording devices in here, I add, "If you so much as look at her again, I'll make sure you never walk out of this city. And that is a fucking threat, you piece of shit."

He scrabbles at the bars and finally puts his hand through, shoving me away. I let the tie slide through my fingers.

I laugh. I enjoy the fear flickering in his eyes, the way he tries to straighten his clothes and pretend nothing happened. It's funny what men will do when they think they're on top of the world, and then they're shown a real predator. It doesn't matter that we're in here and he's out there. It doesn't matter that he has a badge and a suit and a gun.

We have guns, too.

"You okay, Parker?" I tilt my head.

"Threatening an agent—"

"There's no problem if you stay away from her." Well, that's a lie. I think I'll probably cut his eyes out—and other

2

appendages *off*—whether or not he listens to me. This feels a bit like prodding an angry bull anyway. Daring him to stay away is just asking for the opposite. I know this, and yet...

"Wolfe," Apollo mutters behind me.

I wheel away from the asshat and crouch beside Apollo. He's slumped on one of the cots. The doc didn't get to do too much for him before the feds swarmed inside. He started an IV treatment to flush out the meds, but besides that... he just has to sleep it off.

Apollo reaches out and grabs the front of my shirt. "Don't do anything stupid."

I scoff. Me? Stupid?

A buzzer at the end of the hall goes off, preceding the door unlocking. Sheriff Bradshaw strides in, followed by the suit who hauled us in with Parker.

And last through the door is another man I haven't seen in years.

My brows hike.

The suit stops beside his protégé and frowns at us. Parker has made himself presentable again, like the whole thing never happened. He probably doesn't want his boss to know that he has a connection to us. The sheriff is much more relaxed, unlocking our cell door and swinging it open. He goes to Apollo first, uncuffing him, then releases me.

I rub my wrists. "What's this?"

"You get time with your lawyer," Bradshaw says. "Unless you'd like to refuse it..."

My attention flicks to the man. He's the Hell Hound lawyer, known for... well, the better question might be, what *isn't* he known for? He'll do whatever he has to in order to keep my father happy. He stays away from the clubhouse, and from most Hell Hound business. But he's here now.

And he's paid handsomely for pulling any and all strings for my father.

"No," I say evenly. "We'll meet with him."

I help Apollo stand, and the sheriff escorts us to an interrogation room. Interview room. Whatever the fuck they're calling them nowadays. There's a mirror on one wall, and a camera with a blinking red dot in the corner.

"You'll turn those off," the lawyer says to the sheriff. "And no one will be in the observation room."

"Of course."

Apollo and I take the two chairs on one side of the table, and the lawyer takes the other. He sits and flicks open his briefcase, pulling two stacks of paper from within.

"You remember me, boys?"

Apollo's gaze sharpens. "Richard Jacobs," he says. "Hard to forget."

"Here's the deal." His eyes lift to the camera, and he nods to himself. "Cerberus is willing to help you out of this bind."

"For a price." I cross my arms. "Right?"

"Of course," Jacobs says evenly. "Your release is conditional upon you rejoining the Hell Hounds."

I snort. I can't help it.

Damn my father. This is what he's been working toward, isn't it?

"Why?"

Jacobs narrows his eyes. "You haven't heard?"

"Heard what?" Apollo leans forward, gripping the edge of the table.

"A few hours ago, the Titans attacked the Hell Hounds' clubhouse." His brow lowers. "It's an act of war. Cerberus won't let them get away with it."

"Wait." I hold my hand up. "They attacked the clubhouse?"

Where Kora, Jace, and Malik were. My blood runs cold. Did they get caught up in it?

"And Cerberus made it out," Apollo guesses, seeming to miss that *Kora and Jace* were there. "That's why he sent you here. Is he holing up somewhere?"

I try to imagine how many Hell Hounds the Titans would've caught unaware. Only a fraction stay on the premises round the clock. There are guards, security. The whole road to get into their territory is patrolled.

Kronos knew this would be war.

"Sign here." He pushes the stacks of paper—one for each of us—in front of our noses. "This is a plea deal that has been brokered on your behalf."

"What are we admitting to if we sign this?" I take the pen and tap the end against the paper, immediately suspicious. My father likes to operate both outside and within the scope of the law—and I have a feeling this is just another part of the web built to trap us. I scan the first page, then flip to the second. It's a whole bunch of legal shit I don't understand.

"You will be confessing to transporting drugs under duress. That you were going to turn yourselves in when Wesley Graves, aka Kronos, discovered your plot to deceive him." Jacobs frowns. "You'll testify that he was holding Kora Sinclair against her will, as well, and that was a particular motivation for you to traffic the drugs."

Seems like a serious charge... and the timeline is a bit screwed up. But, naturally, Dad would use this as an opportunity to point the Sterling Falls DEA toward the Titans. I'm just not sure it'll stick. Whose side are they on after all? Whose money lines that prick Parker Warton's pockets?

"In return for this plea, you will not do any jail time. You will not be on probation. Your testimony will be required when Mr. Graves is brought to trial."

If he's brought to trial.

"Fine by me," Apollo grumbles. "And this is going to... indenture ourselves to Cerberus, is that it?"

The lawyer smiles. "That is the cost of business, gentlemen. It's this or prison."

I glance at Apollo, then back to the lawyer. "What happened to Jace? And Kora?"

Richard Jacobs shifts in his seat—the only hint that something else is amiss. "They'll join you," he says.

Something raises the hair along the back of my neck.

He's lying.

Still, we don't really have a fucking choice. The only way to the truth is to be out of here. I lift the pen and scrawl my signature over my name. Apollo follows suit.

Jacobs rises and gives us a big smile. "Welcome back to the fold, boys."

CHAPTER 1
KORA

SIX MONTHS LATER

M y version of Hell is quiet. Dead-end streets framed by fields and forests and blue skies. Not a kid or neighbor in sight. No cars, no traffic, no visitors.

Just a house at the end of the road, silent except for the creaking that accompanies my footsteps. And the tick of a clock that echoes in my brain long after it's stopped functioning.

Tick, tick, tick.

This is where my ghosts live.

It's where my demons anchor themselves to my skin.

Around every corner is something that wants to remind me of who I was, and the man who made me that way. He lurks in the shadows of my mind.

The red-eyed god who haunts my dreams once said he wanted to see what my version of Hell was. He was eager for it. But I don't think he could've predicted I'd be back in it without him. I'm caught in fear's tide, being dragged out to sea.

In my dreams, I tell him, *This is nothing, sweetheart.*

Don't speak too loudly.

Don't make a fuss.

Never dredge up the past, because it's stickier and bloodier than you could imagine.

And then, one day, it happens.

The past does rear up out of nowhere, and it wraps its hand around my throat. There's nothing I can do to save myself. Nothing to stop it from consuming me. The death, the pain—it's all on my shoulders. Weights that keep me from escaping this fate.

What was it Shakespeare said?

These violent delights have violent ends.

Well, I've had my fill of violent delight. Tasted blood on my lips, enjoyed the spoils of my gods' triumph.

It seems only fair that my end should be violent, too.

CHAPTER 2
APOLLO

I've got my gun trained on the window long before the intruder hoists through it. Their feet hit the carpet softly, and the figure straightens.

Tem pushes the hood off her head and gives me a look. "Were you going to shoot me?"

I grimace and stow my weapon. "I take precautions. What are you doing here?"

I grab her arm, pulling her away from the window.

She watches me close and lock it, then draw the blinds. Then the drapes.

Can't be too careful nowadays.

I go to my bedroom door and lock that, too.

"Apollo."

I stare at my twin sister. She's been keeping her distance from us for months, only coming when she's sure no one will witness it. I hate that our relationship has become *this*. Some big secret.

Her hair is braided, out of her face, and she wears black clothing that helps her blend in with the shadows. There's a gun in a holster under her arm, and the hilt of a knife protruding from her boot. I never wanted this life for her, but she chose it anyway.

"Did something happen?"

"I found her." Tem steps forward, catching my hands and squeezing tightly.

I sink onto the edge of the bed, staring at her. "How?"

She shakes her head and sits beside me. "I have no idea. I followed a hunch and got really fucking lucky."

Kora's been... *gone*. Not in Sterling Falls, not in Emerald Cove. God knows Tem and Nyx looked. They've been the only ones able to get out of the city—and back into it. Sterling Falls is locked in war, caught in the crossfire between the Hell Hounds and the Titans. Roadblocks make escape, especially for gang members and wanted fugitives, impossible. Everyone who enters is under suspicion, but somehow the girls have found a way out past the normal routes.

Sterling Falls University just let out for the summer. The college kids have all left, fleeing the violence, and I don't blame them. Innocent people are dying because Kronos and Cerberus are hell-bent on destruction.

North Falls is limping along. Nowadays, it's the only place keeping the city's economy afloat. It seems that even the gangs realize there are some things they can't mess with —and the rich side of town is one of them. The trickle of tourists undeterred by the roadblocks and checkpoints has been steady, especially as the warmer weather arrives.

So the Titans and Hell Hounds have been limiting their fighting to the rest of the city. They still patrol the north side. They still have people planted on street corners, lingering, watching for signs of trouble—or staking their claim.

But when the sheriff comes rolling through, they move along.

"Where is she?" I rise again, but Tem pulls me back down. "We can—"

"You can't do anything," she whispers. "You're more stuck than anyone."

That's a sobering thought.

My phone buzzes on the nightstand, and I reach for it on autopilot. Cerberus inducted Wolfe and me back into the Hell Hounds the night his lawyer got us out of the charge Kronos tried to hang around our necks. Since then, I've only seen Wolfe sparingly.

Seems his father isn't making the same mistakes of the past—letting us stay together, plot, scheme. He's acting wiser in his old age.

A text from Malik came through earlier. They intercepted a Titan lieutenant, who gave them the route of an armored truck taking their money to their camp. We're going to meet tonight to attack it, and now I have a meeting time. In five minutes.

What is Kronos without money?

What are any of us without war funds?

Nothing.

We have suspicions that Kronos has completely transformed the church outside of Sterling Falls as his own personal base camp. He does go into West Falls—he frequents his bar, Descend, and gives his men morale—but when the going gets tough, he evacuates.

Cerberus is the same way.

Willing to get his hands dirty, but not at the risk of his own life. He'd rather sacrifice ours. Too many Titans and Hell Hounds have died on the streets for their stupid war. Cerberus has the former neutral zone in his grip, Kronos is pushing farther into South Falls, toward the harbor. Neither of them will let it go without killing all of us.

"And Jace?" I ask my sister.

He's been gone, too.

Richard Jacobs, the lawyer, lied to us. Of course he did. We only found out later, once the dust had settled and we were back with Cerberus, Malik, and a few others, that they saw a man in a snake mask put Jace in the trunk of a car. He had Kora at gunpoint, and he put her in the car, too. And then the Titans overwhelmed the clubhouse, and they were distracted until they could flee.

Jace and Kora haven't been seen again.

My sister's face falls. "There hasn't been so much as a whisper of him."

I stifle the grief that wells up in my chest again. I've been mourning my brother and Kora for six fucking months, and the pain hasn't lessened.

"Can you talk to Kora? See her?" I tighten my hold on Tem again, trying to keep my voice from pleading. "Is she safe?"

"She's..."

When Tem tries to word something carefully, that's my clue that something's wrong.

"Spit it out," I demand.

"She's fine."

She's lying.

But... I don't think I could bear the truth. If it's that bad. I don't think I can carry the weight of anything right now, because I'm barely holding on to reality. These meetings with my sister keep me sane.

Someone pounds on my door, and we both jump. "Apollo. Meeting with Cerberus in five."

"Got it," I yell back.

Tem stands, then glances around my small room. It's a far cry from the house, but it's private. Four walls, a window. A bed, a dresser. Better than what we used to have.

"It'll be okay," she says.

I nod once, not sure if I believe her. I hand her a small journal, and she gives me a grim smile in return. She tucks it into her pocket and turns back to the window. She'll deliver it to Wolfe, and then, on her next trip around, she'll bring it back to me.

We can't text. Our phones are being watched. If I didn't inspect my room for listening devices on the regular, I'd think Cerberus was spying here, too. As it is, we limit our aloud conversations to general things. It's why Tem won't tell me where Kora is, or *how* she is. It's why she doesn't say anything about the journal or what to do with it.

Better safe than sorry.

"Love you, brother." She kisses my cheek. "Stay safe."

"You, too."

She unlocks the window and heaves it open. After a moment of watching, waiting, she draws her hood up and climbs out.

I'm tempted to stand at the glass and watch her go, but I can't bear it. I just close it behind her and redraw the drapes. Then I slide my feet into boots and flick on the light. I've been summoned, and I can't afford not to answer.

The hallway is empty. I stride down it quickly and emerge into the large, cavernous central room. It's been transformed into headquarters for Cerberus. This place isn't what it used to be—taken over by the Hell Hounds when their clubhouse was attacked six months ago—and their stench has sunk into it.

There's no escaping them.

Cerberus, Wolfe, and Malik stand around a table. There's a map on the wall behind them with red pins, flagging areas of Sterling Falls that are prominent, that are held by the Titans and us. It's one thing to be here, looking at the war on a map.

It's another to go outside and experience it.

"There you are," Cerberus snaps. "We've been waiting."

"Sorry, sir." My teeth grind every time I call him that.

I'd have thought time would lessen my anger. Make it easier to manage. But instead, it's just amping up. Every mission, every innocent person caught in this senseless warfare, makes me want to... do *something*.

But I can't.

"Come here," Cerberus snaps.

I approach the table and stare down at the second map.

"We've located him. *Finally*. He's hiding out here." Cerberus taps one of the buildings.

It's on the edge of South Falls, close to the marina. An old warehouse. Kronos has been moving around while in town, taking over as he sees fit. This is the first time we've had the upper hand. We've known he's been pushing into South Falls, and this is just more confirmation of that. If he succeeds in taking South Falls, he'll be able to cut off our supplies entirely. He already owns the highway into the city. If he gets the harbor, too?

The fact that we can catch him now, off guard, is a good sign.

"What do you want us to do?" Wolfe asks, his voice steady. If not for the journal that passes between us, detailing weaknesses in the Hell Hounds, in his father, and ways of exploiting them... I'd think he was fully invested in the Hell Hounds. That he'd been brainwashed. He's so good of an actor, even I can't see the cracks in his mask.

"I want you to go in there and kill the son of a bitch,"

Cerberus snaps. "Tonight. Before he gets the chance to escape."

Wolfe nods. "Who's going?"

"You have Apollo and five others. Surround the building and blow it off the fucking foundation. I don't want attention on this one, boy." His eyes narrow. "Can you handle that?"

A team of seven.

"Of course," Wolfe says evenly.

I swallow and nod. Wolfe steps away first, and I cast a lingering look at the building now marked with a black X. Already blown off one map—and soon to be rubble in the streets. The Hell Hounds assigned to Wolfe meet us at the armory.

If you asked me who they were six months ago, I wouldn't have had a clue. We were away for five years—plenty of time for Cerberus to induct new members and for old ones to die off. Now, I know their names, their personalities. Their distinct hatred for the Titans.

Most of them hated us when we arrived, too.

Wolfe has proven himself, and his father is smug about it. He gloats to Malik about the fine lieutenant his son has turned into. Malik, in turn, just shakes his head.

Because there's something about Wolfe that creates chaos.

Chaos. My heart squeezes. Jace called Kora that. My sister did, too. It wasn't until recently that I discovered Persephone went by more than just her name in Greek Mythology. Kore. Chaos. They were all interlinked.

And now they're linked in Kora, too.

We load up on weapons. Wolfe gestures to two of the guys to take bombs. There's a little receiver attached to the front of them, designed so they'll go off with one call to the right number. It activates... something. I don't know.

I don't want to know about bombs, if we're being honest.

"Ready?" Wolfe asks.

"Yes, sir," they say.

I roll my eyes and jerk my chin down in some sort of nod. I'm not fucking calling Wolfe sir, that's for damn sure.

He lets out a breath, half of a laugh. "Okay, let's go kill this bastard."

CHAPTER 3
KORA

I stare at the ceiling. Someone stuck glow-in-the-dark stars up there, which was a fantastic idea. They're a toxic green in the dark—not exactly *star*-colored, but I digress—and in the daylight, they look like blobs of sharp-edged gum. The point isn't that they look good. The point is that they're a needed distraction.

At midnight, or a little after, my door is cracked open. I pretend to be asleep. A flashlight sweeps across my face, blinding for a split second, then away. The door closes.

I flip the blanket back and swing my legs over the side of the bed, crossing the dark room to my desk. I make another tally mark in my notebook. Another day gone. Then I get ready, and I'm lacing my sneakers when something taps my window.

When I open it, Ben grins up at me.

"Ready?" he asks.

I nod once and climb out. His hands briefly touch my waist, guiding my feet to the ground, then he releases me. He's been doing that a lot. Avoiding touch like someone is going to come out of the shadows and deck him.

But... I haven't been exactly open to it either. Even though I haven't had anyone fucking touch me in six months. He's picked up on my slight flinches, the way I step away whenever anyone gets too close to me.

I'm not the only one here who reacts like that. He's not on some body language genius level—he can just read the room.

"Ready?" he repeats.

"What are we doing tonight?"

I know the answer, but I figured I would ask anyway. Hoping for a different response, I guess. He just smirks and takes off into the woods. I let out a sigh and follow him at a jog, picking out the trail as my eyes adjust to the gloom. There are low-hanging clouds tonight, with the moon peeking through as they shift. The weather has been mild for May. The ground is a bit wet from a recent rainstorm, and it smells like it might rain again.

Soon enough, the woods thin on our right. The water, visible through the trees, is calm, barely moving. Miniature waves lap against the shore ten feet away, and it's the only sound between us. And our footsteps. This side of the island doesn't get hit with the larger waves coming in off the ocean. If I squint hard enough straight through, I can make out the lights of Emerald Cove in the distance.

We're too far from Sterling Falls. But sometimes I imagine the ships that pass our island are heading for the marina in South Falls, and my heart aches. I daydream about swimming out to meet the giant ships, of being hoisted aboard and stowing away to get back to them.

Wherever they are.

My heart tells me Jace is alive. I refuse to believe otherwise, even though the last time I saw him... he was in a trunk. My parents' friend, whose identity is still unknown to me, took him away. *Took care of it*, whatever that means.

My parents brought me back to their house, but I wouldn't stay. The claustrophobia was too much. Every time they closed their eyes, I tried my best to leave.

Dead-end streets and open fields.

There was nowhere to go. Nowhere to run. I cried every day for a week, convinced that Jace was dead and Apollo and Wolfe were rotting in prison. And I lived with the fear that any day, Parker would show up.

And then...

I don't know. The stress got to be too much. I wasn't docile or folding back into their life like they expected. I think I broke on the inside. Saw someone who might've been Parker, or it could've been a total stranger. I'd been having crazy dreams about death and bloodshed and snakes, and my parents didn't understand any of it. They didn't know what I went through, and I wasn't going to tell them.

Their friend didn't mention what he dragged me out of either.

All they knew, all they *thought* was that the guys I was living with fucked me up.

So, they sent me away.

Isle of Paradise is a tiny island off of Emerald Cove. Half the island is for the occasional tourist and the few residents. The other half has a camp of sorts. Some well-meaning people founded it to help trauma survivors cope and heal. The idea is that getting away from regular life is a sort of reset. However, over the years it's transformed into something more than that. The rules and regulations constrict its residents. They don't release us until they think we're ready... whatever that means.

And everyone on the other side of the little island *knows* us as the camp kids. They avoid us, they lock their doors or pretend we aren't there if they see us in the little town. Like we're dangerous.

Maybe we are dangerous.

There's therapy, there are monitored computer sessions for online courses—college, high school, whatever. They teach trade, too. And a self-defense class that feels paltry to what would've kept me alive in Sterling Falls. More therapy. Groups and private. Meals are all together in a cafeteria-esque room with circular tables and chairs that are bolted to the floor.

It's a new sort of suffocating.

They do night checks. Curfew. Everything is structured in an attempt to heal people. To me, it's a prison. I didn't come here because I wanted to—I did because I had no choice.

Two weeks into my stay, after a particularly brutal melt-down in the cafeteria, I met Ben. His story is different from mine. He's here because he wants it—he wants to be away from home, which is where his trauma lies. And I guess there's nowhere else for him. Here or there. No middle ground. No dreams of *away*.

He's closer to the guys' ages—about four years older than me. Shorter than Jace and Apollo. Maybe the same height as Wolfe, with short dark hair and angry eyes. More muscular, though, if that's even possible. Wider in the shoulders.

We don't trade personal details. Besides his first name, and mine... nothing. It's easier that way. If I don't have to think about the shit I've done, and *caused*, then it's easy to pretend it was just a dream. I don't have to worry that he's going to search my name and find that press release the mayor and Cerberus did, or the article about the fire.

Ten months ago, I was chased through similar woods. Barefoot, terrified.

I'm not afraid right now.

I pick up my speed, stretching my legs, and catch up to Ben.

He casts a quick glance over his shoulder and laughs. "There you go, K."

K. My parents' friend called me that. Another mystery to unpack at a later date. I haven't stopped Ben from calling me it, although I don't necessarily like it. It's just one of those things that I allow to remind myself that I'm not going to be here forever.

My lungs burn. I relish it, though. After a full day of dullness, of the therapists trying to pry my secrets and emotions out of me, of classes I don't give a shit about, I need this. An adrenaline rush.

We automatically slow when we reach the edge of the small town center. The rentals are on the other side of Main Street, situated with a good view and an easy walk. The homes of the folks who live here are scattered around the peripherals... but not too close to scare off the tourists.

I stick to the shadows, as does Ben, and we make our way to the brick library. He has a bump key—one that works on most of the doors, so long as they have that style of key—and the door to the basement swings open without a sound.

We descend into the darkness, him in front of me.

I still don't like basements.

He doesn't let me consider that for long. With almost no warning, he comes at me. I only have a split second to register the attack. His quiet intake of breath, and the sensation of movement.

I duck and spin away, not wanting to get caught up in his arms. We've done that before, and it reminds me too much of Jace bear-hugging me from behind, daring me to escape. I have to be eased into that one. And besides—if I can't see, Ben can't either. He only knew I was on the stairs because he heard my footsteps.

The basement is empty. There's another room beyond this one that houses important books, but we ignore those. Everything this library has is already on display on the first floor, for the public.

I quiet myself. My breathing, my steps. I blink rapidly in the darkness, waiting for my eyes to adjust enough to see his form.

He rushes me again. Somehow, he knows where I am.

I take the hit. His padded hand skates across my jaw, knocking me sideways. I go off-kilter, and my breathing hitches. My arms pinwheel.

"Focus," he calls. "You're not going to always see your opponent coming. But you know *yourself*."

I do know myself. I know I'm stronger than I've ever been. I know that Ben was a fighter before he came here, and what he tells me is good information.

My mind flashes to Hestia, the Olympus fighter in all-white, up against a guy taller and stronger than her. And then Artemis. And Nyx. They can *fight*.

I want that, and Ben knows it. Without me asking, without confirming, we started training. It's been five months of this. He's not teaching me the basics—we're going with survival. I learned how to throw a punch in that self-defense class, how to strike a soft spot and run.

But here's the thing: there are times when you can't run. When you can't escape the big, bad thing that's trying to kill you.

So you have to kill it first.

Ben doesn't flinch at my ruthlessness. He grins at it, goads it, fans the flame that keeps me going. And in truth, if he didn't help me, I would've self-destructed long ago.

I catch a glimpse of him. He moves in front of one of the windows, sidestepping. He's still nothing more than a shadow—and somehow, I stand out like a beacon to him. But this is my chance, so I take it.

I strike first.

And, to my surprise, I catch him off guard. My knuckles graze his skin.

"In and out," he says, moving out of the way. "In, attack, out. Protect yourself."

He gets in a hit to my stomach, and I wheeze as I stagger backward.

"Don't leave yourself vulnerable."

Now that I've seen him, I can't *unsee* him. I track his movements, pivoting. I can hear Jace in my ear, telling me to focus. Wolfe by my side, pointing out Ben's weak spots. Apollo, flipping his knife head over hilt, egging me on. I want to be with them so badly it hurts, but I can't. I'm stuck on this island, and I'm fucking pissed about it.

I launch myself at him. He isn't expecting the fury, and we both go down. Pain lances up my arms with each hit—and he lets me get in two across his face before he flips me off him.

I land hard on my back. The wind leaves my lungs, and my mouth opens and closes as I try to take a breath in. Finally, I inhale. The rush of oxygen just makes me madder.

"Better." He hauls me up. "But save your anger for the real fight. Come on. We need to get ice on your jaw."

"Yours, too."

His teeth flash with his grin. "You didn't hit me that hard."

I shrug and tap the padded gloves he wears when we spar. "You didn't either."

"You didn't see it coming. It's worse that way." He always calls off our sessions at odd times. When my temper is on the verge of breaking or already halfway gone. Like he knows exactly how far he can push me—and the boundary keeps inching further along.

We leave the library, and I stand watch as he locks up.

Someone moves out of the shadows across the street. They step into the light, and recognition floods through me.

Recognition—then fear.

CHAPTER 4
WOLFE

I eye the Hell Hounds my father gave us. Apollo stands at my shoulder, his expression flat. At the end of the day, I can't risk their lives. I won't. They're... not quite innocent, but they didn't ask for this either. I can almost picture us in their shoes. Inducted, indoctrinated.

My father has that effect.

"Stay here," I tell them. "Give us five minutes. If we're not out by then, blow it. Apollo, with me."

The guys nod, and one of them sets a timer on his phone.

My best friend makes a noise of affirmation and follows me across the street. I set a timer on my watch for four minutes—can't be too careful. Especially with idiots in charge of blowing up a building.

The warehouse is painstakingly familiar, but the Hell Hounds don't know that. There's no way my father would know it either. But months ago, Kora and I came here. It's *our* warehouse. But it seems like it's been broken into and ransacked. Broken glass litters the sidewalk, and one of the doors has been blown off its hinges. Someone put plywood over the gaping hole.

"Why would Kronos come here?" Apollo asks.

I lift my shoulder. "No fucking clue. Maybe because it's been abandoned for months."

We abandoned it. It was emptied of product, sure, but it's been inactive since Cerberus dragged us back to hell.

I mean, back to the Hell Hounds.

Same thing.

He grunts.

I hop through the broken window and land lightly on the concrete, immediately dropping into a crouch. Apollo follows a moment later. I tap his arm and point for him to go in the opposite direction. We set the bombs.

Once they go, it'll be quick. A chain reaction that should bring the whole place down. Although I'm getting a serious case of déjà vu, moving quietly through the stacks. This place was once a smooth operation for us. A way to keep the gangs from feuding because we could've shut down the city with a snap of our fingers.

But look at it now. The city *is* shut down, and smuggling things in has become a commodity in and of itself. A new business sprung up in this one's grave.

I shake my head at our foolishness and keep moving. We shouldn't have tried to control the whole city. Two gangs under our thumb? It's no wonder everything fell apart.

Once the rest of the bombs are set, Apollo finds me.

"We should confirm he's here," he says under his breath.

I check my watch. The lookouts probably won't blow it until we come back. Unless they've got orders I don't know about.

Either way, Apollo is right.

I nod. "Office?"

He inclines his chin and stalks forward. I pull my gun. It might be easier to just demolish the whole building, but I prefer a confirmed kill. Besides, would there be any better satisfaction than seeing the surprise on Kronos' face when I pull the trigger?

Apollo grasps the door handle to the interior office and slowly twists it. It swings inward, and he takes two quick steps in, his gun raised. The darkness almost swallows him, and all I can see is his back—and then he stiffens. I click my flashlight on, illuminating the back of his head... and the gun now pressed to his temple.

Shit.

"You kill him, and you're a dead man," I growl. "But let's face it, you're a dead man either way."

Apollo's shoulders hike. His hands float up, his gun dangling from a finger.

The damn door is in the way, blocking my shot. I step forward quickly and flick the light on, pushing the door open the rest of the way.

It slams against the wall.

"Holy shit," I whisper.

Jace blinks at us. He still has a fucking gun to Apollo's head.

Apollo swivels to see him, and his expression says it all. *Fuck you*, and *thank god you're alive*. I'm as mad at him as I am relieved to see he's not dead. Apollo knocks the gun aside and lunges forward. He throws his arms around Jace, pounding his back.

"You bastard," Apollo whispers. "We thought you were dead."

It takes a minute for Jace to unfreeze. He seems as stunned to see us as we are to see him. He finally hugs Apollo back, though. They break apart, and he meets my gaze. I don't know what I want to say to him. The last time I saw him was after Apollo had been drugged. After our fight... which I still haven't told Apollo about.

He didn't need to know. It didn't really matter either.

My phone goes off. A text from a lookout, asking what the hell is taking so long.

"We gotta go," I say, reaching for Apollo. "This whole building is about to go."

Jace doesn't question it. He grabs his bag, shoving stuff from the office into it, and together we run for one of the windows. I look away as Apollo breaks the glass, sweeping the frame clear and hopping through first. We follow, landing in an alley.

I shove Apollo ahead of me, then Jace, and we go through another doorway. Another warehouse. This one is still operational, but we ignore the machinery and product. We get another fifty feet before the bombs go off. The bastards outside blew it without waiting for us to get to safety.

Maybe *that* was their true order.

The detonation shakes the walls, the ground. It's like a localized earthquake. It knocks all of us off our feet, and we go flying forward.

Dust and debris float down from the rafters.

Jace is the first up, and he curls his fingers into the back of my shirt. He hauls me up like I'm a newborn kitten. Haven't missed that.

He sets me on my feet and gets in my face. "Did your father send you to kill me?"

I glare at him. "He told us it was Kronos—"

"Did he?" Apollo asks, pushing himself up. "He never said his name."

I stop. "You've got to be fucking kidding me."

My phone goes off. I grab it from my pocket and answer.

"Hey, boss, where are you? The building is coming down, and we didn't see you come out." One of the Hell Hounds. "You said to blow it—"

I swallow my annoyance. "We're fine. Meet us two blocks north with the cars." I hang up and turn back to Jace. "If you have any brilliant ideas to get us out of this, we're all ears."

Jace just shakes his head. "My efforts have been in vain. No one will see me."

Apollo narrows his eyes. "Who have you tried?"

"The sheriff, the mayor. Anyone who has some fucking sway." Jace sighs. "I'm basically acting as a vigilante here. There are too many civilians in the way. I've been doing what I can... Staying off the radar, trying to disrupt things on both sides."

I imagine he's been successful at the disruption. Whatever else he's been doing, though, hasn't been enough. The obituary column is one of the thicker parts of the paper these days. But the true story has remained out of the headlines. The city has gone on lockdown, and if you don't *know*, then you don't know.

"We've got to go." I step back. "Keep surviving. And if you can get us out—"

"Wait." Apollo holds up his hands. "Fuck, it's nice to finally be able to say something out loud to both of you. Jace, find Artemis. She knows where Kora is."

Jace and I stop. I glower at my best friend, wondering when the hell he was going to share that information with me—and then it hits me that there might not have been time. Artemis is due to deliver the small journal to me sometime this week, if she managed to get to Apollo before this stupid mission. We've had a loose schedule, the three of us, but it remains unpredictable.

Just in case.

Jace squints at Apollo. "Where would Tem be?"

He scoffs. "I didn't ask where she'd be staying. And I didn't get any more information about Kora in case our conversation was overheard. Try Antonio."

The chef who works at the restaurant Jace owns—the one named after Antonio—and Bow & Arrow. Tem's club. He's a straight-laced dude, but he also pays attention. That's why he's on our payroll. Because no one thinks the short, older man, who mumbles to himself in Italian on a regular basis, is collecting information for us.

He has a wife. Three kids. He can't afford to open his mouth and draw attention.

But listening? No problem.

He's got one foot in the underworld and one foot in the light. Just the way we like him.

"I'll find her," Jace promises. "I'll bring Kora back."

I ignore him. I don't know if *back* is any better than where she is. And I don't know if she'll even want to come. It's been six months. She's stayed away—for good reasons.

Hell will freeze over before Kora returns to Sterling Falls.

CHAPTER 5
KORA

B en grabs at my arm when he notices we're not alone, trying to shuffle me behind him.

It's too late, though. I break into a run, dashing across the empty street. I've got tunnel vision, and I don't stop until I'm right in front of her. That isn't enough, though. I throw my arms around Nyx's shoulders, pulling her into my embrace.

She lets out a low laugh and hugs me back.

Hard.

"Has something happened?" I demand in her ear. While I'm *so* happy to see her, the fear squeezing my chest won't let up until I know why. "Are they okay? Alive?"

She draws back slightly, her brows drawing down. "They're alive," she finally says. "Well, Wolfe and Apollo are—"

"Where is Jace?"

"Who are you?" Ben stops a few feet away, his hands in his pockets.

My expression must be guilty, because Nyx snorts. Her expression is light but guarded. She wears a black long-sleeved shirt and black cargo pants. Dark tattoos peek out of the collar of her shirt. Her hair is in two braids, and her makeup is dark, too. Just the way I remember her.

"Nyx," she introduces.

"Oh, we're going by fake names?" Ben nods. "Guess you can call me Chiron, then."

I flinch.

Nyx lets out a hoarse laugh, understanding the reference immediately. "I don't suppose you've been training Kora, then? You've got two few legs to be him, though, my friend."

Chiron... the centaur from Greek Mythology. If I'm not mistaken, the centaur trained many of the famous heroes. And he just knew that offhand?

I narrow my eyes at Ben. For the first time, I question if I should've been more curious about him. His past, why he's here. It's been five months, and we've kept the conversation pinned to shallow, meaningless things.

"Maybe you're not looking hard enough." He smiles and tips his head to the woods. "We should get out of view if we're going to continue this conversation."

Nyx eyes him, but she doesn't protest when I loop my arm through hers and lead her down the path we ran not too long ago. Once we're engulfed in shadow, she stops me.

"What is going on?" she asks me. "What is this place?"

I don't know how to answer her in a way that won't make her angry.

Ben answers. "They say their mission is to help trauma victims."

"Uh-huh." Nyx frowns. "But...?"

"But it's a little more complex than that." Ben shrugs. "Whether the program actually works or not is anyone's guess. But Kora probably should've been on her way out months ago. Something else is keeping her here. Someone else, rather. The program will graduate you, essentially, but they haven't done that for her."

Well, *yeah*. I've been hiding from the truth.

I rotate to face Nyx. "Tell me the truth about what's going on in Sterling Falls."

She takes my hands. "Listen, it's... it's not good."

Ben tilts his head.

"The Titans attacked the Hell Hounds' clubhouse," she starts.

I nod sharply. "I know. I was there when they blew up the front room." I've spent the last six months trying to figure out if there was a sign we missed. If Kronos waved a big red flag in front of our faces before he did *that*. "My parents have a friend in Sterling Falls. He... *rescued* me, I guess. And he took Jace with him. Forced him into the trunk..." I somehow keep breathing. "They talked about handling him, like he was a problem."

Nyx's face contorts, and my heart stops.

"God. Have you not seen him? Is he not okay? I thought..." I don't know what I thought. That he was dead? That he figured out a way to get out of it? That *handling* him just meant setting him free, versus the worst-case scenario.

She shakes her head. "I don't know. I haven't seen him, haven't heard from him—and not for lack of trying. We've been looking."

"We?" Ben asks.

She narrows her eyes.

I squeeze her hands harder, pulling her focus back to me. "Where's Saint?"

She takes a breath, and an uneasy sensation washes over me. That she's about to say something bad—and suggest something even worse.

"The Titans have him," she says. "I don't know where.

They grabbed him early on, when the fighting was at its worst. The city was dripping in blood, Kora. And I don't know when it happened or how they managed to get him." Her voice is small. "We've been trying to track everyone down. You, him, Jace. It's been a nightmare."

God. *Saint.* A war prisoner? I know how Kronos treated *me.* I can't imagine what they'd do to someone who openly supported Jace, Wolfe, and Apollo. And Jace? Is he missing?

"I may be able to help with that," Ben says. "Saint, I mean. If you want him back."

We both turn to him, and my mouth falls open.

He picks something off his shirt sleeve. "Didn't I mention? I grew up with the Titans."

Nyx grabs me and hauls me behind her. Her vitriol is immediate. "Did Kronos send you?" she spits. "Trying to get to Kora—"

"Whoa, whoa." Ben raises his hands. "I've been here long before Kora arrived, and I had planned to stay long after she was gone. Do you know what growing up in the Titans is like? Mayhem. None of those fuckers are sane—I'm glad I got out when I did."

"Which was when?" Nyx questions.

I step out from behind Nyx, giving her a look. "He's had plenty of opportunity to do whatever the hell you think he would've—take me back to Kronos or kill me. We've been here for almost six months, and he's been *helping* me. A lot more than the people in charge of the program."

She scoffs. "And I'm just supposed to believe—"

"He doesn't know anything about me," I snap. "Do you want to get Saint back or not?"

She strides toward Ben. They're about the same height, although he's got some muscle on her. Still, I've seen her go toe to toe with bigger men and come out on top.

It makes sense, though. How he knows to fight. The trauma that might've driven him here. I've been vaguely curious about his life prior to Isle of Paradise, but now that curiosity kicks up. I want to know how he ended up with the Titans—and specifically, growing up with them.

But more than that, I'm desperate to get back to Sterling Falls.

"Where are Wolfe and Apollo?"

She winces. "Um... back with the Hell Hounds."

My mouth drops open. "Excuse me?"

"It was that or prison," she mutters.

"How did you find Kora?" Ben asks. He tips his head back in the direction of the dorms, and we follow him down the trail. "This place isn't well-known."

"Artemis found you," she says, smiling slightly.

Ben rolls his eyes. "You really don't trust me, huh?"

"That's her real name." Nyx frowns. "*Anyway*. Artemis tracked you down through your parents. Did they call you recently or something?"

I pause, digging my heels into the dirt. "Um... they sent me a letter." One that I skimmed and then tossed in the trash.

"She's been determined. She confirmed with someone on the island that you were here, and then she told me. And Apollo."

I brighten. "She's been in contact with him?"

Ben huffs ahead of us, probably completely lost. And honestly, I'm not sure how I feel about him overhearing all of this. My trust wavers, but I lean into Nyx's side. I pitch my voice lower. "How are we getting off the island?"

"I chartered a ship," she says. "You don't understand what it's been like, Kora. Sterling Falls isn't the same. I just want you to be prepared when we go back, because it's a hell of a lot worse than when you left."

I nod slowly. "There's just one thing."

She meets my gaze.

"I didn't choose to leave. I was dragged out kicking and screaming."

She squeezes my hand. "I know you wouldn't have left unless you were forced."

We arrive at the edge of the woods. The dorm building, and my cracked window, are a short distance away. Ben lingers in the shadows, eyeing both of us. His attention goes from me to Nyx and back again.

"You trust her?"

"With my life," I answer. The guys trusted her and Saint, and I do, too. "What's the plan?"

He lifts one shoulder. "Pack a bag. In and out. Nyx will stay with you. I've got to get something from my room, and I'll meet you back here in ten."

Ten minutes. I nod, and he takes off around the side of the building. Nyx makes a noise under her breath. I ignore it and hurry to my room. She follows, giving me a boost to get through the window. She hops up and swings her legs in after me, stopping short.

"This is basically a broom closet," she whispers.

I look around. It's a small room, yeah. "I didn't spend much time in here."

Why am I making excuses?

I dump the trash—just paper and a lone tissue—on the floor and yank the plastic liner up. The bags I had when I arrived are elsewhere. Locked up, probably, to try and minimize the chance of someone running away.

Nyx watches me throw my clothes into it, then my

toiletries. It's not even half full when I tie it off and straighten.

"Ready?" I prod.

She jerks, then nods. She goes out of the window first. I hop out after her, landing lightly in the grass. We make a break for the woods, and I set down my makeshift pack. I lean against a tree, inspecting my knuckles. They're a bit sore from my mock fight with Benjamin. My cheek aches, too. I don't think he meant to hit me that hard, and it was with a padded glove, too. But it's tender to the touch, and it might be bruised by morning.

"What has he been teaching you?"

I eye her. She leans against a tree opposite me, her hands in her pockets.

"To fight," I eventually say. "Something better than the amateur self-defense class the program boasted about."

She inclines her chin. "Anything else?"

"Patience. Another thing I wasn't good at in the beginning."

"No one is good at patience in the beginning."

"I taught her how to shoot, too," Benjamin says, seeming to materialize out of the darkness. It's spooky how silently he can move. His outfit has changed to match Nyx. Dark clothes, a black bag slung over his shoulder. He holds out an empty bag to me, and it takes me a second to realize that he must've retrieved mine out of storage. There's still a tag that has my name written on flimsy piece of cardboard.

I take it and quickly shove the plastic bag inside it, zipping it shut.

Nyx is still squinting at Ben. "How did you learn to shoot when you were hiding your training?"

How, indeed? The first time he handed me a gun with an

47

unfamiliar, cylindrical object screwed onto the muzzle, I didn't know what to do. How to react. On some level I *knew* how to shoot. I had pulled the trigger before. Checked a weapon over. But something in my mind had glitched, making it impossible for me to move forward. Maybe it was because of the Hell Hound I killed and everything that resulted... But he walked me through the mechanics of it, explained that the suppressor wouldn't silence it completely, but it would make it so I could shoot and not draw unwanted attention. That I could shoot and not kill anyone—unless I wanted to do so.

And then we started, and I absorbed it like a sponge.

Having lived with Jace, Wolfe, and Apollo, I know the importance of weapons. My chest tightens again. Wolfe and Apollo... if they're with Cerberus, then they're alive. But Jace? Is he missing or just hiding?

"Ready?" Nyx asks. She checks her watch, the face glowing at her for a moment, then raises her eyebrows.

"As ready as we'll ever be," I answer.

Sterling Falls, here we come.

CHAPTER 6
SAINT

The lights flicker on over my head. I open my eyes as much as they can—which isn't much—and roll onto my side. Heavy footsteps precede the rusted metal door scraping open. The hinges squeal, and then the door slams into the wall.

Two Titans enter and stop just inside the small room. I blink hard, trying to clear my vision. A fruitless endeavor. Someone else comes inside, and their shoes draw my attention first, at my eye level on the floor. Polished snakeskin with little hourglass tassels. They've been dyed dark green, almost black. My gaze goes up his charcoal-gray suit pants, to the vest and white shirt, to the shoulder holster that matches his shoes.

Up to his face.

Kronos.

I let out a laugh that comes out more like a huff, my ribs aching. "Come with more questions?"

He snaps his fingers.

One of the Titans at the entrance moves and yanks on a chain. It rattles through a pulley on the ceiling and down to the metal handcuffs locked around my wrists. I'm yanked upright brutally, my shoulders popping at the sudden strain. My body sways until I can get my knees under me, then my feet. They keep pulling until my arms are extended over my head and my weight lifts off my toes.

"Tell me where you think Jace King is hiding."

I let my head fall back. My shoulders are screaming, but I stay fucking silent.

"Here's the thing." Kronos leans in, like a co-conspirator. "A building went down in South Falls. A warehouse. I don't think Cerberus is foolish enough to think *I* would hide out there, so close to their territory... do you?"

Fuck. *Fuck.* The guys' warehouse? Jace might've been there, I don't know. I don't know anything. I've been out of the game for too long—and my loyalty has been tested before. Not quite like this, though. Not by a man set on breaking me.

He tsks, then makes another motion to the guys behind him. They step out of the room, and the door closes. Locking us in.

I swallow.

He reaches out and presses his thumb into the center of my chest. Into the lines of the ugly, inflamed brand. It flashes me back into awareness, sending shooting pain down to my toes. He chuckles at my suppressed groan.

"Where has Jace King been hiding?" he asks again, digging his nail into the wound. "The next step is to give you another one of these... It's a shame, your tattoos were quite intricate. I wonder if your girl will still love you if you're marred? If she survives this ordeal..."

My eyes roll back, the pain blinding for a moment. I don't know how to do this. My breaking point is on a long approach. I can see it in the distance, and I wish that I could change course.

Nyx and I hid away together for a month after the war broke out. And then the Titans grabbed me one night and swept me away.

Kronos doesn't visit that often. The guards regularly beat me for my disobedience—and other than those smug bastards, I haven't seen anyone in days.

Weeks?

Months?

Sometimes the questions are different. The layout of Olympus, the business the guys—Jace, Wolfe, and Apollo—had outside of their precious fight club, where their money is stored. What Jace did on the side, outside of Olympus. Who is most important to him.

No secrets have passed my lips, and I've paid dearly for it.

There's no light in my cell except for the artificial sort. The fluorescent bulb that flickers on over my head with the buzzing that is reminiscent of a fly circling to its death. Loud, obnoxious, irritating.

When they don't have use for me, I'm in the dark. The only light that comes in is under the metal door that I can't reach.

But when he mentions Nyx...

I fling myself forward. My forehead collides with the bridge of his nose. I can't see for a moment, the room exploding with white blossoms, and I swing backward on the chain. My toes lose purchase of the floor, and I twist around.

Kronos stumbles away, hissing under his breath. I manage to stop my movement again and watch him. He touches his nose, which has a distinct crookedness now. Blood gushes out his nostrils.

"You'll pay for that," he growls.

A *boom* crashes in the near distance.

The walls tremble, raining dust down on us.

"Sir?" one of the guards questions, the door opening. He sees Kronos' face and steps farther inside. "You—"

"Go check on that," Kronos yells, spit and blood flying with his heaving breath. "And leave us the fuck *alone*."

The door closes. Kronos strides to the chain on the wall, looped around pegs, and hoists on it more. I'm lifted off my feet entirely. The cuffs around my ankles pull at the chain bolted to the floor, keeping me from swinging. I got those after I kicked at them, catching one of the assholes in the groin.

Kronos leers at me, and his gaze drops to his hand.

To the knife he flicks open.

"I'm going to enjoy this so much more than you."

I meet his gaze. It's too much to ask that he put me out of my misery immediately—but if I'm lucky, today will end with my death. I've been no use to him. But he's brought up Nyx, and that means she's still out there. Still alive, unless Cerberus caught her.

I would've liked to see her one last time. To tell her I'm sorry or kiss her. Make love to her. That girl owns my soul— so I'm not afraid to die. But I am afraid to leave her alone.

Kronos steps within reach. His fury is radioactive.

"Don't worry," he says, patting my cheek. "You'll see your girlfriend in Hell."

I should've seen it coming. The blade. The end of me.

He punches his fist forward, driving the knife into my torso. Right between my ribs.

Pain like I've never known crashes over me, and this

time—*the only time*—I let it out. I scream, and it mixes with his laughter. My blood gushes over the handle, his hand. The blade is intrusive, invading me in a way I've never felt before. It's white-hot, and yet, outside of that, I feel clammy.

Like I'll never be warm again.

And then he rips it out, and the pain triples. He leaves me there, striding out and closing the door behind him. In the flickering light, I wonder how much longer I could possibly have. It's hard to breathe. My chest is so fucking tight, I can't seem to take in another inhale.

Unconsciousness is right there, waiting for me.

The door crashes open, and someone gasps. I manage to see who waits for me, and my already tired heart skips a beat. My light stands there like an avenging angel, but it's too late.

I fall backward into a darkness I know I won't wake up from.

CHAPTER 7
KORA

Ben and I lie on the rise above the chapel. The tall grass between the trees gives us some cover. The night helps, too. Dawn is approaching. Another hour, maybe, but the sky hasn't begun to lighten.

"He kept you here?"

I glance at him, then look back through the night-vision binoculars. "Yeah. Then he auctioned me off to the highest bidder. And then he tried to kill me."

He grimaces. "Radio them. It's time."

I pull the radio up to my mouth. "In position?"

"Ready," Nyx responds, her voice crackling.

He nods to himself, then readjusts his grip on the long-range rifle. He doesn't hesitate—his finger moves, gently squeezing the trigger. The weapon recoils into his shoulder. A split second later, the propane tanks set a few dozen yards from the chapel explode.

The noise is deafening, but the sight—beautiful. My breath catches in my throat as the tanks go up in a huge ball of fire. Immediately, the chapel door opens, and someone rushes out.

S. MASSERY

Ben slides the bolt back, reloading, and tracks the man. He shoots again, and the Titan falls. Then another. Nyx and Artemis should be in by now. I scan the other doorways, and I freeze.

"Kronos." I barely speak the word. "Eleven o'clock."

If he can take the shot...

Ben angles that way, but it's too late. Kronos is out of the building and sliding into a car before we can get him in the scope. The red taillights gleam in the dark, and the squeal of tires reaches us. His car takes off, finally finding purchase on the gravel and vanishing from sight.

"Let's go," Ben says.

We hop up and half run, half slide down the hill. I keep my arms out for balance, but Ben runs without fear. He beats me to the base of the hill, past the burning trees that caught from the explosion.

He rips open the door Kronos exited out of, only waiting a moment for me to catch up. There's a long corridor. It's familiar—it might've even been the same hall I walked down. But instead of drywall, it's been painted a dark color. The lights even feel grimier, dimmer.

A Titan comes around the corner. He yells and raises his weapon.

I shoot.

I just do it without thinking. He was going to kill us, and the small handgun jerks in my grip. But my aim is true, and he falls back against the far wall.

"Keep moving," Ben orders.

I glance at the Titan on our way past. He's gone already, his eyes open but vacant.

It's a maze, but eventually we find the stairs to the basement. We went radio silent for fear of giving away positions —if Nyx or Artemis had to hide, for example. My fingers

58

twitch, eager to call for them. To see where they are, if they're okay.

We did our job. We drew them out.

But they had the harder job of finding Saint.

"Nyx?" I call.

I get an elbow to my ribs for that one.

"Here," comes the faint reply.

I raise my eyebrow at Ben, who finally nods. I take the lead, hurrying down the steps and into another narrow corridor. Artemis comes out into the hall, waving us down, and we follow her into one of the rooms.

Cells, more like.

Nyx kneels next to Saint. He's flat on his back in the middle of the room, lying in a pool of blood. His own, judging from the wound in his chest. His arms are extended over his head, bound together and attached to a long chain that drapes from the ceiling. She must've undone it when she found him, lowering him to the floor.

I go up and manage to break open the handcuffs, sliding them from his wrists. His skin is dark purple where the metal sat. His fingers flex, barely aware that he's no longer restrained.

"We need to get him out of here," Nyx says.

Her voice is steel. She sheds her shirt and presses it to Saint's side. A stab wound, maybe? It's high, almost under his armpit. I don't know if it's wrecked his lungs or heart, but he seems to still be breathing.

"On three," Nyx says. We all take position around him. "One, two, *three*."

We lift Saint, and he lets out a groan without opening his eyes. He's fucking heavy, but the three of us don't falter on our way out the door. Artemis and I each have a leg, with Benjamin holding the bulk of him under his arms.

Nyx has remained at his side, keeping pressure on the wound.

We shuffle our way upstairs and down the deserted corridor. I guess Kronos decided that, if the place were to come under attack, it wouldn't be worth keeping.

Which means this isn't his only hiding place.

I swallow and let my head swing around, trying to keep everything in my line of sight at once. I take both his legs when we're outside, and Artemis runs for one of the vehicles. She throws it into reverse, speeding backward toward us, and the tires screech to a halt. Ben and I quickly slide him into the backseat, Nyx going with him.

Ben gestures to the passenger seat. "Go."

I glance back at him, but he's already shutting Saint and Nyx in the back. "Aren't you coming?"

He points. Down another road, a flicker of headlights between the trees shows at least two cars moving toward us at high speed. Maybe Kronos wasn't prepared to abandon this place, then. But he wanted everyone out in order to defend it... or catch us.

"*Go*," he urges. "I'll hold them off."

I grimace and climb into the front seat. As soon as my ass touches the leather, Ben slams the door shut. Artemis hits the gas.

I stare at her, gripping the handle. "Are you kidding?"

"He said if worse came to worse, to leave him behind." She glances at me. "This is worst-case scenario, Kora."

I twist around. Saint's extended on the seat, his head in Nyx's lap, and she's pressing on the wound. Behind us, one of the cars has broken off and speeds after us. Ben is out of sight, but the rapid patter of gunfire isn't far off.

"Holy shit. Are we taking him to a hospital?"

"No," Nyx snaps. "Absolutely not."

I blink. "What? Why?"

"The hospitals are owned by Cerberus now," Artemis says quietly. "It's not safe."

I blow out a breath and face forward. I strap myself in and check my gun, then rest it on my lap. I shot someone without even hesitating—a remarkable difference from when I shot the Hell Hound. That was out of desperation. This was calculating.

"Have you seen Wolfe or Apollo?"

The corner of Artemis' lips quirk. "Yes, I've seen both of them."

"And Jace?"

She sighs. Nyx does, too. It seems impossible that I was the last one to see him. *Six months ago.* We break out onto the main road, and Artemis lays heavier into the gas. The engine whines in protest, and our speed increases. We cross back into Sterling Falls, specifically West Falls territory, then head north. The stretch of road is familiar. Apollo and I rode it, I think, before everything went to shit.

I twist around ahead, but the Titan car is gone.

"That's weird," I mumble.

"What—"

"There was nowhere—"

Suddenly the car *does* reappear, its headlights turning back on mere yards away. It somehow escaped my notice in the dark, riding our light to stay on the road.

"Go!" I yell, grabbing on to the seat as the car turns into us.

Their front hits our back bumper, and our car swerves. Artemis shouts, swearing, and we fly forward. We're approaching a residential area on the outskirts of North Falls. In a minute, we'll be on a quiet suburb street filled with huge houses and Sterling Falls residents who have so far probably avoided the gang war.

"Hang on," she shouts.

A second later, she twists the wheel to the left and slams on the brakes. We skid sideways, our back end swinging around, and the Titan car sails past us. She floors it again, and we fly back the way we came.

I lean forward and watch in the rearview mirror for the headlights to come back around and catch up.

"What the fuck?" Artemis takes her foot off the gas.

My attention snaps to the road ahead of us, and the person who steps out into the middle of it. They heft something up onto their shoulder.

Wait.

"Jace?" The words have left my mouth before I can stop it. I don't know that it's actually him—but for a second, I thought I recognized him. And then we're sailing by him, and the metal tube on his shoulder lurches.

A split second later, the Titans' car behind us explodes.

"What was that?" Nyx yells.

"Stop the car!" I scream at the same time.

Artemis jerks the wheel and hits the brake. We skid to a halt, and I throw open my door.

She grabs my arm. "Think for a second, Kora. If you get out... I can't wait. Saint needs help."

"I'll catch up with you."

"Antonio's restaurant," she says. "Go in through the back."

I nod and rip free, throwing myself onto the pavement. The door closes, and the car accelerates away. The night is cold, at odds with the fireball of a vehicle a quarter of a mile away. I can feel it from here. And the person now staring at us like he doesn't quite know why we stopped.

He has to know.

I sprint at him. He has barely enough time to toss the weapon aside, and then I'm there. He catches me, his arms locking around my ribs. I push the hood off his head and look up at a very confused Jace King.

Just the person I thought.

"Hey," I breathe.

And then I do what I've thought about for *months*. I pull his head down and kiss him.

CHAPTER 8
JACE

K ora. Kora. Find Kora.

She's haunted my thoughts for six fucking months, and here she is. She's in my arms, and I don't know if she's real or not. I've had nightmares that felt as solid as she does right now. I've replayed seeing her again over and over—as well as my epic failure to keep her safe.

Because I *completely* failed.

I was lost. Everyone I cared about was out of reach. Wolfe, Apollo, *her*. Every day, for months, I tried to make things right. I tried to staunch the wounds of Sterling Falls, but it's an impossible task to do alone.

It may be impossible to do with allies, too.

I got *lucky* that Wolfe and Apollo didn't blow up the warehouse. That I heard them enter and went to investigate instead of hide and wait. If I hid, I'd be under a pile of rubble. My fingers flex on Kora's shirt, and I wonder again if this is just a figment of my imagination. If maybe my last, feeble attempt at taking down the Titans backfired on me.

"Hey," she whispers, and it still doesn't register.

In my dreams, she's berated me for letting him take her. For getting stuffed into a trunk. For being weak.

But my imagination has never grabbed the back of my head and pulled me down to her. She's never brushed her lips to mine either.

My lungs expand, inhaling her scent. It's mixed with smoke and gunpowder, but I don't question it. Her teeth snag my lower lip, pulling me deeper into her.

God. I only got this once, and I'm immediately drunk on her again. She's a hit of heroin straight to my bloodstream. I pick her up and kiss her deeper, sliding my tongue into her mouth. She tastes sweet.

She cups my cheek and finally leans back. Her smile turns shy. "Hi," she says again.

I realize I've picked her up, her legs winding around my hips. She puts her feet back down on the ground, and I take her hand. Unwilling to let go, I guess. She has a weapon in her other hand. I didn't realize it before, but now I grab her wrist and check out the handgun she got ahold of. It's an impressive piece, although I'm not sure *who* would've let her take it. A Glock 21. It's a good gun for shooting at people... which is worrying.

A siren shrieks in the distance, and I wince. "We need to move."

She nods and follows me off the road. She tucks her weapon in the small of her back, and the move reminds me of Wolfe. The easy way he conceals weapons on his person. I grab the RPG—a rocket propelled grenade. The handy weapon that just took out a Titan vehicle.

We climb down a short embankment and through the brush. My bike waits in the shadows, out of sight. Just in case.

I didn't know they were going to be here. I thought I'd be

intercepting a bank run, which Kronos is fond of doing in the middle of the night. I waited for them to pass, and I was going to take out the rear one from behind. So they'd never see it coming.

But the way the vehicles were moving looked more like a chase than any sort of routine... And then the front one spun around, coming back toward me. The second followed, its engine whining as the driver probably put the pedal to the metal.

I took a chance. One that heavily paid off.

What if I had shot the wrong vehicle?

I strap the weapon to the front and hand the helmet to her. "Ready?"

"Where are we going?"

I point to the sky. The clouds catch the blue and red flicker of lights. "Don't want to get caught by the sheriff, do we?"

They've started using the air siren for the big calls, but this is just regular car sirens, screaming at us from a rapidly closing distance.

Kora frowns. "Whose side is he on?"

"Seriously?"

She raises her eyebrow.

I have so many fucking questions. Where did her parents take her? Why is she back? I looked for her. I *tried*. And then getting out of Sterling Falls became harder, and I ran out of leads. I literally didn't know where to search. It was barely enough that I kept myself safe.

Artemis found her, though. Her and Nyx got through. Somehow.

"Listen," she says, taking my hands. "I know I've been gone for a while, and everything has gone to shit. I'm sorry."

I pause. Why is she apologizing?

And then I remind myself that I can't fucking hesitate if I want us to survive.

So I shut off my emotions and thrust the helmet at her. "Put that on."

"We're going to talk about this later," she grumbles, but she thankfully obliges.

I turn the bike around and climb on, then offer her my arm. She ignores it and swings her leg over. Her chest presses into my back, and I suppress a groan. She has no trouble wrapping her arms around my abdomen this time. Her fingers grip my shirt. It's far different from the last time we rode together, when she didn't want to touch me at all.

The engine turns over on the bike, modified to be quieter, and I glance back at her. She meets my eyes through the visor and offers me a short nod.

Okay, then.

Branches whip at us as I navigate the game trail. It's best to stay off the roads, especially if the sheriff is coming to inspect my damage. I didn't want to tell Kora this, but he's been worse than usual. Arresting anyone and everyone, even if they walk a day later. Someone higher up than him is pulling strings. The mayor, the city council... I don't know.

There are rumors that he's interrogating everyone about the same thing.

What that is, though, no one will say. They get squirrely when I ask. Shifty, like there's some big secret they've been looped in on. Big fucking dead ends.

Kora's legs tense against mine as we jostle over tree roots and around rocks. It's almost pitch-black here, even though the sun should be rising soon. The sky is lightening over-head. Barely. It's going to be one of those cloudy, dreary mornings where night and day seem like they've bled together.

It smells like rain.

The sirens haunt me. Too many nights I've been woken up by the sheriff's hunt. I know it isn't him—Cerberus painted me as the villain. He took my disappearance as lack of loyalty. Wolfe and Apollo are as safe as they can be in the monster's den, but me? I became a liability the second he lost control of me—and he acted the moment I lost my leverage.

Everything was fine... until it wasn't.

"Go to Antonio's," Kora calls.

I grunt. "It's not safe."

"It's where the Artemis and Nyx were taking Saint. He was hurt."

I swear under my breath. I knew he had disappeared—but I didn't know who had him. I didn't get a chance to ask Wolfe and Apollo the other day either. But now the answer is clear: Kronos had snatched him. Presumably tortured him to get information.

This is my fault.

Kora's hand slips under my shirt, her hot palm pressing to my abdomen. "Steady."

I don't recognize her.

That gets me worse than anything else. It's been six months, and I don't recognize the girl on the back of my bike. She's not the scared little lamb who we first met in the woods. She's not the same girl who traded barbs with me up until the moment I betrayed her.

We hit a rock, and the bike lurches sideways. Her body hits mine harder, her sharp grunt loud even over the engine.

Or maybe I'm just fucking attuned to her like no other person.

I shake off my thoughts and take a swift turn. We crash through underbrush, narrowly avoid a tree, and bump back out onto the main road. I gun it, leaning forward to urge the bike faster. Kora leans with me, holding tight and not protesting.

We've managed to get through the last bit of West Falls without incident, and now the industrial South Falls warehouses rise around us.

Of all Sterling Falls, this area has been the most affected. It's become the overrun playground of both gangs—the free territory that they both want to take. With Cerberus' tight hold on the neutral zone, the center of Sterling Falls, Kronos wanted to strike big. He wanted South Falls, the harbor, the marina.

If he controlled South Falls, he'd be set. The road into Sterling Falls already comes through the southern part of West Falls. I'd imagine his goal might be to pinch off the Hell Hounds from their supplies.

Pinch off everyone else, too, and get rich in the process.

We pass the remnants of our warehouse, and Kora gasps. It's just a pile of rubble and some free-standing walls. It's settled since the explosion a few nights ago, but it haunts me. Absolutely disgusting. My stomach turns, and I force myself to glance at it as we continue on.

The streets are empty, save from patrolling cop cars. The cops shine lights down alleyways, check car windows, slow-crawl up and down the roads.

Just another reason to hurry up and get to a safe house.

We reach the marina, and I pull over long enough to open a rolling metal gate. We slip through, and I kill the engine. Kora stays on the bike as I hop off and close the gate, then thread a padlock through and click it shut.

"Come on," I say in a low voice.

She climbs off and removes her helmet, shaking out her

dark-red hair. She combs her fingers through it, then sets the helmet on the seat. "Where are we?"

"My backup plan." I push the bike over to its hiding place, a shrub that has seen better days. I fashioned a black tarp with branches and leaves to mimic the rest of the bush, a sort of camouflage, and I pull that out and cover my motorcycle.

She's staring at me with a mixture of horror and awe.

At least, I think it's awe.

I ignore it and continue down the gravel driveway.

Once upon a time, this was the private entrance to some of the richest people in North Falls' boats. They didn't mind trekking down to South Falls for the marina—the pier on the north side is too rough for their precious yachts.

But in the last six months, it's been all but deserted. Most of the boat owners have relocated to Emerald Cove or elsewhere. As far as they can get from the madness—because even Emerald Cove isn't far enough to some.

She tags along behind me down the hill and into a run-down boat house. I've fixed it up as best I could, but the worse the outside looks, the better. I *want* it to look abandoned when the patrols roll by.

I unlock the door and step aside, letting her in ahead of me. I catch sight of the gun handle in the back of her jeans and resist the urge to snatch it away from her. And then my resistance breaks, and I wrap my fingers around it.

I pull it free, and she whirls around, surprise flickering across her face. She snags my wrist and twists sharply. The pain opens my fingers, and the gun leaves my grip. She doesn't stop, though. My arm torques, and my elbow strains. I bow to the pressure, giving up any ideology that I'm going to be able to resist.

I can't help it—I laugh. Even as she folds me over and shoves me away, her gun back in her possession.

Because this is *Kora*. Who couldn't escape my hold, who froze at rough contact. But now she has a gun and she knows how to defend it?

She's moved on, though, my hand sliding from her loosening grip. She turns and inspects my little hiding place, and I stay by the door. She looks healthier. Stronger.

The thought rankles. I don't *want* to be glad that she was gone for six months, but the change in her is undeniable, and I have to bite the inside of my cheek to stop myself from interrogating her about it.

Her gaze goes over the cot in the corner, my blanket folded at the foot of it with the thin pillow on top. I had put down a threadbare rug that stretches across most of the floor, because the splinters were getting old. Fast.

There's a generator out the back door, facing the water. A small fridge that doesn't house anything perishable, because I don't run the generator unless I need something. It draws attention.

Everything draws attention.

I have a case full of weapons on the floor at the foot of the cot. A range of guns, knives, bigger stuff that can take out vehicles. A stockpile I managed to salvage.

"You look like you're waiting for me to run," she comments. She picks up my mug and sniffs, her nose wrinkling. "Whiskey?"

I incline my chin.

It occurs to me, kiss aside, I don't know where we stand. Or how she feels.

She tips the mug back, swallowing a mouthful. She wipes her lips with the back of her hand and sets the mug back down, grimacing. "Tastes like smoke."

I know.

Kora in my space feels... intimate. And not for the first time, I don't know what to fucking do with her.

She sits on my cot, crossing her legs and leaning back against the wall. She pulls her gun out and sets it on the floor at her feet. Her gaze lands on me, and I'm struck by how fucking *steady* she is. She's a mess, to be sure. There's something dark on her chin, maybe blood. Her hair is wild. But she's not trembling or crying or asking a million questions.

"What happened to you?" I finally ask.

She tips her head to the side. "Better pour another drink, King. You're gonna need it."

CHAPTER 9
KORA

W*hat happened to you?*

So, so much.

He collects the mug and takes another cup from a cabinet, rinsing it out before pouring more liquor into both. He comes over and sits beside me, mirroring my stance. Back against the wall, legs kicked out.

I can't believe he's real.

I can't believe I kissed him.

It was an impulsive moment, to be sure. But not a bad one. But then he nudges me, reminding me of his question, and I sigh. I take another sip of whiskey, the burn ever so slightly diminished.

"He put you in the trunk of the car." I stare out. We should be doing other things. Going to the restaurant and meeting up with Artemis, Nyx, and Saint. Maybe going back for Ben. Sitting here and talking feels... pointless. Useless.

"That part I'm aware of," he says.

I roll my eyes. "Right. He took his mask off on the drive, but I didn't recognize him. Did you?"

Jace exhales. "I didn't see him."

"What?"

"The car stopped a final time, and then... nothing. It took me some time to get out of the zip ties, and then another few minutes to get the trunk open. When I got out, we were on the outskirts of Sterling Falls, but there was no one around." He glances at me. "I learned that the car was stolen. Dead end there. And the guy was gone."

"Shit. It's been bugging me."

"I wish I saw his face."

I reach out and lay my hand on his forearm. His muscles jump beneath my palm, but I hold on tight. "He took me to my parents."

"Your father's friend," Jace guesses.

I nod. "My parents kept me home for a month, trying to... assimilate me, I guess. I saw therapists, but other than that I didn't really leave the house. I was a wreck, knowing Parker was in Sterling Falls and Wolfe and Apollo were sitting in jail..." I swallow, now knowing that they *weren't* sitting in jail. They were starting their sentence working for Cerberus. "Anyway, they thought I needed professional help."

"Where did they send you?" Jace's voice is low.

I gulp another mouthful of the whiskey. I stare down at the liquid in the bottom of the mug, then drain the rest of it. It burns a path down my throat, heat pooling in my chest. "Isle of Paradise," I say on a laugh. "Have you heard of it?"

He makes a face.

"I'll take that as a yes." I stand, shaking out my limbs. "I was there for five months before Nyx found me last night and helped me get off that stupid island."

"And your parents?"

I look away. They tried to visit, but I wasn't having it. "The facility won't know I'm missing until mid-morning.

Then they'll probably search the island before calling them and letting them know I'm gone."

He stands, too. My heart skips a beat when he stops in front of me, and he reaches for my hands.

"Do you forgive me, Kora?"

"That's a loaded question." I grip his fingers tightly. Physical contact is a funny thing. You think you can survive without it. Without affection. But then you go months without anyone touching you, and suddenly...

We move forward at the same time.

He must feel it, too. Sterling Falls has been under siege. Sex tends to get taken off the table for vigilantes. Because that's what he is. On his own, isolated. My chest aches for him.

Our lips crash together. I wind my arms around his neck, and his slide down my sides. He grips my ass and lifts me. I wrap my legs around his hips. Our mouths open, tongues tangling. I taste whiskey and inhale the smokey flavor.

He sets me down on the cot, my head on the pillow and blanket stack, and his hands rove up and down my body. Trying to touch everything at once.

I pull his shirt off, our lips separating long enough for me to get it over his head and toss it away. He removes my sweatshirt, then shirt. He stares down at my chest for a moment, and my heartbeat thunders in my ears.

But he's just admiring, maybe, because he ducks down and kisses my collarbone. He grinds his hips against mine, his erection not quite enough between the layers of clothing.

We separate again, yanking our pants off, and then he comes back. I grip his cock, sliding my hand down it, before he captures my wrists and pulls my arms away. He holds them hostage above my head and lines up his cock with my entrance. He's *right there*, but then he pauses.

"Tell me you want this," he says, his face right over mine.

I arch, trying to get him to go deeper. "Show me how much you missed me, Jace."

He lets out a breath and shifts. He thrusts his monster cock into me, and my eyes close. Fucking hell. He stretches me, almost painfully, but he doesn't give me time to settle. He moves at a furious pace. His forearms frame my head, his hands gripping my wrists still.

I gasp. He's hitting a spot inside me that feels too good to be true. I writhe, fighting the sensation. Pointless, though. He plows through my orgasm, his lips swallowing my moans. I shudder, and my vision goes white.

My hearing goes out for a second. Like all I can focus on, and absorb, is the feel of him inside me.

And then I'm back.

He grunts, nipping my lower lip, and he rolls his hips. Then again. He's chasing his own high, and I can only admire the way his body flexes against mine. I lean forward and kiss his neck. Then bite. My teeth catch his skin, and my tongue soothes the spot a second later. I work my way higher, until I get to his ear.

He stills inside me, coming with a groan. He pumps a few more times, then stills.

"We should've done that sooner," I say, my tongue flicking his ear. Because... *wow*.

Talk about bad timing, though.

He chuckles and lowers more of his body weight onto me. He meets my eyes. "I'm glad you're back. But maybe you shouldn't have come."

I narrow my eyes. "You're really out to ruin a good thing, huh?"

"It's dangerous."

"Fuck your danger, Jace." I tug my arms down, but he holds me fast. Pinned... in more ways than one. "I can keep myself safe."

He rotates my wrist and brushes his thumb over the brand. It's settled now, still silvery white but no longer raised.

"I forgive you for that," I whisper. "Stop beating yourself up. We have a lot of people counting on us."

That snaps him out of it. And it might backfire on me, because the walls slam down behind his eyes. I was *so close*. He almost let me in. I had his trust for a second, and now he's gone. The reminder that we're not alone did it. Wolfe and Apollo—I won't just forget about them.

And neither should he.

"Right." He withdraws.

I immediately miss the weight of him, but I don't say anything. He disappears outside, butt naked, and then the soft rumble of a motor drifts in. He reappears and frowns. "Should've started the generator before. It'll take some time to heat up the water."

I rise. The camp believed in *invigorating* showers. Meant to cleanse—not comfort. Their showers were timed and lukewarm at best, if the sun had been kind to the tanks of water outside the dorms.

Jace watches me move across the space and into the tiny bathroom. The shower is no more than a spigot on the ceiling and a drain on the floor.

The weight of his eyes is a lot. It flushes my skin—that could also be the whiskey, but I think not—and knots my stomach.

He turns me inside out without even trying. And he doesn't have to say what he's thinking. I can guess. That he'd rather shuffle me out of the way. Maybe lock me in this shack while he goes off and fights the big bad monsters of Sterling Falls.

"You've had six months," I tell him. "It's my turn."

He watches me through the doorway as I turn on the water and step under the icy blast. I tip my head back, letting it sluice through my hair and down my back. Goose-bumps rise, but I ignore it. And the urge to shiver.

He's staring at me like he doesn't know me. And maybe that's true. I'm different. I'm not afraid anymore.

He can watch all he wants.

Eat your heart out.

CHAPTER 10
APOLLO

Sheriff Nathan Bradshaw sits in front of me. He kicks his legs out into the aisle, taking his time to settle in. Of all of us, I can't say he's fared the worst. He has circles under his eyes, and I think he's probably been running on empty for a few months. But he still looks like himself. His hair is still brushed and trimmed, his beard taken care of, his pallor... normal. Unlike some who have been wasting away under the pressure of this war, he's surviving.

Once he's comfortable, he pulls the waiting mug of coffee closer to himself and doctors it with cream and sugar.

I wait in silence.

"Okay, Apollo," Bradshaw finally says. "Why am I here?"

"Something happened."

His jaw tics. "A few somethings, actually. It would be more unusual if something didn't happen. Can you be more specific?"

I take a sip from my own mug, then set it down. The waitress comes back with two plates of apple pie. I take one from her, smiling, and the other goes in front of Bradshaw. He stares at it for a second, then her. I wonder if he recognizes Wolfe's family member. A cousin on his mom's side, I think.

She eyes the sheriff's badge on his chest but doesn't say anything else.

"You should try the pie." I take a bite. It's the perfect combination of sweet and crisp. Apple pie can definitely be eaten for breakfast. It's just one of those things that works at any time of day. "I'm referring to the burning car in West Falls that your men responded to a few hours ago."

"You have interest in that?"

I smile. "You don't?"

His expression hardens. "Don't be smart with me. I was there. It was hit by a fucking rocket-propelled grenade. A bazooka or some shit in Sterling Falls." He shakes his head, finally succumbing and trying the pie. Once he's chewed and swallowed, he adds, "It has Hell Hounds written all over it."

"Cerberus doesn't have that kind of fire power." I lean back in the booth, casting a glance around. It's not often that I'm let off my leash long enough to do this. But Cerberus thinks I'm on patrol three blocks away. Morning shifts are the worst—and this is his punishment for the warehouse issue the other day. "Were they moving cash?"

Bradshaw sighs. "No. We don't know what it was. Only two Titans were found in the vehicle—burnt to a crisp—and no other evidence. No witnesses. No other vehicles. Nothing."

"The DEA still in town?" Parker Warton, specifically. I was drugged the last time I met him, but I couldn't forget his face. Not after Wolfe filled me in on who he was.

I can't seem to shake the memory of his smug expression that the news crew caught when they led us out of the house. They're the Sterling Falls Drug Enforcement Agency, but they operate mainly out of Emerald Cove. Because some say this city is a lost cause, and they like to win cases.

Some say Sterling Falls is overrun by savages, too. But that's not the whole town. There are parts that make this place seem glossy and clean. A destination. North Falls, the university, the financial district. Well—it's mostly gone to shit now, but *before*.

Bradshaw grunts. "They've overtaken my office—the actual police force has had to relocate. So I don't think they're leaving anytime soon, especially with new drugs on the scene."

My phone chirps. I glance at the screen, then shift to pull my wallet from my pocket. I toss a twenty down and rise. I drain the last of my coffee and shoot him a smile. "Pleasure doing business with you, Sheriff."

Bradshaw grunts. "You didn't give me anything helpful."

I lean down, tapping the table. "Sure I did. I just told you the Hell Hounds didn't cause that wreck. That should narrow down your suspect list considerably."

But who did do it?

Jace, maybe. Or someone trying to cover their tracks.

I stride out the door and into the cool morning. It's still gloomy as shit, and the sky is threatening rain. It smells like it when the wind picks up, and I think I might just be unlucky enough to get hosed on. I walk past the frat row, toward Sterling Falls University. No parties lately, but there are people out and about. College guys sitting on their porches, smoking and watching.

They all fall silent when I pass. I'm only a few years older than them. If my life was different, I might've been one of them. Artemis could've been a sorority girl. I'd have gotten my degree in marketing or business and strived to wear a fucking suit all day, every day.

Maybe it's for the best that things happened the way they did.

The campus has been operating as usual. Cerberus got the go-ahead from the mayor to protect and patrol—and that's exactly what we're doing. Under the guise of keeping this section of the city safe, we've made it ours.

There's a new restaurant that opened up a block over. It's a front for drugs—both cleaning the money and distributing product. People come in and order anything on the menu *deluxe* style, and they get a baggie of drugs with their plate. There's a real chef, of course, and if the server gets a whiff of cop, the drugs disappear. It's a tight operation.

Who knows if the sheriff is aware *that's* going on. It seems his leash is being jerked just as much as mine, although he'd never admit it.

He's too proud for that.

He knows there's new drugs on the street, and I know there's a good chance it came from the Hell Hounds' restaurant.

A car pulls up beside me, the windows completely blacked out. I stop and face it, my hand settling on the gun at my hip. Gone are the days of pretending we aren't carrying. The only people who give a shit don't have the power to change it.

After a moment, the window scrolls down and Malik scowls at me.

"What are you doing?" he snaps.

"Patrol. As ordered."

He narrows his eyes. If he doesn't believe me, he doesn't say anything. I'm three blocks from where I should be after all. "Get in. Boss wants us back at headquarters."

"Why?"

Malik scoffs. "Are you dense? You know what day it is."

Ah.

I let out a sigh and circle to the passenger side, yanking the door open and sliding in. Malik and I were never friends. Friendly, maybe, in a vague sort of way. But he didn't forgive us for leaving the Hell Hounds in the first place. He's all about loyalty, and he thinks we betrayed Cerberus.

We did. But that doesn't really fucking matter nowadays. He can't be trusted. No one can.

CHAPTER 11
KORA

L eave it to Jace to ruin a good thing. I stew over his abrupt change on our way to North Falls. Did he think I was going to forget about Wolfe and Apollo?

Did he think we could just ride off into the sunset or something?

It takes us longer than usual to get to the restaurant. We dodge police cars and foot patrols in the center of the city—men who are clearly Hell Hounds. They don't wear badges, but they walk with authority. And their weapons are visible for all to see.

At one point, Jace pulls into an alley and kills the engine, waiting for a blacked-out SUV to pass. We're near campus. A flapping poster catches my attention, and I hop off the bike before Jace can stop me. I go to the mouth of the alley and flip my visor up, and find a photo of...

Myself.

"What is this?" I yank it down to read it better.

Wanted: Kora Sinclair

It lists bogus charges under it. Homicide, burglary, kidnapping.

There's a reward, too.

I stare at it in disbelief. My heartbeat is loud in my ears, blocking out all other sound. Just a rushing, *whoosh*.

Jace grabs the paper and crushes it in his fist. He tosses it to the ground. "We need to keep moving."

I pick up the paper from where he dropped it and smooth it the best I can, tucking it in my back pocket. My mind is reeling. There are three others on the wall, too. Two of my face, but one of Jace. Just a sketch of him. I pull it loose and tuck it into my pocket, vowing to question him more thoroughly about it later. But there's one pressing question that I need answered.

"Who set this up?"

He doesn't so much as look back at me, and it sets my teeth on edge. My boots crunch over broken glass and debris.

Sterling Falls is coming apart at the seams.

"Did the sheriff?" My heart skips. "Parker?"

Jace's shoulders rise.

I'm poking at a sore subject, I think. It should be the other way around—I should be the one aggravated by Parker's name. But it doesn't, so I guess that stupid camp therapy was good for something.

"Cerberus? Kronos?" I keep asking, stalking after him. "Jace. Who—"

"I don't know," Jace snaps. He wheels around and stops just shy of touching me. "I don't fucking know, Kora. It could be any of them."

I reel back.

"Up until a few nights ago, I hadn't talked to my best friends in months," he continues, coming into my space. "I didn't know where the hell you went. I've been this *fugitive*. On the run constantly, in hiding. I've managed a quarter of the things I wanted to accomplish, none of which actually had any impact."

His chest heaves.

I automatically reach out and press my hand over his heart. "It's okay," I say. "We'll figure it out." I glance over my shoulder, to the empty street. "But you're right—we should go."

He grumbles but doesn't disagree. We get back on the bike and make it the rest of the way to Antonio's without incident. He pulls me back before I can reach the door, and he slides his gun out of the holster. I press my lips together but ultimately stay silent as he steps softly through the doorway.

I catch the heavy metal door so it doesn't slam. We're in a tight hallway lined with wire shelving. We creep forward, where voices come out of the kitchen.

All of a sudden, a flash of movement comes from in front of us.

Nyx aims a gun at us, a flashlight in her other hand blindingly bright.

"It's just us!" I call.

The light disappears, and Jace swears. "I almost fucking shot you."

Nyx shakes her head, meeting us halfway. She hugs him tightly, keeping her hands—which are still stained red—off his back. She releases him and comes to me, and I raise my eyebrows. A silent question.

"He'll be okay," she tells me, cinching me to her side. "Thank you, Kora."

Jace doesn't say anything, but he slips past her into the commercial kitchen. I follow him, Nyx taking up the rear. Antonio is leaning over Saint, tending to a wound on his chest. Not the stab wound, which seems to have been stitched closed.

Artemis leans against the wall opposite, watching him. Her arms are folded over her chest. Her gaze lifts to Jace, and her scowl deepens. "We've been searching for you."

He shakes his head. "I couldn't risk it."

I scoff.

"You've always got to be the lone wolf, huh?"

Jace looks at me. "No, Kora. I just wasn't going to endanger them—"

"Safety in numbers, Jace." I mean, *come on*. Who willingly stays out in the cold? "You've obviously done such a terrific job on your own."

I can't help but press on wounds he bared to me earlier. Now who's the one who has to ruin a good thing? And the way Jace is glaring at me, we're slipping back into our old ways.

"Okay, okay," Antonio says quietly. "No fighting. Please. Quiet."

Tem tips her head toward the door. I nod once, and she pushes off the wall. Jace and I follow her out. She goes behind the bar and grabs three glasses, filling them with water. At Jace's expression, she snorts.

I take it and drink it all, then set the empty glass back down. I wander away, toward the front of the restaurant. The windows are tinted, the lights off. A closed sign hangs in the door. From the front, it looks like the restaurant is just closed for the morning.

Easy.

I turn back around. "Tell me about Wolfe and Apollo."

Artemis closes her eyes. "It's... not great."

"Details." I drag a chair out from the nearest table and sit. I point to the other two, and Jace and Artemis join me.

"They were arrested," she begins.

"I saw that on the news before the Titans hit the clubhouse."

She winces. "Yeah. You're not the only one. Cerberus has a lawyer on retainer, so the guy went by and schmoozed a deal. They go back to the Hell Hounds and plead to carrying the drugs under duress. No jail time, and they agreed to testify..."

"That worked?"

Jace snorts. "Temporarily. The judge threw out the plea deal. Said it was too easy for them to pin it on the one man who wasn't in town at the time."

I connect the dots. "Cerberus wanted Kronos to take the fall for the drugs."

"Made sense. Kronos was the one who planted them to keep the guys busy while he tried to auction you off." Tem lifts her head, eyeing the ceiling. "I'd bet Kronos just didn't count on the justice system moving so slow, it rendered his plan useless."

"Until the attack." I tap my fingers on the table. I'm itching to *do* something. I want to see the rest of Sterling Falls, to catalog everything that's different and make sure that when we do fix it, it goes back to being the city I fell in love with.

An impossible task, I'm afraid.

"Until the attack," Jace says. "Then, it seemed like his timing was impeccable."

His voice is bitter. Understandably.

"This is for you." Artemis pulls a small notebook out of her pocket. It's thin, worn. The edges are folded over, the black leather front crinkled. She slides it across the table to me. "First page."

I open it. It's a guy's handwriting, cramped and tight. I

don't recognize it—but that's not surprising. I haven't examined the guys' handwriting. Didn't think that was necessary when I was with them.

There's just enough light in here, coming through the tinted front windows, for me to make out the words.

I flip to the end and see a scrawled -A. Apollo.

My heart skips. I go back to the beginning and read in earnest.

I DON'T KNOW if I can take this anymore.

Dramatic, much? I'm well aware. I don't know what happened. My ears are still fucking ringing from the bombs that went off. And now we're here. My sister is the wise one, bringing us a way to communicate.

But this first note isn't for you, asshole. It's for Kora. In case Tem finds her.

So unless your name is Kora, stop reading.

THE PAGE BLURS. I swipe at my eyes, unsurprised that they're filling with tears. Damn, I miss Apollo so much it hurts. There's a knot in my chest.

KORA, *baby. I don't know where you are, and it's driving me insane. I want nothing more than to escape these shackles and find you. You know I'd search every inch of this country if I could.*

I hope you're okay.

I hope whoever took you had your best interests at heart.

Ironic, is it not, that they managed to get you out of town right as this stupid fucking war breaks out? If Kronos is behind this—

No. Sorry. I want to think positively. I want to imagine you whole and healthy and happy without us.

And I never had a chance to say it, but I'm in l—

I SLAM THE NOTEBOOK SHUT.

My head is a mess.

My *heart* is a mess.

Did he just write out that he loves me? In a notebook that may or may not ever make it to me? *That's* how he wants the first time he says it to be?

When I next see him, we're having *words*. About how to declare your love for someone in literally any other way than a doomsday notebook.

"You okay?" Tem asks.

I look up. Jace has left the table, the door to the kitchen swinging shut behind him. I frown and shake my head, that damn pain in my chest worsening. I thought I'd be stronger than this.

"Do you want to see them?"

"What?" I lean forward and grab her hands. "See them?"

She shifts. "Tonight. I can… make arrangements."

"No." Jace has returned, followed by Nyx. "Absolutely not."

I glare at him. "You're not the boss."

He's not. He stopped being a leader when he let them be taken back to Cerberus. *Ouch*. I didn't realize how much I'd resent him for that move until right this second. And it might get worse before it gets better.

"Like hell I'm not," he mutters.

I rise. "You know what? I regret sleeping with you. The orgasm seems to have addled your brain."

Nyx snorts. "Oh, shit."

Jace glares at me. "I wouldn't have fucked you if you didn't throw yourself at me."

My mouth opens and closes. "Trust me, Jace. You've seen me *throw* myself at someone before. Wolfe. Apollo. What happened between us was far from that." I glower back at him. "Desperate times..."

His expression darkens, but I ignore it and brush by him. I go into the kitchen and past Antonio, who mumbles to himself in Italian while he cleans up around a prone Saint. I pause and stare at them.

Unlike the last time I saw Saint, he looks malnourished. Each rib stands out in sharp relief under the harsh overhead lights. He's got a welted burn in the center of his chest in the shape of an hourglass, plus countless bruises and cuts.

He survived *months* of this sort of abuse?

My heart hurts. I rub my wrist.

"Stairs," Jace finally says, guiding me past the kitchen. "Go on."

I glance back, but he's not looking at me. Still, I nod and murmur my thanks.

The stairs are around another corner, tucked out of the way of the back door. I creep up them and discover an apartment. My bag is sitting on the coffee table. I snatch it and find an empty bedroom, the bed untouched and drawers empty.

Exhaustion hits me. I haven't slept in over twenty-four hours. At the same time, it seems laughable that twenty-four hours ago, I was going about my day on the island. Getting ready to spar with Ben—

Fuck.

How did I forget about Ben? With no way to contact him, and no way for him to find us... what happened to him? Why the hell did we leave him there?

Because he said we didn't have a choice?

There's always a choice.

I let out a breath and lie down on top of the blankets. I keep my shoes on and roll onto my side. When sleep comes, the dreams stay away.

CHAPTER 12
KORA

"This seems ominous," I mutter to Tem.

She woke me up an hour ago and proceeded to make me, in her words, "fit to leave the apartment." When she finished her work, she turned me loose to look in the bathroom mirror.

And, sure enough, I barely recognized myself.

She glances at me now, her lips pressing together. "It'll get worse before it gets better."

We're in Antonio's car, heading east. Jace was gone by the time I left the bathroom. Nyx and Saint were shut away in one of the bedrooms. Antonio gave us a lingering look on our way out the door, then finally nodded at us.

Tem put me in a tight, long-sleeved black shirt. Black jeans. Black boots. My makeup is dark and smokey. Even my lipstick is such a dark red, it's almost black. I feel Gothic.

Except for the blonde hair.

She had me braid back my hair, and then she brought out *the wig*. She looked from it, in her hands, to me. Hopeful.

I didn't really feel like disappointing her by putting on

the brakes at that moment. Besides, my red hair is notice-able. If anyone is searching for me, they're going to be expecting dark-red hair. A nose ring. An hourglass brand on my wrist.

All the things listed at the bottom of the wanted poster, plus my height and weight, eye color, skin tone...

The blonde bangs brush my eyebrows. They tickle, and I fight the urge to scratch at it.

We come down a familiar road.

I have a bad feeling in the pit of my stomach. "Here?"

She grimaces. "It's Friday night."

"I didn't think—"

"It's different. Trust me, it's not what you're expecting."

She pulls into the long driveway for Olympus. I lean forward, my heart in my throat. It doesn't seem too different from the outside. The cars are parked haphazardly. There are fewer cars, too. Not the crowd that fight nights used to bring.

We get out of the car, and Tem pops the trunk open. She grabs a lacy black mask and tosses it to me, then withdraws a matching one for herself. It seems strange not to put on a mask of flowers—but that's the point. I'm undercover.

"How often do you come?" I ask in a low voice.

There are more people milling around outside. The doors of Olympus are still closed.

"I've been once before." She frowns. "I didn't want to risk coming again. In case."

There's a loud boom, and the huge doors creak open. Dim light spills out across the lawn.

"That's our cue."

We, along with others, make our way toward Olympus. I have that same fluttery feeling in my chest that I had the first night. Nerves, anxiety. I don't know what to expect.

There's no masked men at the entrance. Just a giant man with a Hell Hounds leather jacket on, collecting an entrance fee. The people ahead of us don't make eye contact with him. They seem in a hurry to escape his gaze. Artemis hands him cash for the both of us, and then we're inside.

The atrium is nothing like before.

The last time I was here, the guys had transformed it to include me. A wall of flowers and ivy. The staircase that goes to a landing, then splits into two, is no longer bathed in light. The steps where Apollo, then Saint, gave their welcome speeches.

My boot catches on a piece of loose stone, and I glance down. There's a circle on the floor that people are avoiding. We avoid it, too. Moving away from the circle of sand and cut glass, toward the far wall.

"They fight in here," Tem whispers. "There are rumors that Cerberus will grant favors like the guys used to do. Sometimes they use the fights as auditions to join the Hell Hounds."

I glance around. No one wears finery. No dresses, no suits. Everyone here seems to be prepared for a fight. Boots, dark pants. Clothes for fighting—as if they've prepared just in case.

We're the same. Artemis wears a similar outfit to mine, the only difference is an olive-green shirt under a black vest. A little pop of color. And her brown hair is braided back but ultimately unchanged.

"They've taken over Olympus," she continues. "Since their clubhouse is gone, they needed somewhere to stay. And with Wolfe and Apollo back under his control—"

Bile rises up my throat. I swallow hard and look away. I don't want to think about what else Cerberus has made them do.

I just want to *see* them.

Has he treated them okay? Wolfe is his son. His only son. Apollo—

Don't think about that.

"You saw them recently?" I ask.

A group of guys passes by us, lingering at our backs.

Tem shoots me a look and stays silent. I understand. The time for talking, for questioning, has passed.

I glance up again to the landing. There was once a statue perched on a throne on the second floor, directly above the landing. My first visit, the forlorn man was coated in black and gold paint. A crown on his head. Then, a wreath of flowers replaced the crown.

Now, the statue is gone.

Well, not *gone*.

Toppled. Broken.

I see it on the edges of the staircase, broken bits of stone. A hand, the side of his face. The rubble lines the lower half of the stairs, kicked out of the way by use. Where the statue once sat is now one of the thrones. Hades' throne, if I'm not mistaken.

The doors shut with an ominous crash.

Someone cheers. *Yells.* My heart jumps, banging against my ribcage, at the awful, violence-saturated noise. These people want a fight. More than any Olympus of the past. They're wild, unhinged. There's no order.

Cerberus approaches out of the shadows. He steps in front of the throne, looking down at us with a bare face.

He seems the same as he did six months ago. Time did not affect him the way it does normal people. In fact, he seems better. Healthier.

This war might very well be swinging in his favor.

"Are you ready?" he asks.

The sound spikes again. Artemis nudges me, raising her fist and jeering along with the rest of them. I follow along, opening my mouth. No sound comes out. It's trapped in my throat.

"Clear the ring." He makes a motion with his hand. "Who's up first?"

He shifts forward on his throne, his gaze moving over everyone. A dare.

Artemis pulls me forward, closer to the circle, just in time to see someone step into it.

The crowd roars.

"Our first contender," Cerberus says. "What's your name, son?"

"Simon," the man calls. He keeps his gaze on the man in charge.

"Simon," Cerberus repeats. "And what will you ask for if you win?"

"This is how he rigs it," Tem whispers in my ear. "First person in the circle gets to ask for whatever he wants. Second person in has almost always been a Hell Hound, fighting for a better rank."

Simon's throat moves. Behind his black mask, he seems angry. His brows are drawn. There's a scar peeking out from under the bottom of the mask, continuing through his twisted lips. Tattoos on his biceps.

"I'd ask for entrance into the Hell Hounds," he finally says. "To belong to something worth fighting for."

Cerberus nods. "We *are* worth fighting for," he agrees. His gaze lands on someone else in the crowd. "Who will fight him?"

His gaze slides away, like he was asking the whole crowd. But that person, the one chosen by Cerberus, steps over the crushed-glass-and-sand border. He lifts his chin.

"Name?" Cerberus drawls.

"Logan, sir."

Tem snorts. "See?"

She's got a point. I shiver and slip between two guys. Artemis sticks with me, creeping forward. I just want a better view, although I don't want to risk Cerberus recognizing me. Or anyone else, for that matter.

"What will you ask for if you win?"

Logan sneers. He's got a few inches on his opponent, his hair buzzed short. He strips off his shirt and tosses it outside the circle. "I want a promotion."

Cerberus chuckles, nodding. "Okay, son. Let's get on with it, then. We've got a special guest here tonight. Some of you sorry lot might remember him." He points down, and the crowd automatically parts.

My heart stops.

Apollo strides out. He wears a plain brown mask with ugly horns protruding out of the forehead. There's gold smeared on his body, but it's not the same. Someone did it with a lot less care, and a spike of anger crashes through me that someone else was touching him.

But the most shocking thing of all?

The metal collar around his neck.

The crowd murmurs. Some jeer, others whisper. It's an odd reaction—and it makes me wonder if this is the first time he's brought out Apollo like this. If this is some sort of punishment for Apollo. And if it is, what did he do?

Artemis grabs my hand, lacing her fingers with mine and squeezing tightly. I squeeze back, and that's the only way I don't throw myself forward.

He doesn't carry the staff, or anything else. The collar isn't connected to anything—it's just a symbol.

A terrible fucking symbol.

He strides up to the line and steps over it.

He's barefoot.

The crushed glass mixed with sand isn't for the fighters —it's another punishment.

"Look," Tem says, tugging on my hand.

I turn toward the stairs. A figure in red comes down slowly, painfully. He's not wearing a mask. A red shirt under the Hell Hounds leather jacket, unzipped. There's red paint around his eyes, wet and smudged down his cheeks.

His eyes are red, too. The contacts in place, obscuring the green I love.

I can't take this.

I wanted to see them—but this is nearly unbearable. Wolfe continues down and sits on the landing. His legs splay, and his expression is unreadable.

On the floor, Apollo has stepped back again. His collar clinks when he moves. Or maybe that's just my imagination running away with me.

"Ready," he calls to Cerberus.

"Great," the latter answers. "Well? Get to it, then."

I don't know what I should've expected. Not anything with a semblance of manners, I suppose. But somehow this fight is worse than any under the guys' oversight. It's an immediate bloodbath.

Eventually, one of the fighters manages to pin the other. His body jerks with every hit, and blood soaks the floor. The room goes quiet.

Apollo stalks forward and rips the man off the fallen one, shoving him backward. All our eyes are glued on Apollo, who circles the prone fighter, then goes to the standing one. He looks to Cerberus, then grabs the man's wrist. He raises it.

The crowd cheers.

I lean toward Artemis. "He's perverted it," I whisper.

She makes a face.

Cerberus stands, and the cheering fades back down to quiet. No one has moved the fallen fighter—the first man to step into the circle.

"Logan," Cerberus says. "Do you still want to rise in the ranks of the Hell Hounds?"

"Yes, sir," he replies.

Cerberus nods, motioning him to come closer. Apollo drops his wrist and lets the fighter step over the circle, up the stairs. Logan stops just shy of the landing.

"Lieutenant," Cerberus declares. Just like that. His gaze moves past him, to the man still on the floor. "Toss that sorry excuse for a fighter."

A buzz goes through the crowd, and Artemis and I are pulled along as everyone begins to move to the door. It doesn't stop there, though. We head outside, along the side of Olympus. Toward the cliffs.

My stomach twists.

This is what happens to the losers?

The guy wakes up when he's three feet from the edge. He has just enough wherewithal to struggle against the two Hell Hounds gripping his arms, but not enough strength to fight the inevitable.

They push him off. His scream mixes with the rushing wind.

I squeeze Tem's hand and struggle against the bile rising up my throat. "I need to leave," I whisper.

She nods. "Fine by me."

CHAPTER 13
JACE

I stand in the room where Kronos kept Saint. There are chains on the floor and a pool of drying blood. I came out here for clarity, but all I have are more questions.

Why did Kronos abandon this place so easily?

It was a good spot. Outside of Sterling Falls, barely. Perfect to avoid the sheriff, if he's not in the Titans' pocket. He kept Kora here, too, I guess, when he auctioned her to the highest bidder. We failed to find her then, and we nearly failed again.

I guess I've done nothing *but* fail in the last six months.

No, farther back than that. Ten months. Five years going on six.

Since the day we left the Hell Hounds and tried to put an end to the violence in Sterling Falls.

I laugh quietly, my self-loathing at an all-time high.

What the fuck are we supposed to do now?

From what Nyx said before I left Antonio's, there was a shoot-out. An explosion. A crafted plan to rescue Saint that worked out pretty well... but she left something out. And she wouldn't say what it was.

I leave the cell and go the opposite way I came, finding another set of stairs. The rest of the rooms down here are empty. Some have cots. Others just have thin mattresses on the floor. Buckets for piss, if the prisoners were lucky enough.

Who else have they captured and interrogated?

I find the destroyed propane tank outside. Whoever shot it had good aim. One bullet to take it out. There's blood on the sheet-metal walls around head height, but no body. No bodies anywhere.

I crouch beside a deep tire tread, then look around and try to visualize what the fuck happened.

"Kronos fled first."

I jump up and pull my gun. The man who spoke raises his hands in surrender, a small frown marring his face. He has blood on his jaw, and a bruised cheek, but otherwise seems whole. He's ten feet away, on the opposite side of the driveway. Close enough to the tree line that he might've been there all along.

A Hell Hound? Someone left to guard the place or watch for who swooped in after the attack?

"Who are you?" I demand. I'm furious with myself to have allowed him to get too close.

Sloppy.

He steps forward, and I tilt my head.

"I wouldn't take another step closer if you want to keep breathing."

He goes still. "I know you."

"Most people do." I narrow my eyes. "I asked you a question."

He sighs. He's got dark, short hair. A fighter's build, a good mix of bulky and lean. I don't like the way he's positioned himself, like he could spring forward or back at a moment's notice.

It puts me on edge.

"Ben," he finally says. "I'm a friend."

I stiffen. "Yeah, fucking right."

He lifts one shoulder. "You're here because you want to know what happened. Right, Jace King?"

I don't lower my gun, but I do incline my chin ever so slightly. "Start talking."

Ben moves to the side and points up the hill half obscured by trees. "Kora and I waited up there."

Fuck.

"I shot the propane tank, causing an explosion. A diversion. It drew out the Titans and gave Artemis and Nyx a chance to get inside." He eyes my weapon again, then seems to make a conscious decision to ignore it. He strides past me. "They went through a door on the other side, but Kronos came out here. I tried to kill him, but he got into his car too fast."

I scoff.

He shoots me a bland look, then continues, "War happens fast, Batman. Surely you're aware of that."

"Fuck off."

He smiles. "Anyway. Kora and I approached this door—"

"You let her go in?"

"She's stronger than she seems." He raises an eyebrow. "Maybe I'll let her prove that to you. *Anyway*, we found Saint, but there were inbound Titan vehicles. We got out of there."

"*We*? You weren't in that vehicle. No one mentioned you." I contemplate shooting him. I've got a bad feeling. But what if he's telling the truth? What if he knows Kora? She'd probably kill *me* if I touched him. Not because that's logical, but because she likes to do whatever the fuck she pleases with no regard for anything else.

"You're right—I stayed behind and diverted their attention." He shrugs. "One vehicle got past me. Now, will you put that gun down?"

"No. I don't trust you."

"Kora does."

"She's not here right now, and I'm not about to take your word for it." This infuriating guy. "How about you go run back into the woods and I'll forget this conversation ever happened."

"Don't you want to know where Kronos is hiding now?" He tilts his head. "A new foxhole, so to speak."

"And you know where that is."

"Of course." He shrugs. "My assault could only last so long. I hid in the woods while they burned their dead a half mile west of here. Then followed them to Kronos."

I don't trust it.

I don't trust him.

"You could take me to Kora," he offers. "She'll vouch for me."

Those are my options, then? Take him to Kora or follow him to Kronos? Darkness is falling, and I shift on my feet as I try to decide what the fuck to do with him. I can't just let him go—if he does know, then Kronos might be targeting him.

Or it could be a trap.

But I will *not* risk her. Not after knowing exactly how painful it was to have her ripped away from me once.

"Fuck it," I mutter. I stow my gun and gesture forward. "Lead the way."

CHAPTER 14
KORA

Tem and I stand in the forest beside Olympus. The same forest that Jace, Apollo, and Wolfe chased me through once upon a time. She's got a flashlight in her teeth and a hand-drawn map in her grip.

Our plan borders on crazy. We got in her car and left after the fighter was chucked over the cliff, but she didn't take us back to Antonio's. She circled around and found a narrow, two-track lane that led into the forest. We got out and hiked the rest of the way, my disguise still in effect—plus a handgun now strapped to my thigh.

I ignore the itchiness of the wig and my cramping stomach. My anxiety is taking over. We waited for the fights to break up. Honestly, they went on longer than I thought they would. But only one other person was pushed over the cliffs. I don't know what that means for the other fighters. If they lived and made deals, or if Cerberus did something else to them.

Something worse?

"Got it?"

I jerk back to reality.

Tem looks at me, her eyebrows raised. "Maybe I should run through it one more time."

I wave her off. "No, I've got it. He's expecting you?"

She shrugs. "He won't shoot you, if that's what you're concerned about. But, yeah. He knows I'll be coming some-time this week. So it's perfect timing."

Okay. Great. I take a deep breath and pull my hood up. Blonde hair or no, I don't want to take any chances. In the gloom, everything is encased in darkness. Tem kills the power on the flashlight, and I follow her along the trail to the tree line.

"Stick to my route and don't do anything crazy," she reminds me.

"Right." I swallow, then step out. I cross the lawn in a crouch, and part of me keeps expecting... I don't know. Sirens? Alarms? A giant spotlight, at the very least.

It seems quiet, though. It's almost three o'clock in the morning—we waited an hour after the last car had driven away. My skin prickles, but I don't stop until my fingers brush the cool marble of Olympus.

I let out a little breath.

From there, I stick to the deeper shadows, following the building around to a familiar entrance. It's on the corner, close to the cliffs, and leads into a hall that goes to the main room. Where the guys hosted the fights, and what I now imagine to be a war room of sorts.

I press my ear to the crack in the door, listening care-fully. Tem said to wait for a patrolling Hell Hound to pass, count to ten, then enter. It seems to take an eternity for the footsteps, the muffled thump of each boot hitting the marble floor.

Count to ten.

Enter.

I open the door and slip through, keeping my back to the door as I gently close it. It clicks shut, and I glance around. I'm in the corner of the building. The hallway goes in two directions from here, straight and left, toward the front atrium.

I go straight, then grab the second sconce on the wall. I pull it. Immediately, a grating noise comes from an alcove farther down the hallway. The candelabra goes back into place, and I hurry to the alcove. The marble has slid back, revealing one of the hidden staircases.

If Wolfe hadn't showed me a similar one, I wouldn't have had as much faith in Tem's plan.

As it is, I step inside, and the marble wall slides back into place.

I put my hands out, one on either wall, and make my way up the spiraling steps. I'm in here, and my heart is being torn in two directions. Wolfe. Apollo. I want to see both of them, but Tem insisted that staying any longer, especially moving around inside Olympus, increases the danger tenfold.

Imagine what might happen if Cerberus found me?

How he'd use me to manipulate them even further?

The masked man, my father's friend, is the only reason Jace didn't end up arrested... and then enslaved.

I shiver. I reach the top of the stairs and wait another moment, although I can't hear anything through the thick stone. I find a little latch on the wall and pull. There's another grinding noise, louder on this side, and something gives. A sliver of low light comes through a new crack.

It pushes open, and I step into a shadowed alcove. It

shields me from the hallway that overlooks the old fighting room, with the closed-off balconies that everyone flocked to for the best views. Now for the hard part: getting down the hall unseen, to another staircase four alcoves down.

I take a deep breath and am about to step out when someone calls out.

I jump backward, pressing my back to the stone. A man strides past, his focus elsewhere. On someone else.

"Wolfe. Your father wants to see you."

My heart skips.

"Does he not realize well-rested soldiers perform better?" Wolfe asks, just out of sight.

The man scoffs. "If I had the authority to question him..."

"Yeah, yeah. Fine. Where is he?"

I'm desperate to creep forward and catch a glimpse of him without that red paint on his face. To see the *real* him. But I know if I do see him, I'll see the mask that he wears— not my Wolfe.

"He's downstairs."

Wolfe grumbles something, and their footsteps lead away from my hiding place. I wait a minute, then inch out again. The hall is empty, so I take my chance and run— admittedly, on tiptoe—to the last alcove. It's opposite the direction Wolfe and the other guy went. I pull the sconce, and it clicks down about three inches. I slip into the spiral staircase, unfazed when the wall closes behind me.

These stairs are familiar. They lead up to a hallway with little grates in the wall close to the floor, giving a grainy view of the main room far below.

Tem said third door. They're only on the left, with nothing but open space on the other side of the right wall. I touch the dark-stained wood, running my fingers down the grain until I touch the handle.

Another door, farther down, cracks open.

I curse my own lingering foolishness and open Wolfe's door. I step inside and close the door swiftly behind me, leaning against it. Not a moment too soon, footsteps sound on the other side. I hold my breath until they're gone.

It's only then that I look around.

A desk.

Some chairs.

A window that lets in the faint moonlight.

The only change is the addition of a cot in the corner, similarly set up to Jace's in his little boat shack. The thin pillow, the bedding rolled up like he doesn't expect to stay very long. And a tall standing wardrobe in the corner, stuffed full of clothes so the doors sit *almost* closed. But not quite.

The last time I was in this room, I was with Wolfe. He went down on me and, quite honestly, changed my viewpoint about men.

My experience leading up to that was... Parker. Who took and took and took, even when my flesh couldn't give any more.

I move away from the door and run my fingers over the top of the desk. I feel like that action, which I find myself repeating in new spaces, grounds me. Touch something real. Solidify myself in this moment.

When I inhale, I smell Wolfe. His spiced scent.

Is he still wearing his red contacts? Or did he get a moment to pluck them out, to wash the paint from around his eyes? To return to some semblance of... normal?

I open the wardrobe and eye the hanging shirts and pants. After a brief inspection, which is mostly by feel in the dark room, I close it again. I double-check that my firearm is still safe in its holster, tucked on the inside of my waistband and pressed against my lower back.

There's a suppressor and an extra magazine in my pocket, thanks to Artemis. She suggested it was never good to go anywhere unprepared—and in war, unprepared means unarmed.

Still, I didn't pull my weapon when I was trying to get up here.

I was going to worry about that when the time came. *If* it came.

After a moment, I go to the window and lean my shoulder against the wall, peering out into the night. His window faces north, but there's not much to see. The moon has shifted behind clouds, muting the glow even further. As I watch, raindrops hit the glass panes. Slow at first, then faster.

It's been trying to rain all day, but it took until three o'clock in the morning for the skies to open up.

Ominous, now.

I wonder if that person survived the fall over the cliffs or if the ocean got the better of him. I wonder how many people Cerberus has had thrown to their death in the past six months. And on top of that, how many people have gotten stuck in the crossfire between the gangs.

How many more people have to die before one of them wins?

And how many will die *because* one of them wins?

I'm too absorbed by my thoughts.

I'm too comfortable being in this room, thinking Wolfe will recognize me. Thinking that I'm *safe* here, in the belly of the beast.

Safety is an illusion. I learn that when something cool

touches the back of my head. It's the unmistakable feel of metal—the muzzle of a gun, if I had to guess.

The door clicks shut on its own, closing us in.

I hold my breath until he speaks.

"Don't move." A demand instead of just killing me.

Maybe there's something human left inside him after all.

CHAPTER 15
WOLFE

The blonde woman at my window goes still. It might be the gun pressed to the back of her head, or the fact that she didn't even seem to notice me enter.

Another trap by my father.

I imagine pulling the trigger without seeing her face—or hearing her out. That's what I *should* do. Cut off any more attempts for him to manipulate me. I've been so surrounded by this lifestyle, like being dragged back into a toxic relationship.

I've been trying, *trying* to keep my head above water.

But some days, I don't know which way is up.

I pull back the safety, and her shoulders hitch. She's still looking out that damn window, which is peculiar in and of itself.

It's raining. Not so strange for May. The bulk of our rain usually comes in April, but it's still spring. Technically. The weather is volatile.

As if to prove me right, lightning flashes across the sky. A great big bolt that illuminates my room for a heartbeat, then fades.

"Did my father send you?" I ask roughly, fighting the urge to grab her shoulder and whip her around. "What did he tell you? To seduce me? Loosen me up?"

My damn father.

He called me down to tell me that he thinks my mission in South Falls was unsuccessful. The warehouse.

"Kronos was spotted yesterday," my father informed me. He sat at that giant table with the map on it. Every time I see it, I can't help but see the scratches on the floor from where his men dragged it in. Just that little thing sets me on edge.

If we ever get free of him, I'm smashing that table to pieces.

He was leaning back, a beer in his hand. He made me stand there while he took a sip or two, his eyes on me. "No bodies were found either."

I shrugged. "Maybe he heard us and got out."

Jace escaped. He's still free.

I continued, "Either way, we'll have another shot at him. *Sir.*"

He dismissed me with a wave of his hand.

The girl moves. She shifts a little, not turning around. I don't know why, except to think that perhaps that's the only thing keeping her alive.

I step back, keeping my gun pressed to the back of her head, and let my gaze sweep down the rest of her.

Black on black, except the hair. There's something under her shirt.

"Put your hands on the window," I order.

She does.

I yank up the back of her shirt and jacket, revealing the black handgun. I toss it onto the desk behind us, silently berating myself. She could've done that ages ago—pulled the gun and shot me, regardless of the consequences. Perhaps she's not sent by my father but by Kronos.

To kill me.

I pat down the rest of her. Her hips, down her legs. Back up her sides. Methodical. Maybe a little cruel in the way my fingers push at her body.

"Turn around," I finally say.

She tips her head to the side, her blonde hair moving to give me a view of her slender neck. Her hand slides across the glass, toward her other one. I watch in disbelief as she defies my order *again*.

This time to slowly pull down her sleeve.

The scar is unmistakable.

An hourglass.

Kora?

"You're not real," I whisper. "This is a trick."

She turns around, seemingly chased by a bolt of lightning—and a moment later, the loud crack of thunder. The storm is almost on top of us, and she flinches ever so slightly.

Not the gun to her head, not my threat to kill her. But from thunder and lightning.

She goes still when she faces me, and I still don't believe it's her. My gun is still up, level now with her eye. She ignores it, meeting my gaze. "Not a trick." Even her voice is exactly how I remember it. Low, seductive without trying. A rasping whisper.

What the fuck does she see right now?

A monster?

Her hair is different. The bangs obscure her forehead and dark eyebrows. The makeup is a new look for her, giving her a devil-may-care aura. And she made it through Olympus. Up *here*.

"You're not real." I squeeze my eyes shut for a second.

How did Cerberus get every detail right except her hair?

She reaches out and touches my face. "Prove it."

I open my eyes, blinking rapidly. Her hand on my face grounds me, cuts through my disbelief—and mistrust.

And I'm pointing a fucking gun at her face.

Horror crashes through me. I don't just drop the gun. I fucking dismantle it. The magazine falls to the floor, then the rest of it in pieces, until I'm left empty-handed.

I almost shot *Kora*. I almost killed her before I knew it was her.

A monster, indeed.

"I'm so, so—"

"Shut up," she says.

Her palm is warm, calloused against my cheek. Her thumb strokes under my eye, her fingers slipping into my short hair. I keep still as she analyzes my face without anything between us. With her other hand, she drags the zipper of her jacket down. She releases me long enough to slip out of it, letting it hit the floor. Then her hand is back on me. Moving down the side of my neck. Lower. My chest.

Her hand presses over my heart.

All the questions I thought I'd have if I ever saw her again vanish. In this moment, I don't care where she's been. I don't care that I let go of her—that I convinced myself she was *gone*. Apollo had said his sister found her, but... I don't think I ever thought she'd come back here.

"Wolfe. Come back to me."

I refocus on her. "I'm right here."

Her lips press together, then smooth out. I don't understand her expression. Or the look in her eyes. She's different, that's for sure. Confident and wrecked all at the same time.

Sad and strong. I don't want her to be different. I don't want her to have gone through something terrible.

"I'm right here," I repeat.

"You're miles and miles away." She steps forward, her chest brushing mine. "What he's done to you—"

"Is nothing."

"Is *everything*."

My heart hurts. Every beat brings me closer to death, I'm convinced. Because what kind of agony is this? Why would she come back to me?

I don't deserve this. "I've done terrible things. You thought you saw that before. You thought you knew my demons..."

She leads me to the cot. Pushes me down onto it, then climbs on my lap. She grabs my face again, harder. She ignores my confession.

"I'm going to kiss you," she whispers. "And maybe I'm being selfish for it. But I'm sorry, I don't think I can go another second without touching you."

And then she's doing it. Leaning in and pressing her dark-stained lips to mine.

I forget how to move. How to breathe.

My chest seizes up.

I just let her kiss me like it's a resuscitation.

When she draws back, her eyes bore into mine. "Demons are just shadows, Wolfe. Your dad has been keeping you in the dark, where they fester. Let's shine some light on them."

Her hands go to my shirt, inching the fabric up. She leans back slightly to get it off. Her hands roam my skin, taking inventory of every new injury. Her fingers find one across my ribs, and I look away.

"I can't fix this in a night." She sweeps her thumb under

my lip, wiping away her lipstick. "But stay strong for me, okay? I'm coming for you."

I nod.

Someone bangs on my door, and we both jump. Her eyes widen, and I pick her up swiftly. She doesn't make a sound when I set her by my wardrobe. There's space between it and the wall, and she turns sideways and slips into it. Not the best hiding place, but it keeps her out of sight from the door.

The person knocks again, and I grumble under my breath. I yank it open.

Apollo stands in the hall, his hands on his hips. He hasn't been up here... well, ever.

"Cerberus left," he says, voice flat. "And he sent me up to tell you that you're in charge while he's gone."

I narrow my eyes. My father has done everything in his power to give us as little time together as possible. I lean into the hall, looking either way.

Empty.

My hackles go up. Metaphorically.

This smells like a trap, and I'm very tempted to slam the door in his face. But I can't do that, so instead I step aside and tip my head.

He strides into the dark room. "You ever heard of a lamp?"

I chuckle. "I've been known to use them on occasion."

It's the middle of the night. I don't point that out, though. These days, we're all running on little sleep—and most of the Hell Hounds are becoming nocturnal. The night is when it's easiest to accomplish what we want to do. What my father wants.

He goes for the light on my desk, and I hurriedly close my door.

The light comes on, blinding for a moment.

The wardrobe door swings shut, and Kora rushes at Apollo. He doesn't have time to prepare before she's on him, jumping and wrapping around him like an octopus.

He automatically catches her.

Bitterness sweeps through me. He's already off to a better start than me.

He holds her tightly, his fingers flexing against her back. He sticks his nose into her neck and inhales sharply, his eyes squeezed shut.

I lean against the door, crossing my arms.

When they finally separate, her feet finding the floor again, they just... stare at each other. Then she touches his neck, and he cringes away. There's no more collar—Dad's choice of punishment, since apparently Apollo went off script this morning. How, I don't know. All I was told was Malik found him a block or two over from where he should've been. Apollo must've taken it off as soon as the crowd dispersed.

I let out a hoarse laugh. Of course she went to my father's twisted fight night.

"How did you get here?" Apollo asks, holding her hands. He leans down, pressing his forehead to hers. "I thought you'd never come back."

Me, too.

She swallows. In the light, it's easier to see what I had missed: she's healthier. Filled out with muscle. And the gun...

Something happened.

With space between us, those questions are coming back.

"Nyx," she whispers. "We rescued Saint. I found Jace—"

"You've been busy," I interject. "What happened to Saint? That he needed rescuing from?"

Apollo shoots me a look. A shut-the-fuck-up look. I raise my eyebrows but fall silent. We both know this is a gift that won't last long. Every minute Kora stays with us, the more danger she's in. It would almost be easier if my father had gone to bed. But he's out, and...

"If you *listen*, I'll tell you," she says. "Saint was captured by Kronos. The bastard stabbed him when we raided his compound—"

"You *what*?" Apollo asks. "You raided—"

"Oh my god, shut *up*." She shakes her head and pulls away, going back to the window. "Do you think I can climb down this?"

Apollo turns and gives me another look. Disbelief, maybe.

"Why—"

"No offense, Apollo, but if he's let you come up here when all you've had in the past to communicate was this..." She pulls our tiny notebook from her pocket and holds it up. "Then something's up. And I don't really want to get caught in it."

His face reddens. "Did you...?"

She doesn't answer.

Oh, crap. He wrote a note to her in the beginning of it. Made me swear not to read it. Of course I did, but there's no way in hell I'd admit it. He'd probably punch me in the face. But *he* admits some things... and she's not saying anything. In fact, she looks vaguely uncomfortable.

Right now is probably not the best time to profess your love to someone, but whatever.

"Go out the way you came," I suggest. "Always worked for Tem."

Apollo groans. "No can do. Tiny's decided to use that hall on the second floor for target practice."

"I don't hear gunshots," Kora murmurs.

"Worse," Apollo says. "Darts."

"And his name is Tiny?"

I snort. "It's one of those ironic nicknames that makes you want to puke when you say it."

"Ah." She's still inspecting that window. "So..."

"I've got another idea." I raise my eyebrows at her, bouncing on my heels. I've got a dumb idea... but it might work. And that's better than anything else, at this rate. "How're your acting skills?"

CHAPTER 16
KORA

This is not going to work.

Of all Wolfe's dumb ideas... actually, I think all the guys have a track record of doing stupid shit. But now my shirt is askew, my gun is tucked in Apollo's waistband, and I'm acting like a drunken idiot.

My lipstick is probably still messy from my kiss with Wolfe—which is why I drag Apollo's face down and kiss him with a viciousness that surprises both of us. It's more of a lip-smear than a kiss, but it makes him groan nonetheless.

The story, if anyone asks, is that Apollo found me in one of the alcoves. I got handsy, and now he's escorting me out. If we run into anyone, he'll say we got carried away.

I've got my arm slung over Apollo's shoulders, and we're walking down the main staircase. Past the broken pieces of the statue Cerberus toppled, past the remnants of the circle that has been mostly swept away. The finer grit, almost dust, is still stuck to the marble floor. The blood is still there, too, drying.

I take it all in while trying to make it seem like I'm not.

I've got half a mind to actually pull Apollo into one of

the alcoves. Olympus is beautiful—and it has many hiding places. But then I spot a Hell Hound in the atrium, leaning against the wall beside the door. He's got a cigarette dangling from his lips and types on his phone, not paying us any attention.

Apollo lets out the smallest sigh.

"We were having fun," I say loudly, leaning harder on him and forcing my gait to wobble. "Where are we going?"

"It's time for you to go home, love. No more visitors after fight night has ended." Apollo's hand tightens on my waist. He's pretending to be uncaring, but I see through it. He's confused, warring between happiness and misery.

I get it. Me being here is a catch-22. He wants to see me, but he doesn't want me in danger. So he's conflicted, and he's trying to hide it.

Oh, yeah, plus the elephant in the room: the letter he wrote in the beginning of that notebook. I don't want to talk about that either. In fact, I don't even want to acknowledge it. So I don't bring it up, even though he saw me toss the notebook to Wolfe before we left.

"What's this?" The Hell Hound stows his phone and comes forward, his gun in his hand inching higher.

Apollo waves him off. "Get that out of my face. You were supposed to do a sweep for fight night attendees."

The man stiffens. "I did. But it's not *my* face that's covered in her lipstick."

I giggle. "I think I would've remembered you, handsome."

The man *blushes*. He's a little older. Forties, perhaps. Graying hair. He's got a grizzly scar on his neck, like he was almost beheaded but escaped that fate... barely. He's not attractive. In fact, he's on the scary side.

"She wanted a taste. What can I say?" Apollo shrugs.

"I'm going to get her in her car, and then we can close up shop."

He stiffens. "You're giving me orders?"

Apollo goes quiet. Just how low on the totem pole did Cerberus put him? I think back to the beating he took outside the clubhouse. The anger the Hell Hounds had for Apollo—and probably Wolfe, too—for leaving them. Did they hold on to that when Apollo and Wolfe were dragged back here?

"You know what would make this place better?" I pull away from Apollo and stagger back to the stairs. I sink down on one of the lower steps and pat the broken face of the statue. "If there was some music."

"Music," the guy repeats.

"Yeah, like while they're fighting." I raise my fists and pretend to box, then start humming.

We've officially reached desperate times.

Unfortunately, the only song I can think of is *WAP*, that Cardi B song that took everyone by storm a few years ago. So here I am, humming about wet ass pussies and shadow boxing, sitting next to a broken statue head. Apollo and the other Hell Hound stare at me like I'm nuts.

I've lost it. I acknowledge that.

"She's drunker than I thought," the guy finally says. "Get her out of here."

"You got it." Apollo crosses the room and offers his hands to me.

I stop shadow boxing and put my hands in his, letting him tug me back to my feet. He escorts me out, although I don't stop humming until the giant doors of Olympus have swung closed behind us.

"Thanks," I whisper.

"Kora—"

I face him. "I really wish I could kiss you right now. For real."

His expression is pained. "Me, too."

I clear my throat. "Listen, about the note. Tem pointed it out to me, but..."

"Now's not the time to declare myself," he mumbles. His eyes are stuck on the ground. "I know. I wrote that out of desperation a week after you left..."

I wince. "Right. So, your feelings have changed."

I step back.

He follows me, then glances over his shoulder.

Time is precious, and it seems we're running out of it. There's a car coming down the driveway, its headlights bouncing across the darkness. He pulls my gun from his waistband and holds it out to me. I take it and tuck it away, unsure where we go from here.

"You have to go," he urges. "Stick to the cliffs until you find Tem."

I nod, my heartbeat picking up speed. My legs don't want to move, but I force myself into motion. Before I can make it another step, though, he captures my wrist.

"My feelings haven't changed," he whispers hoarsely.

My eyes burn. "Good."

Then I tug free and run.

CHAPTER 17
SAINT

I wake with a vicious start. I jackknife up, and pain flares through my body. I let out an unholy groan, and my vision goes white. The room slowly comes back into focus, and the pain levels out.

Bed.

Room.

Bandages wrapped around my upper torso. I touch the gauze.

"Easy." Antonio sits in the chair next to my bed, a folded newspaper on his knee. He takes his glasses off and hooks them on the collar of his shirt. "You gave us a scare."

I lick my lips. My mouth is dry, my throat aches. I slowly lie back down and stare at the popcorn ceiling. "We at your place?"

"Yes."

"Where's Elora?" *Nyx.* Two sides of the same coin. But right now, I don't need her darkness—I want the light. Her real name. Her real self. I never call her that to anyone else, but it just slipped out.

It's a sign that I'm not quite myself.

Antonio nods to himself. "Nyx is sleeping. Finally."

"What happened?"

He rises and uncaps a bottle of water. "Drink slowly."

He has to help me sit up again, a bit more gentle, and I take a few gulps. The water is a balm I didn't realize I needed. I've downed half of it before the older man pries it from my grip and returns it to the nightstand.

"What do you remember?" he eventually asks.

I close my eyes and think back. The past... I don't know how long it's been. I've been living in a nightmare. But I still find myself saying, "The Titans grabbed me in South Falls. I had been following a Hell Hounds' vehicle. Wolfe was in it, and I was trying to get an opportunity to talk to him."

Antonio grunts. "Those boys are lost."

"They're trapped. There's a difference." A big difference. I refuse to believe that people can't be saved. *Some* people can't, sure. Kronos, Cerberus. But us? "They took me to that stupid chapel outside of town. Near the reservoir on the west side."

"And you took a beating," he supplies. "For a long time. What did they want?"

"I don't know. Kronos was always asking about Jace. Sometimes other stuff, but...."

Antonio huffs. "He thinks he has the war settled, then."

I eye him. "What?"

"If he was worried about the Hell Hounds, he wouldn't have bothered with you. He thinks they're not a concern... at least, not a concern enough to see what you knew about Wolfe or Apollo." Antonio shifts in his chair, his gaze dropping to the newspaper. "Perhaps I speculate too much."

"No..." I swing my legs over the side. "You're right, I

think. In the grand scheme of things, me, Jace, Nyx, Artemis —we should be inconsequential."

But he was very interested in Jace.

"How did I get out?" I ask him.

Antonio chuckles. "Nyx launched a full-scale attack to get you back. She even brought Kora out of whatever hole she was hiding in."

After the Titans attacked the Hell Hounds' clubhouse, everyone went underground. Phones were no longer safe— we learned that the hard way, when Nyx and I realized we were being tracked through them. The sheriff tried to round up everyone who might cause trouble.

I spent a night in jail, but they were unable to hold me. My timing didn't coincide with Wolfe or Apollo, unfortunately.

While we figured out the new laws of Sterling Falls, I kept my tattoo shop up and running. It felt a bit meaningless, sitting in a chair and creating art on tired, haggard-looking people. Sometimes it was tourists who wandered in, who hadn't got the memo to get the fuck out of town. Other times it was low-level Hell Hounds or Titans who wanted... I don't know. Skulls and shit to prove their worth in the gang. Their dedication.

That income proved valuable... and presented an opportunity for Nyx and Artemis.

A way to clean the money, I suppose, and buy weapons off-book.

So that's what we were doing. They've been off the radar, and I've been... a tattoo artist.

About as boring as you can get.

Until the day I got grabbed by the Titans.

I never saw Jace. I wasn't able to get close to Wolfe or

Apollo. And it was all for nothing, because the Titans—and Kronos, specifically—were convinced I maintained contact with all of them.

"She found Kora," I repeat.

That was one of their goals. Kora had disappeared off the face of the map.

"Apparently, someone she met while away was familiar with the chapel." He rises. "I don't know him. He was... left behind."

My stomach cramps. "Where is everyone?"

Nyx, sleeping. But the rest? His apartment is too quiet.

Antonio looks away. "Jace went off to see what he could find at the chapel. He texted not too long ago that he had found where Kronos had moved his operation. Artemis and Kora went to Olympus."

"Fuck." I push myself upright, ignoring Antonio's outstretched hand. Blinding pain flashes through my chest, and I press my hand to the stab wound. I won't be forgetting the feeling of the blade sliding inside me, that's for sure. "Where is your phone?"

Antonio rises. "Downstairs."

"Go get it!" I follow him into the hall, my pace considerably slower than his.

He disappears downstairs without a backward glance, the door slowly swinging shut behind him. When he returns, I've made it to the living room. My hand is braced on the wall, keeping me upright.

I dial Jace's number, but it rings through and goes to his voicemail.

Kronos stabbed me—but I'm still here. Kronos questioned me repeatedly about Jace. *Jace* and no one else. Not Cerberus, not Nyx, not Wolfe or Apollo or the sheriff or Kora. One man had his focus. *Why?*

Because he considers Jace his biggest threat.

And Jace has found Kronos... or he's found exactly what Kronos wanted him to find.

Does that mean he's walking into a trap?

CHAPTER 18
KORA

A rtemis and I arrive back to Antonio's restaurant in North Falls to find everyone awake and in his living space upstairs. Nyx and Saint sit together at the kitchen table, a phone faceup between them. Antonio hovers by the sink, cupping a mug. There are two more on the table, although they seem untouched.

It occurs to me that Antonio has a family—I've seen photos of kids on the walls, and a beautiful wife. But I don't know where they are. Certainly not here.

"What's going on?" Tem looks between them. "Saint, are you okay?"

"Jace has gone off the radar," Saint says.

My blood runs cold. "You're kidding me."

His attention lands on me. "He's not answering his phone."

How is it possible that I can't seem to keep track of these guys?

"Is this how it was?" I demand. "When they first left the Hell Hounds, and everything was a mess? Five years ago—is this what it was like?"

"It's worse now," Nyx mumbles. She rests her chin on her fist. "It was the way of life before. The gangs were fighting, but there was still a semblance of order. They've shattered that now."

I let out a breath. "Okay, so... where did he go?"

He was gone when Artemis and I left for Olympus.

It's Saint who answers. "Apparently, he went back to the chapel. He sent word that he had found the Titans' new hiding place."

"And, what?" I snap. "He's just going in alone? Somewhere we don't know?"

They all go quiet.

My gaze goes from Saint to Nyx to Artemis, and they're all *silent*.

He could die, and we'd just... not know.

"This is bullshit." I shake my head and grab the car keys from Artemis.

"Wait. Please." Artemis grabs my arm. "Think things through."

Fine. I wheel back around and point at Saint. "Who was the guy who set up the security for the guys at the house? Was he the one who tried to hack into the auction?"

He squints. "Daniel?"

I snap my fingers. "Yeah, him. He still alive?"

What a world we live in that I have to ask *that* question.

"Probably, but—"

"Find him. See if he can track Jace's phone or something. Or pull up surveillance pods... I don't know. I need to narrow down where he might be." I look around, then settle on Artemis. "Do you have a phone I can use?"

She pulls out an ancient black flip phone from her pocket. She hands it over, her expression grim. "I don't think you're being reasonable."

Now is not the time for *reasonable*. "Saint thinks he's in danger. Walking into a trap. Right?"

He grunts.

"I'm going." I'm going to kill him is what I'm going to do. If I can find him. "Call me when you find something."

The urgency pushes me back outside. Artemis follows, maybe with an attempt to stop me, but I ignore her. She halts just shy of the car door, watching me start the car and back out. I'm so pissed I can't even see straight—the last thing I should be doing is driving.

But their plan—no. They don't *have* a plan. No one has a damn clue what to do, because everyone is scattered. I only have the vaguest idea who the players are. But I have my gun, and I have a stupid disguise, a cobbled-together plan, and I'm desperate.

Hopefully that'll get me close enough.

I head south, toward the center of town. This is the first time I've driven in Sterling Falls, and it's eerie. I don't know what I'm going to do or how I'm supposed to track down Jace. If only I was naive enough to think that intuition—or some sort of bond—would bring me to him.

The phone rings, rattling in the cup holder. I snatch it up and answer the unfamiliar number.

"Kora?" Nyx's voice.

"I'm here."

"Saint has Daniel on the other line. He's been monitoring the police radio for the last few months, and he says he might have a lead." She pauses. "Will you wait for us?"

"How far behind me are you?"

"We need to make a plan." She hesitates. "Kora, it's dangerous. We think he's in North Falls..."

Previously untouched territory, if my understanding is correct. The last stronghold Sheriff Bradshaw holds for the "normal" people. Tourists. The rich residents who can afford the police protection. The same part of town I'm in right now.

Of course it would be here.

"You want to plan." My voice is wooden, but I'm already slowing the car. My foot hovers over the gas pedal, the vehicle coasting. But there's another voice, deeper inside me, that whispers dangerous things. That Jace is running out of time, wherever he is. "Do you have an address?"

She sighs. "Kora—"

"Text it to me." I end the call.

I'm *in* North Falls. I could be there in minutes. Wherever it is.

I grit my teeth. I won't be helpless anymore. If Isle of Paradise taught me anything, it's that I can't be idle. I won't.

The phone vibrates in my hand, and I glance down at the text.

An address.

I can save him.

Movement in the rearview mirror catches my attention. A second later, the lights on top of the cop car turn on, flashing red and blue. I pull over and hope they'll go by me. But they stay right behind me to the shoulder of the road.

"You've got to be kidding me," I mutter, trying to get a view of the driver. And contemplating how I can talk myself out of this. I'm *wanted*. I shouldn't have pulled over in the first place.

I touch my fake hair, grateful I didn't remove the wig when I left Olympus. I don't have a license on me. Or cash, since bribery seems to work so well these days. I glance in the rearview mirror one more time, noting that the cop hasn't gotten out yet, and reach for the glove compartment.

Shit, my gun. I yank it out from my waistband and stow it under my seat.

I barely have time to straighten back up again, glove compartment forgotten, when the cop taps my window with his flashlight. The light is brilliant white, and I squint against it. I roll down my window.

"Step out of the car, miss."

My brows furrow. "Did I do something wrong?"

"You're out past curfew." He steps back. "Please turn off the engine and step out of the vehicle."

I grit my teeth and unlock the door. I climb out and register that his hand is on his weapon. *Great.* "I'm sorry, I was just trying to get home..."

"Where's that?"

I bite the inside of my cheek and give him the street of the guys' house. Not the number, because... well, I don't know whose side this cop is on. It was a gamble at all to have stopped, not that I had much choice. Antonio's car doesn't seem like it would be able to outrun the police.

The cop hasn't lowered his flashlight, obscuring his features. My stomach twists, and I resist the urge to run. I do look away, though, and focus on the ground. I was *so close*. Just a few blocks away from stopping Jace from doing something seriously stupid.

"That's a pretty nice neighborhood," the cop says after a moment, his voice disembodied behind the light. "You'd stick out like a sore thumb."

I swallow. "Yeah, well, this is just a loaner."

"Turn around."

I flinch. "What? Why?"

"You've broken the law being out past curfew. Civilians aren't allowed on the streets until six a.m., which means you might have a possible gang affiliation. I'm taking you down to the station."

I shake my head, but I do what he says. He pushes me forward against the car and grabs my wrists, locking cold metal handcuffs around them. I ball my hands into fists, waiting for him to realize I have the hourglass brand—a dead giveaway to who I am.

"What's your name?" he asks, taking my upper arm and leading me to his car.

I don't answer. My tongue feels thick.

He puts me in the backseat, and I risk a glance at him now that the light is gone. He's unfamiliar. Maybe early thirties. Clean-shaven, with blond hair. He doesn't so much as spare me another look once the door shuts on me, and he sits behind the wheel. He radios in, but I tune it out.

The cop glances back at me. "Not gonna talk, huh? Maybe some time in the box will get answers out of you."

Not a quick and easy visit, then. No slap on the wrist and then pushed out the door... I can't believe I just let this happen.

I'm so stupid.

CHAPTER 19
APOLLO

olfe and I meet outside Olympus. We're close to the cliffs, and the cool spring wind buffs at us. We should've gone farther away, but there's no point. Cerberus is bound to know something by now—how could he not? The sun is rising, the sky getting lighter by the second. Soon, it'll break past the horizon and turn the water from dark gray to gold. If we're lucky.

Wolfe eyes me, then shakes his head. "Fuck, man. Kora?"

"Got away clean."

"One of Dad's guys burst into my room about five minutes after you left." He looks out to the water. "Definitely a fucking trap."

"How'd we lose his trust?" I sit and let my feet dangle over the edge. We used to have those plastic Adirondack chairs out here. We'd sit out all night, sometimes. Back when times were simpler and we thought we knew what we were doing.

Wolfe joins me. He lies back and folds his arms under his head. "I don't think we ever had it."

I grunt. That's true. He tried to get us to kill our best

friend. He's been keeping us separated. But with Kora back, everything is different.

"What are you up to, Apollo?"

I glance down at Wolfe. His eyes are closed. He took out those red contacts after the fights, not that they make much of a difference. He's been going dark since we signed over our lives to Cerberus.

Again.

Well—this time, it's more official. The last time we joined the Hell Hounds, we were children. I close my eyes, too, unwillingly dragged back to that time.

I was ten. My father came home one night, drunk and scared. Not his typical combination. Mom could never wrangle him under control when he started drinking, so she was locked away in her bedroom.

Artemis was with me, both young enough to share a room still. Did everything together. I heard Dad fly in through the front door, kicking it shut behind him, at the same time that Artemis slipped into my bed.

He never touched us. We weren't fucked up in that regard. But he liked to yell and throw things, and sometimes he'd get mean that way. Insults were his favorite brand of poison.

Anyway, that night, something had changed. He didn't bypass our room and go to his, or hunker down in front of the television until he passed out.

We knew he was drunk by the way he'd entered the house. We discovered his fear when he came into our room and flicked on the lights. We both blinked sharply, raising our hands to block our eyes.

He spotted Artemis in my bed, and his lip curled. Even now, almost fifteen years later, I can still see that expression. Disgust, anger. He was pretty vocal about us sharing a room, even though there wasn't another space. Just the unfinished basement. He grabbed her up wordlessly, dragged her out of the room and toward that basement door. I heard her yelp, maybe as he forced her down a step. He must've locked her in, the slam echoing in my head. She beat at that door, screaming, but he ignored it and came for me.

"What's happening?" I asked him.

Naively thinking nothing bad would happen to us. That this was an abnormal nightmare, but one that would end soon.

It didn't.

He went into my closet and rifled through it, finally snagging my school bag from the floor and dumping the contents out. Notebooks, my open pencil case, loose papers scattered across the rug.

There was the fear. The whites of his eyes showed, and he roughly shoved clothes into my bag. Underwear. Socks.

"Get your toothbrush," he said in a low voice.

I scrambled to obey. When I returned, he took it from me and stuffed it in the bag with everything else, then grabbed my arm. Like he did with my sister, he dragged me out of the room. Not to the basement, though.

The fear in *me* was so thick, I could hardly breathe. He brought me out to his car, still running in the front lawn, and put me in the passenger seat. My backpack landed on my lap.

I didn't ask any more questions. My throat was closed off, my stomach in knots.

Dad drove recklessly through the city, until we hit the forest. The trees leaned in toward the road, creating almost a tunnel. It was dark out, and the leaves impeded the moonlight. Dad's headlights were old and yellow, and they didn't do much to illuminate our path.

He mumbled to himself along the way. Incoherent words. Drunken words.

Finally, there was a turnoff. A barely visible driveway. Dad took the corner fast, tires skidding against the gravel, and we bumped forward. I gripped my backpack tightly, trying not to show my confusion.

A large building came into view, a huge gravel area in front of it. There were rows of motorcycles parked in front of the wide porch, and the steel door was propped open. It was then that I noticed the men. They wore leather vests and jackets, smoking cigarettes or weed, with beer bottles dangling from their hands.

"Dad—"

"Shut up," he snapped at me.

He parked and got out, motioning for me to do the same.

A man walked outside. He came down the steps and stopped in front of my father, looking him up and down. He was intimidating, with short dark hair and a close-trimmed beard, dark eyes. He was tall. Wide. But he also exuded power, and that's what struck me.

He wasn't someone to mess with.

"What's this?" he asked.

"My son." Dad grabbed my arm and hauled me closer. "He's quick. Smart. He'll make a good—"

"He's how you plan to repay your debt?" The man laughed.

Others echoed him. It seemed like the whole place was laughing at us, but my father just stood there and took it.

"He's all I have," Dad whispered.

The man paused, then gestured to me. I stepped forward, my jaw set. He ripped the bag away from me and tossed it to someone behind him, then leaned down so his face was in mine.

"How old are you, boy?"

"Ten," I managed to say.

He nodded to himself, then straightened. His gaze went back to Dad. "As it so happens, he'll fit right in with my most recent recruits."

His hand landed on my shoulder, turning me around to face my father.

"Say goodbye."

Dad couldn't even look at me. He just shook his head, his throat working. Then he got back in his car. We stood there, this man and I, as Dad threw his car in reverse and shot backward. He swung it around and disappeared down the driveway.

No regret about leaving me behind.

The man made a noise of disgust. "Welcome to the Hell Hounds, son."

"Apollo," Wolfe says.

I cringe. I'd been lost in that memory for who knows how long. My eyes open. I've got handfuls of earth in my hands, and I slowly loosen my grip.

"Yeah?"

Wolfe chuckles, but his eyes remain serious. He's sat up, inspecting my face. "Jesus, man. You okay?"

"Perfectly fine."

"So, are you going to tell me what you've been doing with the sheriff?"

"Oh, fuck off." I stand, brushing the dust off. "I'm not doing this with you."

He rises, too, and shoves my shoulder. "Let me help."

"There are new drugs in Sterling Falls. And that Parker guy is still in town with the DEA." I sigh. "And now Kora's back..."

"He's the asshole who put hands on her," Wolfe says idly. "If anyone deserves to be tossed off the cliffs, it's him."

"He may as well be as far away from our reach as Kronos."

Wolfe ponders that. "Maybe."

He pulls a phone from his pocket. As principle, we both leave our real phones behind when we need to talk. Not that we ever get a chance to... but because we're both suspicious as hell, we assume that Cerberus can hear our conversations. Cloned phones or tapped lines, I don't know.

But this cell must be a burner he picked up somewhere. He has more freedom than I do, so I can see how he'd have more opportunity. He flips it open and dials a number, then puts it on speaker between us. It rings twice, then—

"Hello?"

Jace? I punch Wolfe's arm. The fucker smirks at me.

"What're you up to?" Wolfe asks.

"Kind of in a bind, actually," Jace replies. "You could save me the trouble of bullshitting my way out of something. How'd you get my number?"

"Tem wrote it in our little book forever ago, but I didn't have a spare phone that wouldn't lead back to either of us until yesterday."

Jace grunts.

"So...?" I ask. "What do you mean, you're in a bind? Where's Kora?"

"Hey, buddy," Jace greets me. "You reining in Wolfe's temper?"

"Something like that." I glare at Wolfe.

This must be their first communication—and for that, and *only* that, am I not more angry about it. Wolfe mouths an apology, and I look over the cliffs.

The sun is inching higher still, just barely breaking over the water on the horizon.

"I found Kronos," Jace finally says. "I'm sitting on his place right now, but..."

"Where?" I inch closer, then glance toward Olympus.

The Hell Hounds should all be asleep. Cerberus returned, the guards changed. We're alone out here—it would be so easy to sneak away.

"North Falls." He gives us an address. "But, I've got... company. Eager company."

"Who?" Wolfe's voice is tight. "You know we can't—"

"I know better than to fucking trust a stranger," Jace snaps. "But he wants to go in."

I snort. "Go in, like, to see if Kronos is in there?"

"Wait until he goes in, then blow the place sky-high," Wolfe suggests.

Jace growls. "Can you jackasses get here or not?"

I meet Wolfe's eyes. It would be something, wouldn't it? To go help Jace like the good old days? To pretend, if only for a moment, that we're not all stuck in our own versions of Hell.

Maybe we can make the best of this and kill two birds with one stone.

"We're on our way," Wolfe answers. "Don't fucking move till we get there."

CHAPTER 20
KORA

I've been sitting in an "interview" room for over an hour. The cop who brought me in undid one of the cuffs, threaded it through a metal loop on the table, and resecured it around my wrist.

I consider yelling, just to see if someone actually did forget about me.

Unlike the movies, there's no mirrored wall. There's just a camera in the top corner of the room, pointed in my direction, with a red blinking light.

Ridiculous.

I've given up on panic. The anxiety in my chest, the worry over Jace, settles. It's still there, but there's nothing I can do. I pulled at the cuffs for the first ten minutes, then quit that. I periodically tug my shirt sleeves lower.

The wig is officially itchy.

And if I wasn't in a police station, knowing that Kora Sinclair is a fugitive, I'd have torn it off by now. The need to scratch my scalp is almost overwhelming.

Finally, the door opens and the sheriff enters. He's got a

slim folder in his hand, and his head is bent as he reads something from it. He glances up and goes still. The folder smacks closed.

We stare at each other for a second, and then he leaves.

I look around. Up at the camera. Just in time to see the blinking red light die.

Oh, great.

Sheriff Bradshaw reenters and closes the door softly, then takes the seat across from me. The folder is gone. I raise my eyebrows, not bothering to hide the fact that he and I both know my situation.

Although I have a feeling it's worse than I know.

"Didn't expect to see you here," he says lightly. He reaches out and undoes the cuffs.

I pull my wrists away, hugging my arms to my stomach. There are red marks on my skin that I'd rather not see.

"Didn't think I'd be *here*," I finally answer.

He sighs. "Why did you come back to Sterling Falls?"

"You knew I had left?" I narrow my eyes. "How?"

"An informant," he says. "Someone keeping tabs on everything from the inside."

I don't respond, and we lapse into silence. His hair is longer than I've seen it, combed back with gel or something. He's got circles under his eyes, and he looks like he's lost weight. What sort of toll has this war taken on him?

I motion to the camera. "Why'd you turn that off?"

"Why are you wearing a wig?" he retorts. He leans forward, bracing his forearms on the table. "You're a fugitive."

"Yeah, can you explain that to me?" I raise my eyebrows. "I haven't done anything wrong."

He shifts. "They're blaming you for the start of the war. I

162

don't know if that necessarily makes you a fugitive, but there's a judge... he's working with the Sterling Falls DEA to bring charges against you. Apparently, *you* were the mastermind behind the new drug that's hit Sterling Falls."

I snort. "And yet, I've been gone for six months."

"I know. It didn't come from me."

I watch him closely. He's not telling me something. Never mind that there's a new drug on the streets—I don't think I have the bandwidth right now to worry about that. There were drugs found in Jace's jeep after Kronos took me, too.

The whole thing reeks of Titan interference.

"Shoot straight with me, Nate." It's weird to use his first name, but I'm gambling on his friendliness. That he actually gives a fuck about what happens to me. He tried to warn me after all. That dinner was weird on a bunch of different levels, but I didn't get the impression he was swayed one way or another.

His eyebrows hike.

"I've been hearing different things. What's your take on it? This war?" I need to know what I've gotten myself into—and I'm still holding on to the insane hope that I can help the guys end it.

Step one: put them back together.

Step two: figure out how they did it the first time, and maybe we can replicate it.

I don't have anything beyond that, but it's a flexible plan. I can add to it if needed.

The sheriff rubs his eyes. "Shoot straight," he mutters. "Yeah, sure, why the hell not? I've got two warring gangs going for each other's throats. I've got the mayor and city council in one ear, telling me that we need to get it under control. Arrest everyone. Put an end to the madness the old-fashioned way. But I've got corrupt cops paid off by both sides. They're mangling evidence, delaying response times, letting people get away. And then the DEA—"

Parker.

"They're in the other ear," he continues, "seemingly hell-bent on arresting *someone* for the drugs that have gotten out of control in this damn city."

"They're still here? The two who arrested Apollo and Wolfe?" My voice isn't working right, but I don't know how to fix it. I'm being strangled. I had hoped that Parker was gone. Six months have gone by, and I wasn't here—so why would he stay?

"Yep. They've taken over my conference room."

I jump to my feet. "They're here? *Now*?"

Nate tips his head, trying to get a read on my reaction. "What's wrong? Sit down. They're probably not here yet, Kora. It's dawn."

Dawn. Shit, and Jace—

I grab the wig and tear it off, throwing it to the floor. I back away from it until I hit the wall, then I slide down it.

"Parker Warton," I mumble. "I know him."

Nate comes over and crouches next to me. "How?"

"Dated him. He's not..." I shake my head. "Never mind. I just can't have him see me. And you can't leave him alone with me."

He rises, his brow furrowed. "This is extremely unethical on his part, pursuing this investigation—"

"And you're the expert on ethics?" I hiss.

He doesn't react. But he does hold out his hands to me, and I take them. He takes the wig and brushes it neatly, then hands it back to me. "I have a proposal for you."

I pause and wait.

Proposals don't usually go over well.

Cerberus. Kronos. The guys. Parker.

I should know by now to stay as far away from deals and bargains and agreements, because I'm foolish enough to be burned *every. Single. Time.*

"Go on," I say when he doesn't continue.

"I'll let you go. I'll get your wanted posters taken down, bury your name. Make you invisible."

I laugh. "Make me invisible *again*, you mean?"

He winces. "Yeah."

"And in return?"

"You keep me informed on what's happening." He eyes me. "I think it's a fair trade."

"You have an informant," I say.

"A cryptic one," he replies. "I need someone better. *You.*"

I look around the tiny room, like there's a chance I can escape without his help. This isn't like being the Titans' captive, or under Cerberus' thumb. This is the law, and I'm wavering on a knife's edge. To break it, to not.

"That knife saved my life," I say in a low voice. "You know that? Even though I thought for sure you were working with Kronos. And when he set that basement on fire and left me tied to the chair, I think I would've died without it."

He doesn't respond. Not that I need him to. He's stoic and still, and he's probably had to wear that mask for a long time.

"So, even though I still don't know what you're doing, or why... I think I can trust you enough to know you're not going to kill me yourself."

He frowns. "I'd never."

"I know." I meet his gaze. "So, fine. I'll do it. I'll work with you to end this thing."

"Okay." He holds out his hand.

I shake it.

Another deal struck—I just have to hope it's the right move.

CHAPTER 21
JACE

The mansion sits on the beach in North Falls. Right on the sand, probably with its own private access to the water. It's on the edge of this neighborhood, with just dunes to the west of it. Until the tree line comes back, the shoreline curving to the north once more, and the earth rising to be uninhabitable.

This section of beach is perfect for the elite. The large houses of glass and stone, their wrought-iron fences out front and brick driveways, the extra security systems.

I rode by once, scouting the area, then met Ben on the backside of the dunes. In the dark, we waited. Watched. All the while, I kept assuming he was going to be more forceful about going in—but he wasn't until Kronos appeared in one of the upstairs windows.

"Now or never," Ben finally says, coming back up from his little exploration. He returns to his position beside me.

I thought for sure he'd have gone in and given us away, but no one raised any alarms. The sun is rapidly rising in the east. Within the hour, it'll come up over the top of the house and blind us in our current position. Apollo and Wolfe will be here soon.

"We have confirmation that this is where he comes," I argue. Stalling. "Trust me, I'd love nothing more than to bust in and shoot him in the face, but I'm pretty sure his guards would chew through us before we got close."

"A long-range weapon, then. I have one. I'm an excellent shot."

I've been away for too long. I'm tired. And annoyed.

"You know what? Go ahead and try. I'm going home."

Ben scoffs. He follows me down the dune, back to my bike. It's still in shadow on this side, and so it's noticeable when a car swings around the dunes toward us.

My hand goes to my gun, but I have a feeling I know who it is. Sure enough, seconds later, Apollo and Wolfe step out. I leave Ben behind and go to greet them, a bit of the tension in my muscles loosening.

"Thanks, guys."

Apollo looks past me. "Who's this?"

"Ben." I glance back, then face my friends. "Apparently, he knows Kora."

Wolfe bristles. "Does he now? And where is she?"

"She should be at Antonio's." I keep my voice low. "Should've been there all night."

Wolfe and Apollo both react to that. Wolfe laughs. Apollo presses his lips together.

I narrow my eyes. "What?"

"She went to Olympus. We were with her a few hours ago."

Son of a bitch. I ball my fists to prevent myself from doing something stupid, like taking my anger out on my best friends. They probably didn't have anything to do with it—but Artemis would've.

"She got out fine," Apollo adds. "So she probably is back at Antonio's right now, looking for you."

"Hey," Ben calls, coming forward.

Wolfe glares at the new guy. "What are you doing?"

Ben pauses. "Excuse me?"

"What were you thinking, coming here without backup?"

Apollo nods, frowning. "You could've gotten yourselves killed."

Ben's expression hardens. "I asked Jace what he wanted to do," he says. "And he chose to come here. Not—"

"We got confirmation," I interrupt.

"What's the big fucking deal?" Ben steps forward again, his anger practically vibrating inside him. "We go in. We kill the asshole. We leave."

I shake my head. "Don't you think it would've been so easy to do that before? Sometime in the last five fucking years, when he wasn't defending himself against a rival gang that he's been targeting for months? If it's just a matter of cutting off the head of the snake, yeah, sure, pull the trigger."

Wolfe makes a noise in the back of his throat. He knows. Apollo knows. We've discussed this at length, and the answer has *always* eluded us.

I take a breath. "Killing Kronos doesn't solve anything, because someone else would just replace him. Someone worse. Someone better. We don't know. Same with Cerberus. Killing them only leaves a power grab, and that's when things dissolve into chaos."

We debated taking over the gangs, but that wouldn't stop the violence. And then we'd be the targets.

Our original goal? Disband them. Find a way to settle things once and for all by eradicating the gangs from Sterling Falls. But unfortunately, we got distracted. We fell off our mission because we got swept up in playing gods.

Perhaps it's a good thing we don't have Olympus anymore—so we can focus on what really matters.

A solution.

But Ben is already shaking his head. He goes and grabs his rifle, then stalks up the hill. Apollo and Wolfe exchange a look, but I'm more curious than anything. We wait. Perhaps Kronos will be out of view—how long does this guy want to wait anyway?

The crack of his gun shatters the quiet.

I scramble up the hill, lying flat beside him, just in time to catch his swear.

The upstairs window isn't broken. There's no blood spatter, no signs of a kill.

Bulletproof glass.

And Kronos stands on the other side, just to the left of the opaque impact mark of the first bullet.

Ben slides the bolt back and checks again. He fires without warning, drawing a yell from Apollo. The bullet finds its mark—or it would've, if the glass didn't stop it.

"Pointless," I yell, shoving away from the top of the dune.

Titans are pouring out of the house, armed to the teeth. They leave the property and race toward us.

I haul him up and shove him ahead of me down the hill. I push him at my bike and rush toward the car. Wolfe is already behind the wheel, Apollo in the passenger seat. I don't want to see if that idiot can figure out my bike, or if he's good enough of a rider to follow us. I dive into the backseat and barely close the door, and then we're off.

With Titans close behind.

CHAPTER 22
KORA

W e don't go back to North Falls. The sheriff's office is close to the university, and he takes me there. I sit motionless in the passenger seat as he parks and turns off the engine. He opens his door, then glances at me.

"Coming?" he asks.

I look around, like I didn't notice where we were. "Why?"

"Business." He inclines his chin, fingers tapping the roof of his car. He climbs out and waits.

I let out a sigh and join him at the front of his car. The sun is fully up at this point, the sky light blue streaked with shades of orange. Funny how only a few miles east, there's an unbroken view of the horizon.

Downtown, the university included, is all dark metal and glass and imposing structures. Save the administration building, made of white marble. Rather reminiscent of Olympus and the interior of Bow & Arrow. A lighter counterpart.

Just another piece of the Sterling Falls puzzle.

We cross the quad and enter the backside of the administration building. It's achingly familiar, reminding me why I came here—and what I've lost. I tag along with the sheriff all the way to the elevator.

And then I balk.

I guess it's one thing to be in an interrogation room, or a car, but another to be enclosed in a metal box? Strange logic.

He eyes me, then sighs. "City Council has taken over the upper floors. Sterling Falls University is one of the last safe places for them to meet."

"And why are we going there?"

"Well, I was going to just drop you off, but it's probably best that we get your fugitive status completely removed. Right?"

"Right." I step into the elevator with him and lean against the back wall. "I don't know if I can trust you."

He chuckles. "Yeah, well. Right back at you. Do you think I want to risk my career for a twenty-year-old?"

I roll my eyes. "Twenty-one. Celebrated my birthday on the island."

He pauses. "Oh? When's your birthday?"

"February fourth." I sigh. "It was a real downer. Twenty-one in a camp that doesn't allow alcohol. Even the locals knew not to serve us."

"So you haven't had an official birthday drink," he guesses.

"Right. Legally."

He smiles. "Of course."

The elevator dings on the sixth floor, and the doors slide open. I follow him out, curious. I've never been to this floor. Not that I spent *that* much time on campus, in the grand scheme of things. But none of my classes were above the third floor in the admin building. I'm surprised to find that it's not a replica of the lower floors.

Same hallway, of course. But instead of classrooms transformed into offices, which is what I was picturing, there are offices with glass-fronted walls, letting anyone in the hall see inside. We pass the financial aid office, and it dawns on me that I *have* been up here. Almost a year ago, begging for my scholarship back.

"How is it that they were able to remove my scholarship?" I ask. "The guys. They made me unhireable in the city, too."

Nate stops. I stop, too.

"What happened?" There's real concern in his voice, I think. But then he holds up his hands. "You know what? Don't tell me. They used to have a lot of strings to pull. People who owed them favors, people in their pocket. Their luck ran out about six months ago, though, when Sterling Falls realized the guys holding everything together under the surface weren't actually *that* strong. So they probably pulled those strings to affect you."

Yeah, that's what I figured, too.

But it's interesting that their opinion of them has changed so drastically.

I get it, though. They've had to deal with the consequences.

Wolfe had said they controlled the shipping, and that was one way they steered the narrative. They didn't let in any trucks that weren't their own, and they had the harbor. So one of those must've changed before Kronos acted.

"This way," Nate says, opening one of the glass doors.

He motions me through, following close behind. He takes the lead again, passing the abandoned front desk and down another, narrower hallway. We arrive at a conference room, and he steps inside with a quick rap of his knuckles on the door.

I swallow.

The whole city council is in this room, it seems. There are eight people around the table. I recognize the mayor—who isn't technically on the council, I think—Jeffrey Thompson. And another man, who I had met with the sheriff. Alex Sterling.

Three women, five men in total.

"Sorry to interrupt," Nate says.

One of the men rises. "You've caught yourself a fugitive, Sheriff."

Nate holds up his hands. "Easy, Barron."

"What's this about?" This from one of the women. She has long, strawberry-blonde hair. She could be his age, in her early thirties. She wears a navy-blue pantsuit, white blouse. Gold jewelry that complements her complexion. She's got that sort of timeless beauty that movie stars possess.

"Have a seat, Kora." He grabs the nearest chair and wheels it away from the table. His hands brace the back of it.

I sit slowly, gripping the arms.

"This is Kora Sinclair. She has charges brought against her by the Sterling Falls DEA."

"Yes, we're aware," Barron interrupts.

"However, the SFDEA is biased. One of the men here in our city is her ex-boyfriend."

I flinch.

The woman tilts her head. "Would he have a reason to try and see you behind bars, Ms. Sinclair?"

I swallow. "Yes, ma'am. It's... a long story. But he is the sort to want revenge."

Her eyes harden. "And I presume she hasn't done what she's accused of, Sheriff?"

"Correct." Nate steps to the side and drums his fingers

on the table. "I'm terribly sorry to bring this to your meeting, but with Kora back in Sterling Falls, and completely unaware of the charges against her, I thought it prudent to get this wiped from record."

Alex Sterling clears his throat.

I don't know why he fascinates me so much. Maybe because he's a Sterling and he shares a name with the town. His gaze lands on me, and his eyes soften. Still, his words are directed to the table... and the sheriff.

"I agree with you, Nate. If this ex of hers is out for revenge, and there's no actual evidence of wrongdoing... there's no way an arrest would stand up in court. It would make all of us look bad." He seems to hesitate for a moment, chewing over his words. Or simply letting his previous statement settle. "Kora, you've newly returned to town?"

My turn to talk again. "Yes, sir."

"Yes, sir, yes, ma'am." He smiles. "No need to be so formal."

Nate pulls a paper out of his pocket, smooths it, and goes around the room to hand it to Alex Sterling. The latter takes a moment to read it, then nods to himself. We wait in silence until he's done, then he hands it back.

Nate passes it to the strawberry-blonde woman, leaving it with her and heading back to me.

"All in favor of removing Kora Sinclair's fugitive status, on the basis of no evidence and bias by the agent of the DEA?" Alex eyes the room.

One by one, they raise their hands. A full consensus— even the mayor, who has thus remained silent.

Is he still with Cerberus?

I stand back up, tuck the chair in, and thank them. Then I make a hasty exit.

"Kora."

The strawberry-blonde woman follows me into the hall. I let her catch up, and she extends her hand.

"Nadine Bradshaw."

I blink. "Bradshaw, like—"

"Nate is my brother." She grins. "We keep things professional around mixed company, but it's not a secret."

Now that I know, I can see the family resemblance. Same eyes, same face shape. Their hair is even similar, but not exact. Just different shades of orange.

"It's nice to meet you," I manage.

"Same. I wanted to ask... we don't see very many people moving back to Sterling Falls these days." She makes a face. "I don't mean to be off-putting, I just wanted to make sure you knew what you were getting into. It's been difficult the last few months."

I'm struck by that. Surprised that she cares. But then again, it's her city that's tearing itself to shreds. "Yeah, no... I know. I'm not thrilled about a gang war, but I've got friends here. My family sort of threw me under a bus in Emerald Cove, so there's nowhere else for me to go."

"I'm sorry to hear that." She holds out a business card. "If you need anything, please call."

I take it, reading the front. *Nadine Bradshaw, Alderman for North Falls.* A phone number, an email address. I'm not sure what I'd need to call her for, or why she's offering it. It could have to do with the fact that her brother brought me in and asked for a pardon, or whatever just happened.

"Thanks."

"Ready?" Nate asks.

I nod. He leads the way out. I glance in the room as we go, and Alex Sterling catches my gaze. He gives me a small smile, then continues on with his conversation.

Another facet of Sterling Falls revealed.

"Where to now?" I ask.

He shrugs. "Coffee?"

I look at him. Truly try to *look*. But I don't know what I'm seeing, besides a man who seems to play for every side of the table.

Back into the elevator, down to the first floor. We go across the quad, but I veer left. He shadows me, not asking questions. It feels strange without people on campus. School's been let out for the summer, I guess. The lack of activity makes it feel like a ghost town.

We get out onto the sidewalk. I'm acutely aware that the sheriff is in his full uniform, probably drawing attention. More so than me anyway. I take another turn. Halfway down the block, I stop.

The house is exactly the same.

Still burnt, caved in, with yellow tape across what remains of the entrance.

Nate stops beside me. "You okay?"

I take a breath. "Do you know who pulled me out of the fire?"

"No."

His eyes are squinted, and he remains focused on the house. There's tension in his face.

"You're lying."

He stays silent.

I go forward, all the way up to the yellow tape. My stomach flips, and I recall with extreme ease how terrified I was to be tied to a chair in the basement. How Kronos manipulated the situation to his liking. First by kidnapping me for the auction. Planting drugs in Jace's car. The actual auction. Then trying to kill me when he didn't like who won.

I crouch and dig my nail into the charred wood. The

black ash comes up under my nails.

"Here." The sheriff squats beside me, his knee touching mine. He holds something out to me.

I take the folded knife and flip it open one-handed. The metal has been cleaned. Repaired. But there's no denying this is the same knife he gave me. The knife that saved me.

"I wasn't there because I was on his side," he admits in a low voice. "There's a saying... keep your friends close, and your enemies closer?"

"I've heard of it." Bitterness coats my tongue.

"Kronos and Cerberus both think that I'll do anything for money. And to a certain extent... I will. I diverted police activity from the house when Kronos brought you there. I've pulled strings for Cerberus, including getting the District Attorney and judges to agree to the plea deal Richard Jacobs arranged for Wolfe and Apollo. I've—"

Richard Jacobs?

"Who is that?" I interrupt.

His brows come together. "The Hell Hounds' lawyer? He's worked with Cerberus for over twenty years. He does some straight business, too, but most of it is getting Hell Hounds out of jail time. Plus whatever else Cerberus wants."

Oh my god.

I bolt to my feet. "I need to go—"

"Slow down. What is it?"

I shake my head. "Can you bring me back to the car?"

I give him the street name, and he nods. The phone is still in it, and so is my gun.

I might need both of them.

CHAPTER 23
WOLFE

"Now would be a great time for a bazooka," I yell at Jace.

There are three Titan cars behind us. Every time they get close, I hit the gas and shoot us forward. I can't push this thing much faster, especially as we're coming down through the outer side of West Falls.

Jace laughs. "You know, I thought about bringing it with me."

He rolls down the back window. So far, no one's shot at us. But I think it's more because they have orders to take us alive.

That's just great. To be captured by Kronos and have him string us up by our ankles in his basement.

Apollo cranes around. Jace is leaning out of the window on my side, his gun out. He gets off a few rounds, then ducks back inside. Immediately, gunfire comes our way. We all duck, and my side mirror shatters. The back bumper takes most of the impact, but the windshield doesn't break.

Terrible shots.

Or, they're still not trying to injure us.

Which means... "Are we driving into a trap?" I call.

"What?" Apollo faces forward again. "I don't think so—"

"Yes," Jace yells. "Turn here."

There's a narrow road on the left that'll lead back to the center of Sterling Falls. I jerk the wheel, and the car almost tips over. We're up on two wheels for a moment. My heart hammers as we come back down on all four tires. I punch the gas pedal down.

"Trap?" Apollo snaps at Jace. "Seriously?"

"The Titans like to set up roadblocks. They've been collecting tolls."

"You've got to be kidding me."

They're lagging behind us now, seeming to have given up now that we're venturing closer to Hell Hound territory. Or maybe they're spooked because their roadblock didn't catch us. I take another turn, then swing us onto the main four-lane road to South Falls. We've lost them completely at this point, but I keep switching my attention between the rearview mirror and the road ahead. We'll take the round-about way to...

"Where are we going?"

"My place," Jace says.

I raise my eyebrows and don't comment.

He leans between the seats. "Get off here."

He continues to direct me to the marina and then to a stop at a solid metal gate.

"That guy stole your bike," Apollo says suddenly.

Jace grunts and hops out. He unlocks the gate and pushes it open. I drive through, and he closes it behind us.

We climb out, and I stare around. It's... not much. I can see how he'd gravitate toward this depressing shack, though. He thinks he deserves it after what he let happen.

I march ahead. Part of me is eager, hoping Kora will have

beat us here. The better part of me knows she won't be. If anything, she's with Tem at the restaurant. I open the door and stop short.

It's worse than I thought.

It smells like... sex.

My stomach turns, and I fight the urge to deck Jace. But after a second of trying to breathe through it, I can't. I spin around and beeline for him.

"What—"

I punch him in the face. His head whips to the side. Immediately, Apollo is on me, grabbing my arm and dragging me back.

That's all I needed, though. Just one hit. My knuckles sting, and I shake Apollo off of me.

"He fucked her," I accuse. "While we've been *killing ourselves*, he took her to his little shack and had SEX WITH HER!"

I can't see straight. Definitely can't think straight. I stalk away, shaking out my arms. I kick a forgotten tire and pass it, then head for the water.

Apollo stays behind. As I stride away, he asks, "What the fuck, man?"

I don't catch Jace's reply.

Damn it. I thought sharing her with Apollo was hard. But I guess I've always known that Jace had the appeal, so of course she'd go for it. Their tension... I don't know. I keep my teeth locked, my jaw tense. Otherwise, I'd just go back there and hit him again, or yell more, and the last thing we need is to draw attention here.

She'd already fucked him when she saw us at Olympus.

My head hurts.

I sit on the dock and put my face in my hands.

Apollo loves her, admitted as much to her in that stupid notebook. Jace slept with her.

And what did I do? Hold a gun to her head.

Everything is so fucked up.

"We're not going back."

I lift my head.

Apollo sits beside me, leaning back on his elbows. Similar to our position earlier this morning, on the cliffs. Except now, the water is a hell of a lot closer.

"We can't," he continues. "Kora changes things."

"I know."

"We're going to end things the right way, Wolfe," he whispers. "We have to. There's more at stake now than ever."

I swallow.

Jace lowers himself down on my other side. He keeps his attention out on the water, and the boats lining the docks on either side of our little space. "I love her, too, you know."

A lump forms in my throat. "Is that it, then? Everyone's so sure of their feelings?"

Apollo nudges me. "She knows how she feels about *you*."

I'm not so sure.

"Cerberus will come after us now," Jace says. "We've got to be a united front."

I laugh. "We're back to square one. Six years ago, we were debating the same fucking thing. Did we just waste all that time?"

"This is really like square two," Apollo points out. "Square one was us being stuck with Cerberus in the first place."

"Okay." Jace hops up. "Let's go get the girl, yeah?"

Yeah. *Right.*

His phone goes off, and he fishes it out of his pocket. "It's Nyx."

He answers and immediately presses his lips together. Like she jumped right into scolding him—and knowing her, that's exactly what's happening.

"I had it on silent," he says. "Because the distraction— yes, I turned it back on a few hours ago." He pauses, listening. Then, "Yeah, I saw the missed calls. I haven't had a chance—oh my god, Nyx, *chill out*."

He pulls the phone away from his ear.

His expression drops. "What?"

"What?" Apollo repeats. "What's she saying?"

"Kora tried to come after me. *Fuck*." He hangs up on Nyx and pockets his phone.

Immediately, it rings again. He yanks it back out and snaps, "Why weren't you *with* her?"

I shake my head and move away. Kora went after Jace. Finagled a way to figure out where Kronos was... and now? Where is she now?

But then Jace says, "Kora?"

I wheel back around. His face is stricken, and he puts the call on speaker. Immediately, Apollo and I crowd closer around him.

"I could use a little backup," she whispers.

"Where are you?" I demand.

"Wolfe?" Her voice wavers. "You're together?"

"Yeah, flower. Where are you? Let us help you."

She huffs. "I'm outside your house."

I grimace. Apollo closes his eyes, pinching the bridge of his nose. I know the feeling—this week is just one massive fucking headache. Jace glares at the phone.

"Okay," Jace answers. "Give us ten minutes."

"Fifteen," I mutter.

"By all means, take your time," she answers. "But then you're going to explain what the *fuck* happened. First Olympus, and now your house?"

Anger. Lots of anger.

I don't blame her—I'm angry, too. That my father took advantage of us so fully, we couldn't see our way out of it. But Kora was gone, so what was the point? Looking for her was fruitless. Bringing her back here... none of us wanted that. She has no place in this war.

"Let's go, then." I hurry away, not wanting to say something I'll regret. Because I already have a lot of regrets when it comes to Kora. Insensitive words won't be added to that list.

CHAPTER 24
KORA

I give the guys ten minutes. That's about as long as my patience lasts anyway. Then I climb out of the car and head for the gate. I try the smaller pedestrian gate, and the knob turns under my hand.

Maybe they think they're untouchable?

I slip through and close the gate door softly behind me, then head for the side of the house. Everything is familiar but wild. The grass is overgrown, the hedges are exploding with new growth. There're bits of pollen and leaves everywhere.

The ache in my chest only deepens.

Just as I get to the side of the house, the garage door rattles open. I press my back to the wall, heart pounding, and watch a silver BMW pull out. A man in the driver's seat.

Fine.

I duck into the garage as the door is closing, and I wait for a handful of seconds. Waiting, perhaps, for the guy to realize someone just snuck into his house. Nothing moves. The garage door settles shut, and silence reigns. The car doesn't return. No one bursts through the door to the house.

Are those security cameras the guys installed still here? Still accessible?

I don't think they had a feed to the garage. But still. I pull my gun from my waistband—retrieved safely from under the seat in the car where I had shoved it—and head inside.

The new occupants haven't changed much inside. Same furniture. Same smell, even, with an undercurrent of some sort of spiced aftershave. Male, sure, but different than the guys' smell. I wrinkle my nose and sweep the first floor.

There's music upstairs.

I find a housekeeper in the guys' den, and I watch her for a moment before retreating. She doesn't notice me.

My heart pounds. I get upstairs and go down the hall. The guys' rooms have been tossed. Like, destroyed. Their mattresses are off the frames, the drawers yanked out, clothes strewn about. I continue farther, with the weird sense of déjà vu hanging over my head. How long ago was it that I followed Apollo through the halls in a similar pattern?

I reach my bedroom. The door is cracked, and the music is coming from here. My fingertips brush the cool painted wood, and I slowly add pressure. It swings soundlessly open.

The room has been rearranged. The bed is in the far corner, just barely blocking the fireplace. It's a mess. Clothes... books. Jewelry.

The occupant is on the bed, facing away from me. Typing on a laptop that emits the music.

I bite the inside of my cheek and try not to scream that *I knew it*.

Instead, I stride forward and press the gun to the back of her head. Wolfe and I are more similar than he thinks.

"Don't fucking move," I order.

Marley doesn't listen. Not surprising. She rolls onto her

back, eyes wide. Then she seems to register it's me, and her fear falls away. "Kora? What are you doing?"

Yeah, not this time.

"Get up." I step back, motioning with the gun for her to get off the damn bed.

"Are you going to shoot me?"

"I'm considering it."

She blanches. Then, thankfully, she rises. She pulls at the hem of her tank top, but it doesn't touch the rolled top of her white joggers. "I don't understand."

"This is *my room*," I whisper-yell at her. Trying to control my temper. "This is my life that your father is fucking up."

She rears back. "What?"

I look at the bookshelves that used to house my belongings. The shadow box with the first mask the guys gave me —the one with real flowers. It's all gone. Probably removed on purpose by Richard Jacobs before his daughter moved into it.

"Your shitty father who you were so eager to meet in Sterling Falls is affiliated with a gang." I laugh. "Jesus, Marley. Tell me you didn't know."

Her eyes widen, and her lip quivers.

"For fuck's sake. You live in the house he took from them."

"Who?"

She steps forward, and I jerk the gun back up. I had started to lower it. I'd let my past get ahold of my emotions. Marley and I were best friends, but...

"Did you even try to find me?" I ask.

She cringes. "No."

"No," I repeat. I back away and fight back tears.

"You've been different. How the hell was I supposed to know you were living here?" She sweeps her arm out.

I laugh. I have the urge to burn down the whole fucking world right now—and maybe that's not a bad idea. Burn down Sterling Falls and rebuild it.

"I've missed you, though."

"So much so that you tried to find me," I retort. "Don't come closer."

She stops. Her hands rise up in surrender. I hear what she hears—footsteps on the stairs. Maybe Daddy Dearest is coming to rescue her. Is he the gun-wielding type? Or the talk-it-out type?

Either way.

I lunge at Marley and grab a fistful of her hair. She puts up little fight as I slip behind her and press the muzzle of my gun to her temple. Just in time for someone to step into the light.

Jace. Followed quickly by Wolfe and Apollo.

"What are you doing?" Apollo asks.

"Please help me," Marley sobs. She folds in front of me, hitting the floor hard on her knees. "She's crazy—"

"I'd stop talking if I were you," Wolfe interrupts. "Seeing as how Kora appears to be two seconds away from following through on her threat."

Marley swallows. Hiccups. "You know her?"

"We didn't come here for you," Wolfe replies, wrinkling his nose. His attention switches to me. "Hey there. You going to kill your friend?"

"Ex-friend," I mutter. "Did you know her father is the Hell Hounds' lawyer?"

They all eye me.

"Did you know *they've* been living in our house?"

Marley tries to look at me. "Kora—"

"Shut. Up." I release her and shove her forward.

She catches herself on her hands, then climbs shakily to

her feet.

"Stand against the wall," I order.

She does. It's surreal, having this sort of power over her. It turns my stomach, too. My insides feel like they're being eaten away by acid. I don't like it. I don't like the fear in her eyes. But she... she could've prevented this, right? She could've been a better fucking friend, and then we wouldn't be in this position.

"Kora," Jace says.

I eye him, then scoff. "Not talking to you."

In the distance, the garage door opens. I raise my eyebrows at the three of them. "Well? Are you going to take back what's yours?"

Apollo is the one to slowly shake his head. "We can't."

"Fine." I go to the mantel. I wonder what happened to that first mask. That's the one thing I would've liked to keep. But Marley has replaced any trace of it with rows of candles. I find the matchbook and strike a matchstick against the side of the box. It catches with a hiss, the flame pale yellow.

Wordlessly, I toss it onto the bed.

Jace holds Apollo back, seeming curious about what I'm going to do.

I'm unhinged.

So I don't know what I'm going to do.

Marley remains against the wall, eyes wide. I pull my sleeve up as her bedding catches, the flames climbing. There's a lot of fuel in here. It'll go fast.

"Do you see this?" I show her the hourglass brand.

She just looks at it with a blank expression.

"The Titans," I explain. "And then the Hell Hounds. The gang *your father* works for."

"We need to go," Jace says.

The fire on the bed is emitting a lot of heat. The flames

S. MASSERY

are traveling. I go first, letting one of them deal with her. I stop in front of Apollo and reach up, touching his face.

"I meant to do this earlier." I grip the back of his neck and pull him down. Our lips touch. Too quick, really, for anything, but butterflies flutter in my chest.

He groans when I release him, then slip past. I touch Wolfe's shoulder. He follows on my heels to the stairs, smoke following us.

"You still holding that matchbook?"

I offer it to him.

He grins and lights one, tossing it in his room. Then Apollo's and Jace's. I smile, too.

"End of an era," I tell him.

He shrugs. "We'll rebuild it."

Good.

Downstairs, Richard Jacobs is removing his tie. His briefcase is on the floor beside the table in the front foyer. He freezes up when he sees me, and his brows draw down in confusion at the sight of Wolfe.

"You arranged the deal for Wolfe and Apollo to go back to the Hell Hounds?" I ask.

He jerks. "Yeah—"

Jace and Marley come down next. He's got her in front of him, gripping both her upper arms. Richard starts again.

"What—"

Apollo has located the housekeeper. Must've seen her earlier, because he wordlessly shuffles her out the front door. Smoke is floating along the ceiling from the stairwell, dropping lower by the second.

It doesn't matter, though. Apollo blocks the front door. Jace has his daughter. Wolfe and I are both armed, although I'm the only one with my weapon out. And my finger itches to pull the trigger.

"Answer her," Apollo says.

"Yes, yes," Richard stutters. "Cerberus asked me to keep an eye out for opportunities to bring his son back."

I tense.

Wolfe has gone utterly still, his expression thunderous. "Explain."

Richard raises his hands. "I don't— I just follow directions. We kept an eye on you. Please, just let Marley go."

"Is there a loophole? Some clause that gets us out of it?" Wolfe glances past the lawyer to Apollo. Then back.

The flames have reached the stairs. In the distance, there's a *crack*—and what could possibly be the sound of the second floor collapsing.

My bedroom, my things, *gone*. Same with the guys. It doesn't break my heart the way I thought it might, though. It feels right that, with everything else going up in flames... our physical representation of what we had goes, too.

"Apollo, check downstairs," Jace orders. "Kora, what do you want to do with them?"

I look from him to Marley, still in his grip, to Wolfe. Then the lawyer.

My plan sort of ended here.

Focus. "Loophole? Is there one?"

"No, no," the lawyer shouts. "Please—"

"Get them out of here," I tell Jace. "Wolfe and I will check the rest of the house."

He nods. I grab Wolfe's hand and tow him toward the kitchen. Past that, to the den. We stop in the doorway for a moment. Then...

"Office. Shit. Music room." He's talking more to himself than me.

"Wait." I pull him to a stop. The smoke isn't too bad on

this side of the house. It feels like we have a moment to spare. "I'm sorry."

He stares at me. "Sorry? For what?"

I gesture around.

He shakes his head and comes for me, sweeping me up in his arms and putting me against the wall. I wrap my arms around his neck. He kisses me with a fierceness I'm not expecting. It matches my racing heart.

Our teeth hit, our tongues slide together. He nips my lower lip.

He drops my legs, letting them hit the floor, and undoes the button of my pants. I don't stop him from doing that or pushing them down my legs.

Fuck it. Right?

I undo his pants, too. Freeing his cock. He wastes no time picking me back up and yanking my panties to the side, sliding into me. The stretch is delicious, and I let out an involuntary groan.

"It's been driving me wild, knowing you're back but unable to touch you like this," he admits in my ear. "I couldn't wait."

"Fuck me hard, then," I order. My nails curl in his t-shirt, my back already arching.

He draws out almost all the way, then slams back into me. My spine hits the wall. Pleasure and pain are hand in hand.

I groan. I can't hook my legs around his hips, not fully. My lower legs are still trapped by my pants and boots. He grips my ass and keeps me at the right angle.

"Hurry up," I say, my gaze catching on the orange-and-yellow flames at the other end of the hall. "We don't have time for a marathon."

His laugh is breathy. "The last time I was inside someone, it was *you*, six months ago. Trust me, I'm not lasting long." He lets go of me with one hand and flicks my clit.

My back arches.

It's hard to focus with the heat of the fire pressing at us. Smoke swirls above our head, thick and black. He kisses me again, pinching my clit harder. The fear, the adrenaline—I come suddenly, a surprise attack. My muscles clench around him, spurring on his own climax.

He's still for precious seconds, buried inside me, while we both ride the high.

Then he's slipping free and righting his clothes. I pull mine back up, then drag my shirt up over my nose and mouth.

"Go," he orders. "I've just got one more thing to check."

I scoff. "I'm not leaving you alone."

He glares at me, but then he moves. *Toward* the flames.

I staunch my objections and race after him. We burst into the music room, which is already on fire. The piano is burning, the glossy black top melting. There's rubble every-where—this was where the ceiling collapsed.

It doesn't stop him from rushing inside, though, and grabbing something from the middle of the room. I stare at him and then the instrument case. It's a hard shell case, protecting what's inside it, but the shape is unmistakable.

A cello.

My instrument.

A lump forms in my throat, but that's all the reaction I have time for before Wolfe's taking my hand and yanked me back into the hall.

There's a cracking noise above us.

The ceiling in front of us suddenly gives out, showering fire and debris down into the hallway.

Effectively cutting off our exit.

CHAPTER 25
KORA

I'm frozen. I don't know why my muscles can't seem to work, with fear holding me hostage. I should be better than this. I've fought to survive for so long... and now, with a fiery death staring me in the face, I can't move?

Wolfe doesn't have the same problem. Behind us is fire. Ahead of us is fire. The music room is out of control, the instruments burning. He sets down the cello case and kneels. "Get on my back."

I shake my head. "Are you serious?"

"Get on my fucking back," he yells.

I climb on and hold on to his shoulders. The smoke is almost insufferable now. He doesn't hesitate. He grabs the case and charges through the flames. I bury my face in his neck. The heat sears at my skin, but he doesn't stop. He rushes down the hall, to the room off the kitchen. He keeps going until we're out the back door, bursting onto the patio.

Still, he moves away from the house. Farther. His legs buckle, and he hits the ground hard on his knees. He's coughing uncontrollably.

I release his shoulders and slide off, pulling my shirt

down and taking gulps of air between coughs. I fall to the grass and roll onto my back, trying to regain control over my body. Over my aching lungs.

"Come on," Wolfe finally manages. He sits up and reaches for me. "Are you okay?"

"I don't know what I would do without you," I admit.

He crawls closer. "Kora."

I wrap my arms around his neck and pull him down on top of me. "You just ran through *fire*." My voice cracks. "I thought we were goners. That's not the first time I've thought I was going to die, okay? And you—"

"I'll always save you." His lips touch my ear. "Don't fucking doubt that. Any of us would've done it."

He's got to be burned. I roll us. The move is easy now, having practiced forms of grappling with Ben. In the name of self-defense, of course. But I see now that it has its other uses.

Wolfe lets out a surprised grunt, now on his back. His hands land on my thighs. I ignore our position, straddling him—now's not the time for that. I mean, we *just* had sex. So I shouldn't be thinking of that as I shove his shirt up and inspect his skin for burns. The hem of his shirt is singed, and a spot on his thigh, but it didn't get him.

Somehow.

"You're a miracle." I climb off him. "I don't know how we made it."

"Kora!" Apollo yells.

"Backyard!" I answer.

Wolfe gets to his feet as Apollo comes around the corner. He keeps some distance between him and the house, and he stops in front of us. "Where the fuck did you go? Jace said you didn't come out—" His gaze lands on the forgotten cello case, and his brows furrow. "Wolfe, you didn't."

He shrugs. "I thought she'd need it."

"Need and want—"

"Can be synonymous," Wolfe finishes. "Jace got it for her."

I laugh. "Of course."

"Speaking of." Apollo eyes me. "He's probably getting ready to shoot the lawyer and go into the house after you…"

I turn back to the house I called home for such a short period of time. Black smoke belches out of the upper windows, the pressure and heat breaking the windows. Flames curl under the roof.

Nothing will be left.

"There are no sirens." I follow Apollo, Wolfe behind me with the cello. "Why?"

"No one calls the cops anymore." Wolfe's voice is dark.

Huh. "Why?" I repeat.

"Because you don't know who you're going to get," Apollo answers. "And you don't know what kind of favor they're going to require. Plus—this is Richard Jacob's house now. The whole block knows it. The whole fucking neighborhood is probably aware of his affiliations. So, no cops. If anything, someone would've called Cerberus."

"All the more reason to get out of here," Wolfe grumbles.

We reach the front, and Jace's shoulders lower. He's got his gun trained on Richard and Marley—the former sits with a stoic expression, and the latter is *sobbing*.

"We need to go," I say.

"And them?" Jace glances at the cello in Wolfe's hands, and his face gets red.

Interesting.

I shrug. "Marley comes with us."

Richard leaps to his feet. Tries to anyway. Jace shoves him back down.

"Don't," he says. "She's innocent in all of this."

Marley Jacobs. It makes me *wish* I had asked more questions about her father. I shake my head and turn away. I don't even want to look at her. I certainly don't want to interrogate her.

But the fact of the matter is clear.

She's leverage.

"Marley stays with me." I crouch in front of Richard. "Cerberus thinks he knows who I am. Marley probably does, too. But I want you to know something about me."

He swallows. His throat bobs, and his eyes dart all over. The house is emitting so much heat, I'm desperate to move away. But I stay right where I am, waiting for Richard to acknowledge me.

Finally, he says, "I'm listening."

"This is my city. And I won't hesitate to burn down the whole fucking thing to get rid of the infestation." I hook my thumb behind me. "Do you understand?"

"Yes. But don't hurt her—"

I rise. "Leave him. He knows to cover our tracks. Don't you, Dick?"

The guys are staring at me with a mixture of awe and horror. Probably more awe, since they're not exactly rule followers. They just don't expect it from me.

I've had six months to sit on my anger over this fucked-up situation. Six months to stew over what the Titans, what the Hell Hounds, what this whole town has done to me.

It's about damn time we took it back.

The guys follow me down the driveway, escorting Marley between them. I don't have any more words for them. I can't stick around and watch the house crumble.

The street is quiet. They parked behind Antonio's car, a few spots down on the opposite side of the road. It's midday, and no one else is around. Even at the height of the guys' power, six, seven months ago, it wasn't this quiet.

But there is someone.

I stop mid-step.

Parker straightens up off the hood of Antonio's car. Goosebumps break out down my arms. He pulls his wallet from his pocket and flips it open, flashing the badge.

He found you, one voice in my head whispers.

A sick, evil voice.

Run, another urges.

And oh, how I want to.

Apollo steps up beside me, taking my hand. A silent message. He squeezes, and I grip his hand back hard. Parker smooths his suit jacket and comes toward us. He stops in the middle of the street, his focus never wavering from me. Five, maybe six feet of asphalt separate us.

"It's good to see you," he says.

I can't speak.

There's a thousand pounds on my chest, compressing my lungs.

"You look good." His hands slide into his pockets. He's the picture of calm. Slicked-back light-brown hair, square jaw. He's classically handsome. Perfect for luring unsuspecting girls into his trap.

My throat works, but I don't answer him. There's no question anyway. His blue eyes bore into mine, and I remember every cruel word he said. Every injury I suffered while he looked at me like *that*—like it's my fault.

"Someone actually called this one in," he says, gesturing with his chin to the house. "The address is flagged in our system, so I cancelled the firetrucks. It's a dangerous place, after all, isn't it? Full of gang and drug-related activity."

Run. Run. Run.

I can't move.

Apollo steps slightly in front of me. "How about you back up."

I hold his hand tightly, willing him not to do anything stupid. Parker *would* arrest him—again—if Apollo laid a hand on him. My ex is that level of petty. Still, Apollo's defense means more than I know how to express.

Parker smiles. He doesn't move. "Are you threatening me?"

"You don't seem like the type to need threatening. You're smart enough to read between the lines, aren't you?"

My ex-boyfriend *tsks*. "Last time I saw *you*, you didn't look so hot. But she's forgiven you. And you..." His gaze moves to Wolfe. "You threatened to... cut my eyes out? Well, here we are. Both free men. I don't see you doing much about it, though."

Wolfe laughs. "This is the game you want to play?"

Parker shakes his head. "Actually, I'm here to take Kora in. She's a criminal, you see."

I cast a quick thank you to the sheriff. "I'm not a fugitive."

He pauses, eyes narrowing. "No? Maybe you missed the wanted posters."

"Maybe you missed that the district attorney dropped charges," I answer. "Cleared of all wrong-doing as of this morning. That's your fault, though."

I'm still holding on to Apollo's hand like a lifeline, and I can feel Wolfe and Jace behind me. Jace never met Parker, but Wolfe... I'm afraid if I show fear, Wolfe's anger will get the best of him. He's got it under control right now. Barely.

But it's because we don't have any power.

Parker scoffs. "My fault," he parrots. "How's that?"

"The mayor and city council were very curious to know

why you were pushing so hard to punish your ex-girlfriend." I force indifference—but it's so much harder with him. I can't believe I'm talking to him and not cowering. "How does it feel that I have more people on my side here, Parker? Your game is up. You didn't get me. And you won't ever touch me again."

He watches me for a moment. His eyes are so cold—there's fury under his skin, buried deep down. "We'll see about that," he finally murmurs, then steps aside. "Marley Jacobs. How nice to see you again."

"Go fuck yourself with a stick, Warton," she snaps.

He chuckles, turning on his heel and striding away. It's not a retreat. If anything, it's calculated. There's one thing about Parker that I know to be true: he won't give up so easily.

CHAPTER 26
APOLLO

We lock Marley in Kora's car. Wolfe gingerly sets the godforsaken cello case in the trunk of Antonio's car, protecting it with whatever soft things he could find. We meet between the two vehicles.

"We shouldn't go back to Antonio's," Kora says. "But we need to move."

Jace rubs his hand down his face. His frustration is our frustration. We loved that house. As much as it hasn't been ours in the last six months, I still held out hope that we'd get it back and return to normal.

I look over and watch it burn. The fire has consumed it fully now. There's fire eating at the roof. Pieces fall in, large chunks of it. Our bedrooms, our training room, our cars... all gone. There's a burst of flames as one of the cars goes, the gasoline in the tank causing an explosion. Then another. Another.

Each one hurts.

Kora hasn't let go of my hand. Not even since Parker got back in his government-issued SUV and drove off. She squeezes now, like she knows what I'm thinking.

It's funny how personal things can be such an anchor.

Get away from Cerberus. Come back here. Restart our lives.

"Apollo will ride with me," Kora announces. "Jace?"

"If we bring her to my place, it's burned."

She frowns. "A boat? The one Nyx and I came in on."

That might work. "Sure," I say, then release her hand. I go to the driver's side, not leaving room for debate. Kora doesn't say anything, but I feel her gaze on my back.

Wondering what the hell is wrong with me, maybe.

Don't worry—I'm wondering the same thing. Why can't I just let this go?

In the car, Marley is pouting in the backseat. Neither of us say a word to her. I wait for Jace to pull onto the street, then follow behind them. We'll take a roundabout way— but we're in a hurry. No doubt Cerberus is on his way here, and it isn't just because of his precious lawyer.

We're officially off the map. Wolfe and me.

I don't know what sort of repercussions that'll bring down on our heads.

I glance at Kora. "How'd you get the DA to drop the charges?"

"The bogus charges, you mean?" Her lips quirk. "Seems like I have friends in high places."

And all I have is friends in low places—that hits a little too close to that country song.

Marley makes a noise in the back, and Kora's shoulders hitch. She turns around and looks at her former best friend. *Former* because I'm pretty sure everything Marley has done stacks up to unforgivable.

It's hard to forget the look Kora wore when her so-called friends dragged her to the beach and left her to fend for herself.

That was the first time I felt a strong connection to her.

I'm not like Wolfe or Jace. I'm not drowning in anger or vengeance. But I am suffocating in the past. That's what will kill me.

"What?" Kora snaps at Marley.

The latter sighs. Loudly. "I didn't know you lived there, okay? Dad picked me up from school and said some bad stuff was going down in the city. He didn't want me living on campus anymore, so he asked me to move in. Why the fuck would I think you lived there?"

Kora frowns. "You didn't want me to come to Sterling Falls at all."

"No, I didn't," she snaps.

Kora abruptly sits forward again. Her fingers dig into her thighs, and her brows draw down. That upsets her. Clearly.

Marley leans forward. "I'm sorry. I just... it felt like mine, you know? Then you came in, and my friends didn't understand why I put up with you—"

"Let's not talk," I suggest.

Kora scoffs.

"You've changed," Marley continues. "You just held a gun to my freaking head—"

"Your dad is a gang lawyer," Kora interrupts. "So you don't really have much wiggle room. Your dad gave you those VIP passes to Bow & Arrow, didn't he? He probably got them for Hell Hounds to give out to pretty girls."

She frowns. "You know what—"

"Janet's a colossal bitch." Kora glares straight ahead. "Is she still in town? We'll just drop you off with her. It's best if I don't see you ever again."

Marley's silent. Not that I can blame her. She's on the verge of losing something, too. They both are. It's just one of those things that they might not notice right away.

Like my sister. Did I miss her when Dad sold me into the Hell Hounds? Yeah. But I resented her, too. Until everything changed... then I understood. But that took years.

"Some things can't be salvaged," Kora whispers. "What do you know?"

"Nothing," Marley responds. "Please drop me off—anywhere. Here. I'll make it back to Janet's on my own."

"Fine. Apollo, pull over."

I do. The car lurches when I slam on the brakes, guiding it to the curb. In a flash, Marley's out of the car and stomping away.

I look at Kora. "Happy?"

She glances at me, then away. "What's got your panties in a wad?"

Is she serious? "Oh, just the fact that you burned down our home."

"Apollo," she starts.

"No. *No*." I grip the steering wheel with both hands, my knuckles turning white with the force. "You just destroyed the one thing we were going to go back to—after—"

She puts her hand on my arm. But that's not enough. She unbuckles her seatbelt and climbs over the console, landing sideways in my lap. She takes my face in her hands and forces me to look at her.

"You once wanted change," she whispers.

I swallow.

"You had dreams of making this place better. Didn't you?"

"Yeah." I clear my throat. "Still do."

"Then there is no going back." Her gray-blue eyes bore into mine. "There's no back, Apollo. We're done with that. Done with the way things were before, done with dealing with everything the same way it's been handled for the last five years. There were intentions, and then there were actions."

Her eyes fill with tears.

"If we go back, we'll get stuck. Do you understand that? The way forward is going to be painful. We've got the uphill battle. Barely any ground to stand on. But we've got to fight, and we've got to do it together."

She's... she's right.

Fuck, she's making more sense now than ever.

"We're on the edge of the cliff," she continues. "Are you going to jump with me?"

There's no question. She sees it in my eyes—where she goes, I'm going to follow. I would've, too, if I could've. Before.

She slips back into her own seat. The weight of her in my lap, her palms on my cheeks, it all feels like a ghost. Now she's back to the colder, harder version of the girl I fell in love with—and I don't know how to reconcile those two women. I don't know where she learned how to be so strong.

"Hey," she says into the phone. "Change of plans. Ditch your car and meet us by the university."

I eye her.

She hangs up on them and smiles at me. She runs her fingers through her hair, letting it fall around her shoulders. The wig is in a bag by her feet, the hairs neat. I don't know when she took it off, but I prefer her without it.

Red suits her better.

"SFU," she urges. "We're close."

I lean over and kiss her before I lose my nerve. I can't *not* kiss her, but since I realized my feelings for her, and since she *read* about my feelings, there's been distance between us. She went to Wolfe, not me. But now, she leans into the kiss. Her lips on mine are a warmth I didn't know I was missing. Her tongue slips along the seam of my mouth, and I open for her. Let her take control and taste me.

I've craved her for six fucking months, and now she's here.

But she's not mine.

She's still holding back.

I want to take a sledgehammer to her guard. I want to tear open my skin and let her take refuge there.

If only, if only.

She pulls away, her tongue darting out and sweeping along her lower lip. "We need to go."

I nod sharply, putting the car back in drive. There's nothing else to say.

CHAPTER 27
KORA

I move to the backseat. There's still some weirdness between Apollo and me. Jace slips into the front, and Wolfe wastes no time sliding me across the bench in the back. He hooks his arm around me, and I rest my head on his shoulder.

The truth? I'm exhausted.

Apollo fills them in on what happened with Marley.

Wolfe smells like smoke. I do, too. We probably should've gone to a hospital and been put on oxygen or something. My throat aches. But the thought of being intubated again freaks me out, so I don't say anything.

Apollo seems to drive forever before we wind up back at Antonio's. Jace eyes the front of the restaurant, then the street. He hops out and goes inside. I start to inch away from Wolfe, but his grip tightens on my waist.

"Let him make sure it's okay," he says in my ear.

I nod.

"Should we talk about how you almost shot your best friend?"

"Former," I correct. "Former friend."

He chuckles. "Yeah. Right."

"Richard Jacobs." I sigh. "Jacobs is a common last name, but I *knew* her dad lived in Sterling Falls. Marley Jacobs—she kept his last name."

"Well, you were right about it." Wolfe shifts. "He's coming back."

Jace returns to the car, tossing a bag—mine, I think—into the trunk. He gets into the front seat and scans the area ahead of us. There's a little more activity today, especially in North Falls. More cars on the road, some people walking. He gives Apollo an address, and we pull away from the restaurant.

"Oh." Jace turns around. "Do you know someone named Ben?"

I straighten, alarm shooting through me. "He's alive?"

Jace narrows his eyes.

A knot forms in my chest. I'd forgotten. Honestly, with everything happening, I put it out of my mind that Ben literally sacrificed himself to save us. After all he did for me.

I'm the worst.

The guilt follows a second later. Ben helped me out—and what did I do? Let him stay behind and fend for himself against the Titans.

"Where is he?"

"Not sure. I gave him my bike—"

"Wait, wait." I hold up my hands. "Start from the beginning. How did you meet him?"

Jace makes a face. He explains how he met Ben at Kronos' converted chapel outside of Sterling Falls and that they traveled together to where Kronos is currently hiding. Well—where he *was*, up until a few hours ago. It's a mystery if he's remained there.

Ben tried to kill Kronos, but it didn't work. It *did* draw

out the Titans. Apollo and Wolfe came to his rescue, and then they got my call.

So in a way, it worked out.

Except Ben is still unaccounted for, Jace doesn't trust him, and I'm pretty sure we're going to have both gangs hunting for us. Wolfe and Apollo have abandoned ship, too.

Right.

I put my hand on Wolfe's thigh. His hand comes down on top of mine, keeping it there.

"Where are we going?"

Jace glances back again. "A safe house."

Is there such a thing in this city? "We should find Ben."

"He's fine."

I narrow my eyes at Jace, then glance at Wolfe. He shrugs, leaving me to draw my own conclusions—Jace met him and doesn't like him. It goes beyond distrust. No wonder. From the sounds of it, Ben acted a bit irrationally and almost got them killed.

I let out a huff and lean back again.

"Guy seems to have a survival instinct," Apollo offers. "He probably let the bulk of the Titans chase after us, then made an easy escape on the beach. Over the dunes and into the trees."

That mollifies me... for now.

Wolfe traces patterns on my leg until we reach our destination. It takes forever, with Apollo taking a crazy route through the city. He seems to know what streets to avoid—all the major ones. At one point, he turns us down an alley that's barely wide enough for the car. The guys both have to reach out and fold in the side mirrors just to pass through without scraping the sides.

I alternate between focusing on the road, and the silent guys in the front seat, and Wolfe's moving finger.

At some point, I realize he's writing words on my thigh. I catch an *r* and a *y*. There's a pause, his finger slashing across the letters, and then he starts over. *S. O. R. R. Y.*

"Why are you apologizing," I whisper.

He doesn't answer.

I glance over at the other guys, but the decision is made for me. Wolfe seems truly like he's hurting. More than the burns and the fear.

I climb onto his lap and swing my leg over, straddling him. He makes the smallest noise of surprise.

"Wolfe James. Why are you apologizing?"

His gaze flicks over my shoulder. To Jace? Apollo's eyes in the rearview mirror?

"Don't look at them." I cup his cheek. "Look at me. Why are you apologizing?"

"For doing everything wrong," he says softly. "With you. Holding a gun to your head—"

"Stop."

"Kora, I almost fucking killed you—"

"I knew you wouldn't." I lean forward and press my lips to his. I don't know how to tell him that Ben and I worked through those scenarios. How to get the upper hand once I've been caught off guard. I ran through those scenarios in my head when Wolfe pressed the gun to the back of my head, but I held off. My choice, not Wolfe's.

If he had pulled the trigger, we both would've been at fault.

He deepens the kiss. I taste ash on his tongue, and my heart skips. Here comes the anxiety again, the belated rush of surprise that we almost fucking died fifteen minutes ago.

"They're making out," Apollo mutters.

Wolfe's hands slide along my thighs, gripping my ass and pulling me closer to him. His erection grinds into me.

Desire floods through me. If we weren't in a car with Jace and Apollo, I'd strip and ride his lap for real.

Seems he doesn't have any predisposition against his best friends seeing, hearing—he undoes the button of my pants and slips his hand in, cupping my core. He thrusts two fingers up into me, curling them. I let out a low groan, my abdomen clenching at the sensation.

"Ride my hand," he says in my ear.

I do. Fuck it, right? I squeeze my eyes shut and rock my hips forward. The heel of his palm brushes my clit. I angle my movements for the maximum amount of friction.

"Fuck," Apollo mutters.

Wolfe's free hand runs up my side. He palms my breast through my shirt, then goes down. Slides back up under the fabric, under my bra. My back arches when he rolls my nipple between his fingers.

"Tell us," Jace orders. His voice is hoarse. "Tell us how it feels."

Wolfe pushes another finger inside me. I gasp and grab his shoulders. My movements get more frantic.

"Kora," Apollo urges.

"It feels good," I manage, breathless. "His hand…"

"She's clenching around my fingers," Wolfe continues. "And she's so fucking wet."

"Every time you touch my nipple, it's like electricity goes straight to my cunt," I whisper.

Wolfe smirks and pushes my shirt up. All pretenses lost —it doesn't matter that Apollo's still driving, that it's the middle of the day. He exposes my chest, then folds the cups of my bra down. He leans forward and flicks his tongue against my untouched nipple, keeping the other one pinched.

"Oh my god." I move faster, my hips rocking against him. I can feel Jace's eyes on me. Always watching.

I come like that. With Wolfe's tongue and teeth on my breast and his fingers plunging into me, the calloused heel of his palm rough against my clit. I go still, my head falling back. Wolfe kisses my throat.

It takes me a minute to return to planet Earth. While I sit there in a daze, Wolfe straightens my clothes. Eventually, I slide back over into my own seat. I glance at Wolfe, who gives me a rogue smirk and brings his fingers up to his face.

My eyes widen when he licks them clean. My face gets hot.

We're silent for a moment. Then—

"I'm sitting in the fucking back next time," Apollo mutters.

THE PARKING GARAGE.

The quick walk down an alley and into the fenced backyard.

It's familiar—and not in a good way. My heart is thundering against my ribcage by the time we reach the back deck. The yard is in even worse shape than the first time I saw it. The grass is knee-high, interspersed with thick weeds. There are dying patches, matted straw-colored clumps. Spring hit hard, and it seems like no one was around to take care of it.

Or the deck, which is now sloped away from the sliding glass door. The wood is worn and swayed, and it creaks as Jace goes up the steps. I follow behind, ignoring his motion for me to stay put. Apollo and Wolfe are on our heels.

We enter silently and spread out, Wolfe shadowing me

as we check out the first floor. The kitchen opens into the front room, the large picture window covered by blinds. Light filters through them in streams, narrow little strips of white-gold on the carpet. I check the corners, forcing myself to ignore the bloodstain on the couch.

Apollo.

I swallow and keep moving.

Jace comes down the stairs, and Apollo comes around the other side. We meet at the front door.

Apollo checks the locks—four of them—then shrugs. "Seems fine for our needs."

Wolfe lets out an exasperated scoff. "Our needs?"

"Well, we're not going to find a mansion now, are we?"

"No security, in the middle of West Falls—"

"It's fine," Jace interrupts them. "Kronos wants us dead. Cerberus wants us captured. But only one of them has the motivation to search every hiding place in his side of the city."

"Cerberus," I guess. "Because he wants you back."

Wolfe looks away. Guilty, maybe, because this is his father we're talking about.

"Kronos will think we went back to South Falls, or East Falls. Maybe that we were acting on the Hell Hounds' behalf," Jace says. "That buys us time. And that means West Falls is the safest for us right now."

Titans' territory.

Last time we came here, after Apollo and Jace failed to find and destroy my contract with Kronos, the streets were flooded with Titans. They were knocking on every door...

But they had reason to do it.

"Whose house is this again?" I ask.

"Nyx grew up here." Jace moves away. Toward the kitchen. "Before she became Nyx."

I turn slowly and try to envision a teenage version of the woman I know. I can't really do it. I have no idea what my friend's life was like before the guys entered into it.

"Who was she then?" I ask.

"Elora Whitlock." Apollo leans against the front door, crossing his arms. "Only daughter of a working-class family. She was friendly with the guys at the MMA club a few blocks over, and the owner gave her lessons when he could spare the time. Fighting was her way out of this life."

"What life?"

"Being a Titan." Wolfe's gaze is fixed on the window blinds. "Being... married to a Titan, or dating one, or being used by one."

"This is her story," Apollo says. "You should talk to her about it."

I nod and step back. I wouldn't want them spilling my secrets, so it's only fair that I don't ask them to do the same for her.

"You should get some sleep," Jace says, reappearing from the kitchen. He hands me a bottle of water, then two to the guys. "We'll take it in shifts."

Apollo and Wolfe both focus on me. I narrow my eyes, my attention moving from one to the other.

"What?" I question.

"Do you want company?" Wolfe asks.

Even Jace shifts his weight, like he's ready to anticipate my answer.

I laugh. It's ridiculous, them all watching me with an eager sharpness. The car ride must've got to them. "Sure."

"Who do you want?" Jace asks.

"Oh, no." I gesture between them. "You want *me* to pick? The whole point of this... situationship... is so I *don't* have to pick. One of you wants to join me, figure it out amongst yourselves."

I turn and bolt up the stairs. I'm only halfway there when someone grunts. There's a *thud*, something—or someone—crashing to the floor. I cover my mouth to hide my snicker. But I don't look back as their scuffle continues.

As I said—they'll figure it out.

CHAPTER 28
KORA

Any trace of the young Nyx has been erased from this
house. There are no pictures on the walls, no
personal touches. Just faded magenta-flowered wallpaper,
threadbare carpets, and a collection of furniture. I duck into
the bathroom and take care of business, then find a wash-
cloth and scrub the ash from my skin the best I can. Once
I'm relatively clean, I step into the last bedroom at the end of
the hall.

There are sheets in one of the dresser drawers. I make
the bed quickly, pulling up the blanket that was folded at
the foot of it. Gun on the nightstand, jeans discarded in a
pile beside it. I toe off my socks and pull my shirt off, then
slip under the covers. My eyes are sandpaper, and there are
a million thoughts racing through my mind.

What are we going to do?

Parker. Ben. The Titans and Hell Hounds. The sheriff—
and his sister? Everyone has motives here, everyone wants to
claw through the bodies and come out on top.

Even me.

I close my eyes and fold my arms up over my head. I find

the lip of the headboard and curl my fingers around it, holding on tightly just so I don't lose myself in my thoughts.

The first problem is Ben. The guys apparently left him to fend for himself, and I have no way of contacting him. No way of making sure the guy who saved me on that island is even still breathing. Of course, the guys don't know him. They don't give a shit, and they won't unless I make them.

Then there's Parker.

Why can't he just let me go?

He seemed different. Worse, in a way. My escape from Emerald Cove, and from him, just made him angry. In all honesty, I should've gone much farther away than Sterling Falls to get away from him. Moved to California or Alaska, or hid away in New York City. Big places with lots of people to get lost in.

Too late now.

And my parents. My throat closes up when I think of *them*. The last time I talked to them was weeks ago—surely they know I'm no longer on the island. I wonder if the program has connected my disappearance to Ben's and if that won't work in my favor.

But I can't—*won't*—go back to them. What they did...

I fight my shiver.

The bedroom door closes, and I automatically go still. I don't open my eyes, don't want to ruin the surprise of who decided to come up here. I stay still even when the blanket is lifted and a weight presses down on the mattress.

He doesn't speak either. His body inches down, lying beside me, and lips touch my temple. I inhale and smile.

"Apollo."

"Winner, winner," he whispers in my ear.

I open my eyes and let my head fall to the side, meeting his gaze. "Hi."

"Hey."

"Are you still upset with me?"

He shakes his head. "No, I decided you were right."

"A good decision."

His hand ghosts up my bare side. "We should sleep."

I bite my lip. There's a shadow of a bruise on his cheek. And I can't stop seeing that damn collar Cerberus put on him. Then the whole *love* business. I wish I hadn't read it. I didn't want to hear it from past him, about past me.

I'm different.

He's different.

Who knows if he'll love this version of me, too?

One way to find out...

I roll on my side and reach for him. "Will you do something for me?"

He pulls me closer, his leg slipping between mine. "I could blindly agree, but something tells me your request is going to be wicked."

I push him onto his back and straddle him. The blankets slide off my back, pooling around my hips. I grab his wrists and drag them up over his head, guiding his fingers to lock around the lip of the headboard. The same way I was holding it when he entered.

"What are you going to do?" he asks.

"You're going to let me show you how much I missed you." I move lower, taking his black briefs with me. His cock is already stiff, and I look at it for a moment before I descend. "Don't let go of the headboard."

"Fuck," he mutters, already craning down to look at me better.

I take the tip in my mouth and swirl my tongue around it. I grip his shaft and squeeze, then drag my hand up. When my hand goes down, I take more of him into my mouth. His hips jerk, and his cock hits the back of my throat.

I try not to smile.

"I'm not going to last long at all if you keep this up," he admits.

I'm not bothered by that. I pick up my pace, my intensity. My other hand goes between his legs and cups his balls, earning me another sharp exhale.

Soon enough, his hips are rocking almost against his will. I circle his tip with my tongue, sucking hard, and he mutters some incoherent nonsense—my only warning. He comes in my mouth with a low groan.

I swallow, then lick my lips as I rise.

"That was—"

"Shh," I murmur.

I fix his briefs and climb back up beside him. He covers us with the blanket and sheet, and he wraps me in his arms. I face away from him, my butt against his groin. He shifts a little, moving my hair up, and his lips touch the back of my neck. My shoulder.

"I missed you," he admits.

My heart gives a painful thump.

Same, I almost say.

But the exhaustion is right there, and I can only bare my soul so much in one day.

I WAKE to Apollo's teeth on my shoulder and his erection pressing into my ass cheek. His hand has crept around me, and he cups my breast under my bra... which is suspiciously loose. Someone's been messing with it while I slept.

I smile to myself and shift more, wriggling against his cock.

"Are you awake?" he asks.

"Yes," I whisper.

"Good." He moves my panties aside and thrusts into me from behind.

I gasp. He feels bigger this way, with my legs together. He rolls me onto my stomach and keeps my legs that way, my hips slightly raised. The friction is delicious, with waves of agonizing pleasure crashing through me. I hold my pillow, burying my face in it, as he pulls almost all the way out and thrusts back in.

He fucks me hard. The box spring squeaks with each move, and soon enough, the headboard is bumping the wall rhythmically. He pulls out completely and flips me over, spreading my legs and plunging back into me again. I arch my back and let out a whimper. He braces one hand next to my head, and the other plays my clit like a magical instrument.

I'm sore from all this activity after months of nothing, but I wouldn't trade it for anything. My muscles ache, my abdomen is tight. I reach up and run my hands over Apollo's skin. His abdomen, his chest, his neck.

His dark eyes meet mine. I touch the stubble on his cheeks, then drag him down.

Our lips touch. Slide together. We're not kissing, really, but just breathing against each other. Panting, more like. I catch his lower lip in my teeth and tug.

He pulls free, his eyes gleaming. "You're so fucking perfect," he says, lifting slightly to change his angle. It nearly undoes me. "I don't regret telling you I love you, even if that notebook was the wrong place, the wrong time. I don't give a shit about that. I've known you were the one for us since the day you stole the mask."

I dig my nails into his shoulders. "Then, huh? Not when you chased me through the woods?"

"No." He hooks my leg over his arm and brings it up. This pace is brutal. I reach behind me and press my palms to the headboard, trying to shove back against him. To give him *some* resistance.

"Love at first sight is for morons, then?"

He grins. "No, I'm sure Wolfe felt something for you then, but me? I'm addicted to your fight. To your stubbornness. For your will to do whatever the fuck you want, even when people try to order you around."

I mirror his expression. "Good. Now kiss me."

He does. He resumes his attention on my clit as his tongue slides against mine. The kiss is such a stark contrast to how he's demolishing the rest of me. I savor both sides of that coin. But I miss the possessiveness he had before. His hands on my throat, the way he demanded things of me.

I'll get that back.

But right now—

"Oh my god," I gasp. "I'm going to come."

"Good," he replies.

A minute later, the overpowering sensation blasts through me. I shudder, tensing, and let it ravage my senses. Apollo isn't far behind. He comes with a grunt, his teeth on my earlobe.

Finally, he relaxes. His weight lands on me, and I wrap myself around him like an octopus. He doesn't let me suffocate under him long, though. Still in me, he rolls onto his back and takes me with him.

I put my head on his shoulder, then flick my tongue out and catch a bead of sweat on his neck. "I missed you."

My form of love? I don't know.

I went from not being able to read the words, to not being able to look at him, to being pissed that he was upset about his house burning down. My fault. And now every barrier has been erased, and my mind has settled.

Funny how he can do that to me.

I don't know how he managed it.

"What time is it?" I ask.

"Time to sleep for another few hours," he says, kissing my forehead. "I'm going to go relieve whoever's on watch."

I nod and let him maneuver me to the side. He climbs out of bed, his ass looking *damn* fine. He hunts around for his underwear, which he must've tossed before I woke up. He pulls them on, then his pants. His socks and shoes are next. I watch him, propping my head up on my hand, and try not to drool.

Finally, he tugs his shirt on—giving me a view of those movie-worthy abs—and gives me a cheeky wink. Then he heads to the door and closes it softly behind him.

I sag back on my pillow, letting out a sigh. Then I giggle.

I can't help it.

What's worse? I don't want to help it.

CHAPTER 29
JACE

I try my best not to glower at Apollo when he comes around the corner into the kitchen. It's hard not to, however, since the sound of them having sex traveled through the thin walls with ease.

When it started, Wolfe went out the back, slamming the sliding glass door behind him.

I think I just like to torture myself, so I stayed.

"You need some sleep?" Apollo asks.

I grunt. Me and Wolfe both. We stayed up while they slept... and then fucked. We discussed what we knew of this Ben guy. How Kora seemed genuinely alarmed that we had left him behind.

So... finding him is next on our to-do list.

Lucky for her, I have a GPS tracker on my bike. Unless he ditched it, locating him should be straightforward.

But we're not rushing into anything. I need everyone solid, and that means rested.

"Where's Wolfe?" Apollo crosses to the cabinets, searching them until he finds a jar of peanut butter. There's a heavy layer of oil at the top, but he doesn't seem to mind. He just cracks it open and stirs it back in with a butter knife.

I lean against the counter, crossing my arms. "You expected him to sit through that?"

Apollo has the good grace to blush.

The sliding door opens again, and Wolfe reenters. He's got Kora's bag over his shoulder and the cello case in his hand. He keeps his expression relatively bland when he sees Apollo, but he drops her bag and the instrument to the floor.

"You should take it up," he says to me. "It was your gift after all."

I nod sharply. "Apollo's taking watch. You and I need rest."

Wolfe's got a ghost look about him. I can't quite explain it—but maybe the best way is that he's not all here. He's taken a step back in his head.

And that won't do either.

Guess everyone needs to make their amends with Kora. Her riding his fingers in the car wasn't enough for him?

I grimace and grab the case and her bag. I don't give Apollo another look on my way upstairs.

Wolfe's already shut the door to one of the bedrooms, leaving one open for me.

Kora stands in the doorway of the last.

She eyes the bag and case in my hands, and her brows furrow. "Are those...?"

I stride toward her. Then past her, into her room. I don't know why. I should turn around and walk right back out, but there's something about the messy bed that drills holes in my heart. It's torture. *Again*. I can't seem to stop.

I toss her bag on the bed and step back, but I don't leave. She comes toward me in a t-shirt and gray panties. Her legs are bare—not that she seems to care. She unzips the bag and removes its contents, setting down plain t-shirts and black leggings, white socks, toiletries. She pulls something from the bag with a silver chain and opens her palm.

"What's that?"

She glances at me. Her cheeks are still red, almost matching her wild hair. She steps closer and then holds it out.

I take the necklace from her. At the end of the chain hangs a black stone pendant backed in silver. On the back it says, *To KS, with love*. I have a surge of jealousy that I have to mentally beat back. To be loved that much. To have something to hold on to.

I hand it back, but she waves it off.

"Keep it," she says.

"What? Why?"

"Because my parents shipped me off to a camp on an island, ensuring I couldn't even fucking escape." She steps closer. "Who does that? Who orchestrates... whatever the fuck happened to us? That guy burst into the Hell Hounds' clubhouse. He had no problem killing whoever got in his way. It's a miracle he didn't put a bullet in *you*." She stabs at my chest. "Jesus, Jace, you almost got killed."

I grab her wrists. "I didn't."

"He put you in his car and *tasered you*." She jerks out of my hold and pushes me again. With a lot more force than I was expecting.

I go back a step, then my temper flares. I grab her again and haul her closer, then lean in until we're nose to nose. "I'm so sick of this city. I'm sick of everyone getting the upper hand. I'm sick of Apollo flaunting that he has you, that Wolfe gets to touch you—"

"Newsflash, asshole. You can have me, too."

Fuck. It.

I push her against the wall. Her chest rises and falls faster. Her gaze is glued to my lips. Everything in the whole fucking universe is centered on this moment, and I can't seem to move.

"You can have me if you won't be a dick afterward," she adds. An addendum. A clarification.

"What if I can't help but be an asshole?" I let the pendent swing in front of her face. The engraved side shows toward her, then slowly rotates toward me. "Wear this, would you?"

She makes a face. "I don't even know how it got in my bag."

"So what?" I release her, but I don't back away. If she wants to get by me, she'd have to touch me—and right now, she doesn't seem so inclined to do so. I undo the clasp and reach around her neck. I bring one part of it around and clip it under her chin, then straighten the chain. It's long—it could've probably just gone over her head. The pendant hangs down between her breasts.

She takes it and tucks it under her shirt, out of sight. "Fine," she murmurs. "I'll wear it. But..."

"But?"

"It doesn't mean I forgive them." She gives me a weird look, then touches my cheek.

I flinch.

Her hand doesn't go away, like I thought it might. She just keeps touching my cheek, her fingers finding their way along the bone. This may be the first time she's touched me like this. With care.

My chest is tight.

I don't know how Apollo and Wolfe do this with her.

How they match her softness. I am so out of my fucking depth with her. With affection.

"A deadbeat dad and a dead mom," she says quietly.

I almost flinch again. *Almost.*

"And then you were passed along to Cerberus?"

"Something like that." We're missing a few steps, but I don't want to talk about that. Not now, with her.

She takes my hand and lets the one on my face fall back to her side. She leads me down the hall to the vacant bedroom. I watch her from the doorway as she makes the bed with slow, methodical movements. Then she sits at the foot of it, scooting all the way back so she's leaning against the wall. She points to it.

"I'll keep watch," she says.

I frown, but I sit on the edge of the bed. I lower myself on the foreign mattress, fluffing the pillow and sliding my arm under it. I face away from the door for once, because I'd rather see her.

She doesn't move. Doesn't stretch out beside me, doesn't extend her legs. She takes up a relatively small spot on the bed. And she doesn't seem perturbed that I don't take my shoes off and I don't put the blanket over me.

This life has taught me that those precious seconds can cost too much. And they're just small comforts anyway. Things that are easy to live without when living—surviving —is the goal.

"Sleep," she says softly.

Strangely enough, I abide.

It's dark when I wake up, and I'm alone. The bedroom door is cracked open, the hallway light on and letting in a sliver of warm yellow. I rub my face and sit up, swinging my feet down to the floor.

My body hurts. I don't think I've slept this hard in a long time. My watch indicates that it's the middle of the night— and I've slept for well over eight hours. I take the opportunity to shower in the hallway bathroom, sudsing everything and rinsing under hot water, then stepping out and redressing.

The house is stocked with nondescript clothes, generic sizes that fit all of us. I find a clean shirt and underwear, new socks. Then head downstairs.

The first floor is silent and dark. The sliding glass door in the back is open an inch. I walk toward it, almost afraid of what I'm going to find. Dead bodies?

The photo of Kora with her throat slit flashes in my mind. Even though it was an edited picture, a manipulation, that image has haunted me more than anyone knows.

No dead bodies outside—just Kora. She sits on the edge of the deck, her legs dangling off. I step outside and close the door almost all the way behind me, then sit beside her. Not too close, of course. But close enough to smell whatever's in the mug in her hand.

She glances at me. "Sleep okay?"

"Yeah. You?"

"I dozed until you started snoring."

I frown.

"Always so serious, Jace King. I was kidding. You don't snore." She grimaces. "You just kind of make this moaning noise, like you're in pain..."

"That's better."

"Do you have nightmares?"

I shrug. "Maybe. If I do, I don't remember them when I wake up."

"That's lucky." She offers me the mug.

I take it from her, avoiding her fingers. The ceramic is warm, and I take a sip without questioning what it is.

Tea.

Spiked tea.

The cinnamon whiskey burns my throat, and I fight the urge to cough. It's not like me to not handle my liquor—but then again, this particular variety tends to taste like battery acid. I take another swallow to cover it up, and Kora chuckles.

"Where'd you find this?"

"In the freezer." She tips her head back. "Well, the nip of whiskey anyway. The tea was in the pantry."

I follow suit, mirroring her position. The sky has cleared up, giving us an unblemished view of the stars. One good thing since everything happened: less light pollution. This section of town, so close to downtown, would allow only the brightest stars to be visible. But now, it's like the sky isn't just black. It's a patchwork of millions of other lives.

"Do you know the Greek heroes are in the constellations? Beasts, too. But not the gods."

I glance at her, then set the mug between us. "The gods don't need stars."

"Why is that?"

"Because we're here on Earth."

She lets out an exhale. "You think you're so invincible, Jace. It's going to get you killed."

I reach out and touch her shoulder. She stiffens under my hand, but she doesn't move away. I don't know why I have the inclination to touch her, or why I can't stop fucking thinking about her. I wish I wouldn't. But she's imbedded in my mind and under my skin.

"I want you to understand something, Chaos." I grip her shoulder tighter, willing her not to retreat. "The gods won in the end. Not the Titans, not the three-headed dog. *Us*. And it's because we were born of them. We suffered through blood when we were kids."

"We?"

Maybe.

"What do you want? The war to end? The gangs to dissolve? How do you think that's going to happen?"

She knocks my hand off her shoulder and swivels to face me fully. "How do I *think* that's going to happen? How did *you* plan for it to go? How did you see Sterling Falls when you left the Hell Hounds? And what happened to knock you off your path?" Her eyes are cutting straight through me. "You think you know so much. You think we can make some plan and wrangle everyone back into a truce, then come out on top. But it won't work. Your plan won't work."

"And why's that?"

"Because if you were going to get it right, you would've already." She grabs her mug and hops to her feet. "You had five years. It's my turn."

I wince. She doesn't stick around for my rebuttal—but I don't have one. I watch her disappear back into the house, and then I turn back and face the dilapidated yard.

She's so fucking right it hurts.

Which means we're going to have to do the one thing I really, *really* don't want to do.

We've got to tell her the truth that we've been hiding.

CHAPTER 30
KORA

I come to suddenly, jackknifing upright and swinging.

Except, there's no one around. The living room is empty, although voices aren't far off.

I fell asleep in the chair next to the bloodstained couch. I debated just flipping over the cushion, using the backside, but I couldn't do it. So I curled up on the chair and fell asleep. After the spiked tea, it was surprisingly easy to let my mind go quiet.

Now, it's the smell of bacon that captures my attention first. Then the sizzle of it.

I straighten my clothes and rise, coming around the corner to find all three of them in the kitchen. Apollo at the stove. Jace and Wolfe at the table.

"Morning," I say, tentative.

I'm not sure if Jace is mad at me for what I told him last night, but he shows no indication of being extra grumpy. He looks up, and one corner of his lips turns up. Then he goes back to the map in front of him.

"Good morning." Apollo abandons the stove and comes over, wrapping me in a giant hug.

It's exactly what I need.

I hug him back, fisting his shirt and holding on for dear life. Until I can breathe a little easier anyway. "Where did you get bacon?"

"I ran to the store this morning," he says.

I release him, and he nudges me toward the table.

I almost sit, then shake my head. "I need to brush my teeth. Immediately."

Wolfe rolls his eyes. "Did you pack toothpaste?"

"Umm... no."

He rises and gestures for me to follow him. I raise my eyes at his back, then glance from Jace to Apollo. Neither of them seem particularly worried, so I follow Wolfe upstairs.

"Are you okay?"

He checks over his shoulder. "Me? Dandy."

"Uh-huh."

He digs through a drawer in the bathroom and hands me a travel-sized tube of toothpaste. One I could've easily found on my own.

"Did you want to say something? To me?"

Is he avoiding my gaze, or am I going crazy?

"Wolfe."

"What?"

"What's wrong with you?" I block his exit from the bathroom.

He stares at me for a moment, then exhales. His gaze drops to the chain around my neck, and he wordlessly reaches out and tugs the pendant free. I'd almost forgotten about it, but he inspects it, and the back, before dropping it. It hits my sternum with a dull *thud*.

"I just don't know how you can forgive so easily," he says.

I narrow my eyes. "Are you talking about my parents? Or you?"

He doesn't answer.

I step closer. "To answer your non-question, I *don't* forgive easily. I have a lot of resentment toward my parents. Kronos. Cerberus. Sterling Falls in general. The camp. The island. The sheriff."

"Your list?"

"Yeah." I'm inching closer, and he's backing away. I don't know if he even knows he's doing it. "There are people who need to pay for their actions. But, Wolfe, you're not one of them."

He scoffs. "Tell that to the guy who held a gun to your head—*oh wait, that's me*. I almost fucking killed you—"

"We've been over this," I interrupt. "I don't care. I forgive you. Stop blaming yourself."

"Kora—"

"Wolfe. Shut. Up." I kick the bathroom door closed behind me and reach for him. My hormones seem to be going insane, because I can't get enough of them. I want *all* of them, together, separately. "I want us to be okay. I *need* us to be okay."

He grips my hips and lifts me, setting me on the counter.

Familiar territory.

My knees part, letting him step closer, and I keep my eyes on his face. "You guys are the reason I came back to Sterling Falls. *You*. Apollo. Jace. I love this city, but if you told me the best move is to pack up and leave, I'd do it."

He slides his hands around my throat. His thumbs press on the underside of my jaw, keeping my head up. "I have to ask you something."

"Okay."

"If my father sinks his claws into Apollo and me again... you have to save Apollo."

I swallow. He catches it, he feels it. Of course he does. His grip tightens ever so slightly, and my heart skips.

"Why would you make me choose?"

"He's worth saving."

I push at him, then pull him closer. He rocks, his weight shifting backward, then forward.

"You're an idiot. God, you're the actual worst." Now I do shove him away, sliding back to my feet. "If you think he's worth any more than you, you're out of your goddamn mind."

A hurt expression crosses his face. "Kora—"

"Stop. We're going to beat this, Wolfe, but you've got to give yourself some credit." I don't know how to fix him. I don't know how to put his confidence back together, when he's so clearly been shattered by his father.

Six months.

How can I fix in a day what it took his father months to break?

His father made him feel worthless. His father took his confidence, his self-assured ease, and ground it into the dirt. How many lies did Cerberus tell Wolfe about me? About Jace, about Apollo, and everyone else who gives a damn about him? How long did Wolfe spend in isolation before his father's words started to sink in?

It's clear. It's all so crystal clear now that he's let me peek past his mask. He's put up a front for himself, pretended to be okay for the last twenty-four hours. But he can only fake it for so long—and now, here we are.

My eyes are burning. There's a lump in my throat.

I open the bathroom door, then I reel him in again and kiss him. I walk him backward, into the hallway, then break away. He's got a dazed look in his eyes, like he doesn't know what the hell to make of me. So I step back and close the bathroom door in his face.

Because I can't take any more of this. I might just burst otherwise.

I turn the lock and lean my shoulder against it.

It's only then that the tears fall.

———

EVENTUALLY, I pull myself together enough to go back downstairs. My eyes are *slightly* red, but I've got my fingers crossed that no one notices. My hair is freshly washed, and it was a wonder to use warm water and real shampoo. And conditioner.

Small comforts.

I'm just in time for breakfast. I take the seat next to Jace, who's still got the map in front of him. He chews the cap of his red pen when he's not making little notes.

I crane over and try to read his cramped handwriting, and he gets tired of me peeking relatively quickly. He slides the map toward me and lets me have a better look.

It's a map of Sterling Falls, of course. It's pretty detailed, and it includes outside the city limits to the west, where the reservoir and the Titans' converted chapel sit. Just south of that is the falls where Apollo once took me. Straight across to the east is the center of town, the once-neutral zone... now Hell Hound territory, as gifted by the mayor.

Between the university in the center of town and North Falls is the financial district, with the more expensive neighborhoods of North Falls above that. Then the boardwalk, North Falls main street, and the beaches.

The road that continues from the North Falls main street east, curving along the cliffs that move east, then turn south along the eastern coast, eventually leads to Olympus. Hell Hound territory. Down, down, down to the industrial district in South Falls, and the harbor and marina at the bottom, facing south.

The one main highway in and out of Sterling Falls, which approaches from the southeast, has a red X across it.

"What happened?"

"The Titans have a roadblock set up," Jace explains. "They destroyed our checkpoint outside of the city and have their own men posted there. Anyone who gets in and out of the city goes through them."

"Anyone who goes by car," Apollo clarifies. He puts a plate in front of me, just to the side of the map, and takes his seat between Wolfe and me.

"Thanks," I murmur.

"So," Jace continues. "The harbor is iffy. There are too many vantage points, and it keeps changing hands. For now, it seems like the sheriff's department has put a lock on it."

"Interesting."

"He's upped his game since we last saw him," Jace continues. "But you would know that, wouldn't you?"

My face heats. "Yeah, um, I was arrested."

Wolfe spits out his coffee.

I fix my gaze on the map and explain what happened. How the sheriff eventually came into the interview room and we took a drive to the university, where he made a case to the city council.

"You saw the aldermen?" This from Jace, whose brow is furrowed. "They're at the university?"

"That's where we went, yeah. They and the mayor were meeting. Alex Sterling, Nadine Bradshaw..." I press my lips together. "Probably should've known that the sheriff's sister is an alderman, don't you think?"

"Did you talk to her?" Apollo asks.

"Yeah, she pulled me aside. Seemed nice enough. Gave me her card." Which has since been lost, although it's probably just in one of my jean pockets. "Alex Sterling argued in my favor, too. Although that's not the first time I've met him."

They all stare at me.

I shrug. "What? I had dinner with Nate—"

"Oh god. *Nate*?"

My face is getting even hotter, and I meet Wolfe's horrified stare. "Just because you guys don't get along with him doesn't mean he's evil." A position I didn't think I'd be taking. "*Anyway*, I had dinner with him the night you and Jace fought. Or don't you remember that?"

"I remember something else from that night." Wolfe smirks.

Mask firmly back in place.

I shake it off and lean back in my chair.

Apollo pushes the plate of food closer to me. "Eat."

My stomach growls. It's been a while since I had a meal —which isn't something my body is accustomed to anymore. I eat the eggs and bacon, piling them on the toasted English muffin and creating a sandwich.

"Here are our contenders," Jace says, also sitting back. "The Titans are only as ambitious as Kronos. That bastard will keep poking at Cerberus until he gets what he wants—"

"No," I interrupt, covering my mouth. "Sorry, um, no. Everyone was freaked out because Kronos was more worried about you than Cerberus. That's what spurred us into searching for you."

"That's what made *you* go search for him and then get arrested, you mean?" Apollo snickers. "Brilliant, by the way."

"Oh, shut up." I resume chewing, then reach over and take Apollo's mug of coffee. He drinks it with less cream than me, but it'll do.

"If we go by that theory, then Kronos is a non-factor. Cerberus is the one to worry about." Jace rubs his lips. "So, first we get the Titans under control, then the Hell Hounds."

"Question." I quirk my lips. "You didn't take out the Titans for years. Why now?"

Jace sighs. He glances at the other two, then turns to face me fully. "You've called us out on our bullshit. And in truth, we've been afraid to deal with the risk of the Titans voting someone into power who wants to take over everything— another Cerberus. Someone stronger than Kronos."

"Kronos is an evil dick," I point out. "Who has no problem trafficking humans. How much worse can it get?"

They shake their heads.

"Worse," Apollo says shortly.

Okay, then. "So, we take down... all of them? Find some way to bury the Titans so far down, they never have a chance of coming back."

Nods all around.

"Works for me." I sit up straighter. "And the sheriff?"

"Will hopefully mind his own business," Wolfe grumbles.

We lapse into silence, then Jace circles a house on the map. "This is where Kronos lives."

He explains the layout to me. It's in the neighborhood in North Falls right on the water, about as far west as you can get. So, expensive and secluded, for the most part. Ocean on one side, dunes and forest on the other.

"If he's still there, you want to attack it?"

Jace makes a face. "Well, we discovered the hard way that the glass is bulletproof."

I laugh. Of course they discovered it the hard way. Actually—I think he mentioned that was Ben's plot that went off course.

"Okay, so..." We sit in silence again, and I tap my fingers on the table. "I think I have an idea. But you guys aren't going to like it very much."

CHAPTER 31
SAINT

Nyx's childhood home hasn't changed much. The guys have taken out the ugly, scratchy upholstered couch and put it in the backyard. It's upside down, its wooden feet sticking up into the air. There are cobwebs clinging to them, and the felt pads that her parents might've glued on years ago still holding strong.

There was a time when I slept on that couch. When we feared the gangs would retaliate against us for associating with Jace, Wolfe, and Apollo. That was in the early days, when their rebellion was young. Strong.

Everything ground to a halt in the years that followed. Cerberus and Kronos accepted the space the guys had carved for themselves, grudgingly agreed to the new rules. Temporary rules, with temporary enforcers.

There was a lot of fear that lived in the city, under the guise of a polished exterior. The tourist business boomed, the university grew in notoriety. Things picked up—and the gangs wanted their slice of the profits.

Of course they did.

I touch Nyx's shoulder. She's avoided coming back here

in recent years. The last time she was even in this neighborhood was because of them and her willingness to help.

Help. That's a dangerous word in this godforsaken place.

Until recently, I only *helped* the guys in a legal sense.
Made masks, ran their security team from afar, ran their
staff at Olympus. Nothing that would've put me on anyone's
radar.

But I was on someone's radar. Kronos'. The Titans'. I
don't know if Cerberus is aware of me... and part of me
doesn't want to find out.

I press my hand to my side. The pain is almost unbearable without medication. The stitches Antonio gave me are
clean, neat, precise. Exactly what I would've expected. But
when I close my eyes, I can still feel *everything*. The chains
around my wrists, which have lingering bruises and scrapes,
the strain in my shoulders as they hoisted me off my feet.
The slide of metal into my belly while I screamed...

"Come back." Nyx's hands are on my cheeks, her touch
light. "You're here with me."

I shudder, and my chest releases. I take in a breath and
put a steadying hand on her hip. "I don't know what I'd do
without you."

She smiles and steps closer, pressing up on her toes.
She's tall, but our faces only align when I tip my head down.
So I do, meeting her warm brown eyes. They look like
brown sugar in a certain light, but right now they're nearly
black.

"Okay, okay," Wolfe calls, stepping out onto the back
porch. "Let's get inside."

"Ready?" I ask her.

She gives me a look. *Right.*

Okay. I let her wiggle out of my embrace and go up the
warped deck steps. I follow behind her, skipping the boards

that seem the weakest. We go in through the sliding glass door, into the kitchen, and I hold my breath.

Not sure what I was expecting. Ghosts to come flying out of the cabinets?

Nyx moves ahead of me, through the doorway and toward the front of the house. I stay back with Wolfe, eyeing him. This is the first time I've *seen* him since before the war. In the truest sense of being able to talk to him face-to-face. Freely.

He looks haunted.

I look from him to Apollo who enters the room from the doorway Nyx just passed through. I don't know how I'm feeling—just that we're on the edge of the cliffs.

Wouldn't be the first time we jumped.

"Are we ready for this?" I ask.

Apollo nods. "We've let this go on for too long."

Don't I know it. Kora's the catalyst. Without her, we'd still be in the same ruts. I'd still be in a cell, tormented by Titans night and day. Jace would still be on the run, Wolfe and Apollo would still be under the Hell Hounds' thumb. Nyx, Artemis...

"Saint." Kora comes in and touches my arm. "How are you feeling?"

I shake my head. "Alive is the best I can ask for at this moment."

"Great. Let's sit." She tips her head, gesturing for us to follow her back into the other room.

The living room at the front is now almost completely bare... except for a map spread on the rug. There are still indentations from the couch's legs on one side, and the chair that sat next to it has been shoved back in the corner. A lamp from one of the side tables is now on the floor, pulled as close to the map as possible.

Kora sits on one side. Artemis and Nyx are already there, also sitting. Artemis leans against the wall under the window, her legs crossed and eyes half-mast. Besides the single light, it's dark in here. Cloaked in shadows.

Footsteps pound down the stairs, then Jace rounds the corner. He shakes my hand, then smiles at Nyx. "Glad you made it."

I nod. "Of course. What's the plan?"

I go for the empty floorspace next to Nyx, but she points to the chair on her other side. I roll my eyes, intending to ignore her, but Apollo stops me.

"Injured guys get the good seats." He winks. "Take advantage, man."

I sigh and take the chair. Sure, it's easier to lower myself into the armchair than it would've been to get down on the floor. And infinitely more comfortable. But I don't like the guilty look Artemis gives me or the way Wolfe's weight shifts back and forth. They don't like my injury either—because it doesn't let me help them the way they need.

This is clearly an all-hands-on-deck situation.

Hell, I don't even know the extent of their plans, but I know something big is about to happen. Something that will hopefully set us on a better path.

Jace's phone goes off, and he disappears into the kitchen. The sliding glass door makes a distinct scraping noise, slightly off its track, and then it closes. There are low voices murmuring, greeting each other, and Jace reappears. He steps aside, revealing Daniel—and a man I don't know.

Kora, however, shoots to her feet.

She stares at the newcomers with a mix of amazement and horror.

I glance at Nyx who bites her lip. Wolfe and Apollo are glaring at the stranger. Kora keeps staring, her mouth opening and closing. It seems like she's trying to decide which question to spit out first.

"Someone going to make introductions?" I finally ask.

Kora starts. "This is Ben. Ben—"

"We've met," he says briskly, looking around at all of us. His demeanor is intriguing. He isn't afraid or meek. He has a level of comfort, even in this new place, that rubs me the wrong way. His gaze lands on me. "Met Dan outside. And you... Saint, she said?"

I lift my chin.

His expression stays light. "As most of you know, I met Kora on Isle of Paradise. We became friends."

Ah, fuck. *That's* where her parents kept her? I'm seeing Kora through new eyes. That place... well, it was where my parents threatened to send me as a kid. An island that straightens you out under the guise of getting you over your trauma. They deal with addiction, anger issues... Not the kind of place Kora should be.

And judging from the expressions of the guys, they didn't really know where she'd been either. Apollo turns away, his palm sliding down his face.

"That's all you were," Wolfe murmurs.

Ben pauses, the tiniest little trace of a smirk crossing his face. "Right."

Silence.

Awkward.

I reach down and take Nyx's hand, a warm feeling spreading through my chest when she squeezes my fingers.

"Fill us in," I finally drawl. "You're here because...?"

"You need my help."

Artemis scoffs. "Like you were so helpful in letting Kronos escape last time." Her gaze goes to me. "He assisted with your rescue. Then conveniently stayed behind."

"Nothing convenient about it—"

"Then you happened to meet Jace," Apollo says. "After surviving a night in Titan territory. And took him to the Titans' new lair, which would've gotten him killed if we didn't arrive. How do you explain that?"

Ben shrugs. "We're exceedingly lucky."

Kora groans. "Can you just be serious for once?"

Daniel rubs the back of his neck. "I can wait outside—"

"Sit down, Daniel," Wolfe snaps.

He does, beside me. We're old acquaintances from school, and we've worked together on a number of projects that required his skills with computers. Hacking, security. He's dabbled in all of it. And the guys tend to let me fully handle the legal side of their operations.

Kora goes to Ben and stops in front of him. She seems to be communicating silently with him—something that puts the rest of them on edge. No one wants Ben here, and yet... he's found us. They seem to reach some unspoken consensus, because the cockiness Ben strolled in here with falls away.

She nods and goes to Apollo. Their relationships are fascinating to watch. How she interacts with all of them.

And then I try to imagine sharing Nyx, and it boils my blood. Best friends or no, I'd murder them all for touching her.

"Kronos is not in North Falls anymore," Ben says. He stops at the edge of the map of Sterling Falls and stares down at it. "Hate to break it to you, but he's in the wind."

Jace grunts. "Because you stole our chance at surprising him."

Ben dips his head. "Yes."

Nyx leans toward me, her voice pitched almost too low

for me to hear. "He knew where Kronos was holding you. He grew up with them, supposedly."

"Do you know where?" Jace eventually asks.

Ben shakes his head.

Kora sighs. "Okay, so—"

"But I do have an idea of how to find him," Ben interrupts. He flashes Kora an apologetic look. No one else speaks up, though, so he continues, "Kronos has an inkling that I'm in the city... and we're going to give me to him."

Silence.

Again.

It's less awkward, more horrified.

"Why?" Kora voices the question on all our minds.

He sighs. He slides his hands into his pockets and goes to the wall, leaning his shoulder against it. "I've been hiding from him for a very long time. And if this brings about the end..."

The guys look to Kora. We do, too. Nyx, Daniel, Artemis, me.

It's her decision.

And she knows it. She takes a deep breath and nods. "Okay. Let's do it."

CHAPTER 32
KORA

"Are you ready for this?"

Lowering the bow of the cello, I glance over my shoulder at Jace. I couldn't resist testing it out—the case sat next to the duffle bag in my room, practically begging me to play it. And as I did, I relaxed. For the first time in a while, the tension drained out of me.

Now, I stash it back in the hard shell case and rise, brushing invisible lint off my pants. Am I ready for what's about to happen? That's anyone's guess. There are a million things that *could* happen—and maybe that's what I'm most afraid of. Being unable to predict the outcome.

We have to succeed. If we don't, someone's going to get hurt.

"Kora?"

I shake my head. "I'm fine. Are you?"

He snorts. "Yeah."

They all went to hang Ben out as the Titans' bait without us. Ben argued that Kronos wants him, Jace, and me. Getting all three of us in a room together will be dangerous, and it has to happen on our terms.

The rest of them agreed. They're waiting for Ben to be scooped up, and we'll follow them back to wherever Kronos is hiding now. And then we'll figure out if we go through with my plan, or if we should scrap it and start over.

I cross my arms, drumming my fingers on my forearms. I've got too much energy now the room has gone quiet again. Sitting still hasn't been in my wheelhouse for a while. And right now, I feel... useless.

"What are we doing?" I ask.

He's got his classic bad-boy uniform on. A tight black t-shirt that should be illegal, leather straps of a shoulder holster, currently missing the two guns it can hold. Black pants, boots. His dark hair is damp and messy, like he ran his fingers through it right before coming in here. Dark scruff on his cheeks gives him a roguish appearance.

And those blue eyes just know exactly how to skewer me.

His gaze moves down my body, then back. Sizing me up the same way I did to him. "Everyone can feel when you're not right with someone."

I narrow my eyes and drop my arms. I step closer. "Not right with someone, or not right with one of you?"

"The latter."

I keep approaching. He's tensing, spine straightening, but he doesn't try to stop me from getting in his face. Why do I like prodding him so much? Pushing all his buttons? He does the same to me.

"Who am I not right with, Jace? You?"

"Me, Wolfe. Apollo." He looks away. "Everything is off, and the whole fucking universe can feel it."

I reach for him. My fingertips brush his chest, sliding flat until my palm is pressed over his heart. I imagine I can feel the rapid heartbeat that tells me there's some emotion there for me.

There must be.

"You want to make it right?" I ask.

He inclines his chin. His eyes are burning. I don't know what I'm doing, but I don't want to stop. I don't want to censor my actions around him anymore. Sometimes, I even think I *like* him, against all reason.

So, fuck it.

I curl my hand in the fabric of his shirt, ensuring he can't get away from me. "Tell me how bad it was for you, then. Tell me how goddamn awful it was being *here*, on the run, while I—" My voice cracks. I press my lips together and swallow sharply. Quieter, I continue, "While I was totally alone. I didn't know if you were dead or alive. If Wolfe and Apollo were in prison. I sat on that stupid fucking island and waited for *six months*." I started quiet, but by the end my voice has risen. A lump forms in my throat.

I release his shirt abruptly and back away.

"I was desperate to come back and now I don't recognize anything about it."

He's staring at me like he doesn't know me.

And he doesn't.

I've changed. For better or worse, I couldn't say. But I'm angry.

"Ask me." His expression is hard to read, and he inches closer. "Ask, Kora. Just spit out the damn question on the tip of your tongue. The one you're afraid to ask."

You know what? *Fine.*

"Why didn't you look for me, Jace? Why didn't you save me?"

His lips flatten. His whole body tenses, as if electrocuted. Eerily familiar to how he reacted when he was tased, but there's no one holding the weapon to his skin now. Just a question.

"I didn't want you to come back," he admits. "I didn't want you anywhere near here—"

My eyes fill with tears. Chest tightens. My mind takes a second to catch up to my emotional reaction, and I realize... "That's bullshit."

He rears back. "Excuse me?"

"That's fucking bullshit and you know it. Don't lie to me." I shove at him, furious that for a moment, he had me fooled.

He rocks on his heels, eyes narrowing.

I push again, my palms connecting with his chest. "You didn't save Wolfe or Apollo, either, and that's not because you didn't want them in Sterling Falls. They were stuck, and you just sat on the sidelines—"

He captures my wrists and pushes me against the wall. *Finally.* He crowds in close, and I let my head fall back. He never breaks eye contact.

"You know what the truth is, princess?" His voice is pitched almost too low to hear. "The truth is that I had to pick between saving *you* and trying to save as many goddamn people in this city as I could. You, Wolfe, Apollo. Three people versus stopping a whole fucking war. You tell me how that makes sense."

I shake my head. "Stop it."

"This war is in the city's bones." His lips trail over my cheekbone and pause at my ear. "The *truth* is that I was so fucking miserable saving everyone but you, I almost let it all go."

"But you didn't." Is it wrong to want someone to pick me?

"Because I've demonstrated time after fucking time that I can't save you no matter how hard I try."

His words shoot straight through me.

"I wasn't able to protect you from Kronos. The auction. The fire." He lifts my wrist, running his thumb over the brand. "I may as well have held the iron to your skin."

Ah.

He lets my wrist slip through his fingers, but I only move so I can take his hand. I squeeze, trying to convey... something.

"All I've wanted is honesty. I wanted Wolfe and Apollo and you to just treat me how you feel, with nothing holding you back."

He kisses me.

It's inevitable. I felt it building in my chest from the moment he walked through the door. It doesn't matter how many times we fight, the barbs we trade, the way I want to throttle him. The hurt that assaulted me a moment ago washes away, replaced with hunger.

I only hope that this time, I'll break through the mask he wears.

He picks me up, keeping me against the wall, and I tilt my head. My mouth opens. Our kiss deepens, the pressing need ricocheting around inside me. I want to touch all of him at the same time. Two hands aren't enough.

Still.

I break away, panting slightly. "Fuck me if you promise not to be an asshole about it afterward."

He raises his eyebrow. "Me?"

"Yes, you, Mr. I-Use-Jabs-To-Keep-People-Away."

He snickers. "Fine, I promise to be on my best behavior." He rocks his hips forward. "Now... can I take your panties off, or do you want me to pinky swear?"

I roll my eyes and wriggle out of his hold. He lets my legs go back to the floor, and I quickly yank my pants off. Panties, too. I kick them away and edge around him, giving myself more room to take my shirt off. Then bra. I drop it and raise my eyebrows, unsurprised that he's still in the same position. Staring.

God, his eyes do something to me.

"Jace," I murmur, backing toward the bed. "Are you going to take advantage of the situation... or should I just take care of myself?" I sit and spread my legs. I'm fucking soaked—maybe verbal sparring is our foreplay—and sensation shoots through me when my fingers brush my clit.

I spread farther, leaning back slightly, and thrust two fingers into my cunt.

"Jesus, Kora," he breathes.

"What'd you do while we were away?" I ask in a fake deep voice, mocking. "Oh, I just watched Kora finger herself. Didn't want to join in—"

He growls and lunges forward. In seconds, he's got me farther back on the bed—but he doesn't undress. Doesn't take his cock out and fuck me like we're both dying for. No, he kneels in front of me, between my legs, and pries me open wider.

I lie back. My eyelids flutter at the first stroke of his tongue on my pussy. He explores, tasting me, casually removes my fingers. He sucks them into his mouth, one at a time, and my cunt is *throbbing* as his tongue works around the pad of my index finger.

Fuck me sideways.

His fingers push into me, curling on my G-spot. I arch my back. His little chuckle precedes his mouth descending on me. He licks my clit, then sucks. I groan, grasping at the blankets. My heels come down on his back, my thighs tensing on his head.

He works me over until I'm a writhing mess. I can't stop the babble of noises coming out of my mouth. He's got a magic fucking mouth and fingers, and he doesn't stop even when I tell him I'm coming. The orgasm bowls me over and leaves me weak. If I wasn't on the bed, I'd be in a puddle on the floor. White spots flicker in front of my eyes.

"Goddamn," I whisper.

I don't even care when he crawls up my body and kisses me again. I don't *hate* the taste of myself. But then he's withdrawing, and I manage to open my eyes long enough to see him tear his shirt off. He loses his pants, but then he turns around.

I miss what he does, but he comes over to me and puts his mouth over mine. Cool liquid comes out of his mouth and into mine, the taste registering a second later.

Whiskey.

I swallow, the liquor burning a path down my throat. I don't even know where he got it—and at this point, I don't care.

He moves me farther up the bed and hovers over me. His eyes burn into me. He inches inside me, and his size stretches me deliciously.

I had forgotten about his monster cock. Like, *damn*.

"You take me so good, princess." He rocks out and then farther into me. "Fuck, you're perfect." He cups my breast, rolling my nipple between his fingers.

I can hardly breathe. Last time, he fucked me like he didn't really give a shit if it was painful. Now, he's making *fitting* look like a skill... he's still shallow, thrusting in and out slowly. Torturously slow. My bones are jelly, but my abdomen is clenching.

"You feel like heaven," he admits.

"I need—"

"I know, princess." He thrusts deeper, groaning in my ear. "This is it. There's no walking away from this anymore."

"I know." I close my eyes.

His lips touch my throat. Teeth follow a second later, a pinch of pain. Tongue. He sucks on my throat. "You like that."

"Yeah," I manage.

"You're wetter."

My cheeks heat.

He does it again. Kiss, bite, lick, suck.

Then he pushes all the way into me, and we both make obscene noises. I curve my legs around his hips, locking my ankles. His pace quickens, driven on by my nails raking his back. Every time he pounds into me, it hits my G-spot. It feels so fucking good, my legs tremble. My muscles are obliterated.

"I'm going to come again," I whimper.

"Good," he growls.

He fucks me harder. The headboard slams into the wall, the box spring is creaking. This is loud and unashamed, and I'm so turned on, every touch threatens to undo me.

He bites my breast, and that's game over. My muscles clench around him, and I come with his name on my lips. He follows a few seconds later, stilling all the way inside me. His cock pulses, and we both breathe heavily. He rolls to the side, taking me with him.

I let out a little noise of surprise, especially when he wraps his arm around my back. He positions me half draped over him, our legs tangled. He slips out of me, and his cum seeps out, too.

"What are you doing?" I ask.

His eyes close, and he adjusts the pillows. "Taking a nap. Cuddling. I don't fucking know, but what else should we do while we wait for Ben to get kidnapped?"

I grin. It's true—we're playing the waiting game. I adjust, hooking my arm over his abdomen, and press a kiss to his throat. "Fine by me."

CHAPTER 33
WOLFE

I glance at Apollo. Ben was just stuffed into the backseat of a blacked-out SUV, just like he predicted. It would be easy to let him slip through our fingers and find Kronos another way. Especially if Kronos wants Ben dead.

I don't like how he talked to Kora. How he looked at her. It could be innocuous, but it could be something else. Something more deceptive...

Apollo sighs. "I don't have it in me to be that blood-thirsty today."

I grunt my acknowledgement. I guess if we let him die, I'd never hear the end of it.

My bike purrs to life under me, and I flip my helmet's visor down. Without a word, I hit the throttle and pull out onto the street. The bike is a loaner. Flashy, red. Not the sort of thing I'd be riding... which is precisely the point.

Saint arranged that for us. He also got Apollo a neon-blue bike. My best friend catches up to me halfway down the block. He flips me off, and I grin.

Serious business doesn't always have to be so *serious*.

Besides, we're free men.

S. MASSERY

Maybe not forever... but right now? I'll take it. The way I feel so much lighter is amazing—I haven't felt this good in months. And that's saying something, knowing that we're about to try and take down Kronos.

"We're riding parallel," Nyx says in my ear.

The earbuds and open line of communication were just some of the toys Daniel brought along with him. It's handy, I'll give them that.

"They're heading toward North Falls," she adds.

"Maybe he has another house," Apollo guesses. "Or he decided that mansion on the beach was good enough for him."

"It's defensible," Daniel says. "I've got an overhead satellite image and... it's impressive. A fortress."

"The bulletproof glass is a perk," I add. "That had to be expensive."

"No doubt." Daniel pauses. "The tracker on Ben seems to be heading back to that location."

"We'll confirm with our own eyes." I glance at Apollo. I can't see his face, and he can't see mine, but I have a feeling we're thinking the same thing. That Ben can't be trusted. It's a gut feeling, and my gut has yet to lead me astray.

We slow down, letting the SUV with Ben in it get farther ahead. Saint and Nyx pick it up, turning onto our street behind it. There's not *much* traffic, not enough to remain inconspicuous. Trading off who's tailing, and in what vehicle, should hopefully throw them off.

Ahead, Artemis and Daniel wait in another vehicle. They'll take the last part of our tail. When we locate the safe house, they'll sit on it until we're ready to move in.

Last night, Apollo came clean that he's been feeding information to the sheriff. Then Kora reminded us about meeting the city council. Bradshaw's sister, Nadine. And Alex Sterling offered to help her, too.

That's Kora's plan. She wants Kronos in prison—which means getting the sheriff to actually make an arrest. But perhaps her new friends will have enough sway to make a charge stick.

"Do we have ears?" I ask.

"Not until he's inside," Daniel answers.

Right. That lack of trust I mentioned? We planted a bug on Ben. One of those high-tech ones that can turn on remotely. It won't give us eyes, but we'll be able to hear what's going on. Daniel explained that there's a short burst of frequency, so timing it when Ben is near a radio could give it away. Dormant, it also won't set off any sensors or wands that search for transmitters.

I glance at Apollo again, then pull off onto a side street. We take a back way toward the main street in North Falls, coasting down residential roads. The point is to be inconspicuous. Unfortunately, we pass a patrolling vehicle and catch their eye. They follow us for two blocks, slowly closing the distance.

"We've got a tail," Apollo says. "We're going to split up and lose them."

"Going radio silent," I add.

"Copy," Saint replies. "Stay safe."

I hit a button on my phone, secured to my bike in front of me, and it severs the open line. Apollo glances at me and gestures with a head tilt. He's going west, gambling on who is following us. If it's the Hell Hounds, they'll stop at the edge of the neutral zone. If it's the Titans, well... they'll just keep coming. Which means I'll go south. Same consequences, really. But anything is better than going into my father's territory.

Without a backward glance, we turn away from each other. I hit the throttle, the bike roaring between my knees. I relish the power and lean into the wind, keeping one eye on the car behind us.

It follows me.

Good.

There's a part of me that still carries the guilt over what Apollo has been through in the last six, seven months. So much fucking guilt that he bore the brunt of my father's anger, that he was the one perpetually punished. I couldn't do anything about that—but I can take this for him.

WE HAVE audio on the Titans. We sit around one of the rooftop tables at Bow & Arrow, crowding Daniel and his laptop. It didn't take me long to lose the car, and all of us regrouped at the club. Saint and Nyx are watching the house, which *is* the same one Ben and Jace tried to kill Kronos in. I guess it's too irresistible, too tricked out for Kronos to abandon it.

Or he's staying for another reason.

Originally, Artemis and Daniel were going to stake out the house from down the street. Their car was discovered, however, by one of the sheriff's deputies. He threatened to take them in if they didn't quit *loitering*.

Maybe he was being honest, or he could've been in the Titans' pocket. Impossible to know, so they did the smart thing and got the hell out of there. Saint and Nyx were in a fine position to take over anyway. And so far, their car has gone undetected.

Kora sits opposite me, her gaze on the speaker. Her hair is pulled up in a messy bun. She switched out her septum piercing for a simple silver ring. She's also decked out like she's ready for battle.

I mean... we all are. Black clothing, bulletproof vests, weapons. Jace, Apollo, and I will take in long guns. They rest on the bar, out of the way until we need them. Still, I can't help but eye Kora with a new understanding. She seems comfortable in what she's wearing, and the situation. The gun—a Glock 21, if I'm not mistaken—strapped to her thigh.

God, it's sexy like that. It makes me want to peel her pants down and...

"Benjamin," Kronos booms.

I almost jump. It had been quiet except for a few remarks from the Titans who must've hauled Ben inside the house. Some static. Ben's shallow breathing. The loudness, the crisp tone, has all of us sitting up straighter.

"Father," Ben replies.

I reel back. I'm not the only one with that reaction. Kora looks equally stunned, her lips opening and closing like she can't find the words.

"Daniel," Artemis prods. "Can you figure out if that's accurate?"

He nods sharply. His fingers fly across the keyboard.

"It's been a long time, boy." Kronos again, softer. Closer.

"Not long enough."

Someone sighs. Kronos, Ben, I don't know. There's a scraping noise. Maybe chairs being drawn out from under a table. We wait, tense, for another sound. Another morsel of information—something to answer the goddamn question of how we missed *this*.

"I didn't know Kronos had a son." Apollo looks from me to Jace. "Especially after that fake family shit that almost got us killed. When did that happen?"

"We must've been children," Jace mutters. He rises. "We

can assume Kronos doesn't want to kill him. Ben is his heir—"

"He *helped* me," Kora says. Her expression is pained. Confused. "Why would Ben do that? He said he was on the island because of trauma—"

"Why did you come back?" Kronos asks him.

"Lots of trauma with him as a dad," Apollo mutters.

"I know you want to take over Sterling Falls. You've wanted that as long as I've known you." Ben hesitates. "But... there's something else, isn't there?"

"Something besides power? Besides safety?" Kronos scoffs. "No."

"My mother—"

"Is nothing more than ash in the ocean. She's got nothing to do with this." A longer pause. "So... why did you come back?"

My heart is in my throat.

This is the part where Ben will either keep up our lie or give us up. It doesn't change much to our plan, but...

"I've heard that people are trying to kill you." Ben clears his throat, clearly relying on the fact that his father is unaware that *he* tried to take a shot at him, too. "Just because we don't always get along doesn't mean I want to see you... gone. I was ready to come back. In truth, I've been ready for a while. But it wasn't until this that I *wanted* to come back."

"People are always trying to kill me. It doesn't mean they'll actually follow through with it." Kronos laughs. "I have an insurance policy. It's why I'm still alive after all these years. Either way, I'm glad you're back. I've missed you." He seems to be moving farther away from Ben. He calls out to someone else, who must be outside the room they're in. "Can you show my son to one of the bedrooms upstairs?

Freshen up, son, and we'll discuss your new role in the Titans over dinner."

Jace looks around the room. "Ben went off script. Understandable, seeing as how he had this..."

"Bombshell," Kora supplies.

"Secret," Artemis whispers.

"Yeah, those." Jace frowns.

"Does this actually change that much?" I burst out. I brace my forearms on the table. "I mean, so what? We still take out—"

"Did you forget about the part where he said he had an insurance policy?" Apollo raises his eyes. "Or did you stop listening after he said 'father'? Hits too close to home, does it?"

I glower at him. "Watch it."

"Daddy issues," Apollo grumbles, shoving away from the table. "It's clouding your judgment."

"Or maybe it makes me an expert in Ben's thinking," I counter. "Maybe I have something useful to bring to the table that you're ignoring."

"Wolfe." Kora rises. "Can we... talk?"

"Get him out of here," Apollo says. "So the adults can figure out what to do about Kronos."

Kora makes a face, and Apollo immediately winces. *Yeah*, implying that Kora isn't capable of refining her plan— I lunge at him. I get my hands on his shirt, and we go down. We grapple for a moment, until someone yanks me away.

Jace.

He drags me to the kitchen and shoves me through the swinging doors. I stumble and catch myself on one of the stainless-steel counters. My breathing is ragged, a weight pressing down on my spine. I keep my head bent, but I still catch a glimpse of the gorgeous girl stepping through the doors in Jace's wake.

The doors whoosh closed behind Kora.

Just us again. And again. And again.

Why is each time more painful than the last?

She meanders closer, like we don't have a clock ticking down over our heads. She runs her fingers over the counter, inspecting the equipment of the commercial kitchen. I finally lift my head and face her, resting my hip against the one opposite so I can watch her.

"I told Jace to fix it," she says lightly. "All of us. We're broken, you know?"

I know.

"I don't think he can, though. I think we just need to get through this and heal after." She stops in front of me. "But that doesn't mean we're not worth fixing."

I swallow. "You're worth fixing."

Her palm lands on my shoulder. She seems to debate whether to slide it up to my neck or down my arm. That fine line.

I'm wound tight. Kronos is one beast, and my father is another. He hasn't found us yet, hasn't tried to bring me and Apollo back... it scares me. The fear is new, a chill that has settled under my skin. Because now, if he catches us, he also catches *her*. And Jace. And Daniel. Saint. Nyx. Artemis.

Everyone I love.

I have no doubt my father would string them up by their toes to get me to comply.

"It'll be okay," she whispers.

"I—"

"Got it!" Daniel yells. "I figured it out!"

She rolls her eyes and darts forward, pressing a quick kiss to my lips. Too fast for me to enjoy it.

I snag her waist and reel her back in, giving her a better kiss. One that I hope she feels down to her toes. She relaxes into me for a moment, and I relish the taste of her.

All too soon, though, I'm pulling away. "To be continued."

CHAPTER 34
PARKER

"You arrested my boy."

"I did." I look up from the menu, meeting the steely gaze fixated on my face. "You're welcome, by the way."

Cerberus James—the most ridiculous name I've ever heard—doesn't smile. Doesn't react at all. He reminds me of the serial killers I interviewed in college for my thesis. Stone-cold. They're bottom-line people. Don't care how you get there, just show results.

I admire that.

"Deluxe is an interesting addition." I tap the laminated menu, where the fine print at the bottom declares: *Make it a deluxe for an extra special sauce.* "Sauce is what they're calling PCP these days?"

He leans forward ever so slightly. "Are you threatening me, boy?"

Boy. I should show him how much *boy* there is left in me. I force a smile and relax. Across the room, some gang idiots are lounging at another table. Pretending to lounge. They're strung tighter than a guitar string, ready to pounce on the DEA agent.

The waitress comes over, and I smile at her. She's young, maybe Kora's age, with dark-brown curls and warm, almost golden eyes. She smiles back. Automatic. Sure, it's just part of the job. But she's also smiling because I'm sitting with *her* boss, and he makes her nervous. My looks don't hurt. I'm not a threat—not to her. Add it all up, and she'd be won over in an instant.

"What can I get for you?" She glances at Cerberus first, pen poised above the pad. "Your regular, sir?"

"Quite right."

"I'll take the bacon cheeseburger. Deluxe, if you will." I tap the menu again, drawing her attention—and his—to the fine print. "I'm interested in this sauce."

"Oh." A shadow crosses her face. "We're actually out—"

"It's okay, sweetheart," Cerberus interrupts. "Let's get the man what he wants."

I eye him.

She takes the menu and slips away, and Cerberus and I return to our staring match.

I imagine what he'd look like dead. I find myself doing that more often, now that I've seen a few murders. Junkies with foam coming out of their mouths, chasing a high and ending up dead from an overdose. Dealers caught in gang wars, bullet holes in their head and torso.

He's the sort of man who would die with his eyes open. He wouldn't be caught unaware. As I look at him, I picture the bullet hole in the center of his forehead. The back of his skull would be blown off, brain matter and blood, hair and flesh painted on the back of the vinyl seats.

"I assume if you wanted to arrest me, you would've done so already," Cerberus comments.

I nod. "You're right. I'm not here on official business."

His gaze sharpens. "Then why are you here?"

I take a breath, then reach into the breast pocket of my suit jacket. The men across the room react violently, one of them lunging out of his chair. I wonder what he would do if I pulled a gun and shot his boss in the forehead. If he'd be so shocked, so belated, that he'd let me find cover—or worse, shoot him, too.

But there's no weapon. I move slower, giving them a wry smile, and pull out my slim wallet.

Cerberus watches me open it and withdraw a photo. I put it on the table, turned to face him, and slide it closer to him.

"Kora Sinclair," I say.

He grunts.

"You know her."

"I do."

He does. He knows her, all right. I take out another photo, this one more creased. I've folded it and refolded it, taking out my disdain for the system. Trying to get answers and being stonewalled.

This one is a still shot of their little press conference. Kora just behind Cerberus at the podium, behind a burnt house. I hadn't heard a word they'd said when it had come up on my television. I was captivated by her. The way she held herself. Her neat hair, her bored, blank eyes. The curve of her lips, kept carefully neutral. I'd felt myself leaning closer and closer into the screen, almost like I could fall through it and be with her.

"I wondered where she went," I say, "and then I knew."

Cerberus lifts one shoulder. "She was a means to an end."

Anger zips through me, a quiet flash that sets my nerves buzzing. Kora is *not* a means to an end. Not to me. She's the only reason I'm here—and I won't be leaving without her.

I wave my hand. "I won't pretend to understand your asinine feud or the war currently raging. Bodies are dropping on both sides, I hear. Either way, I don't give a shit. I made the arrests that I wanted to, and you got them out."

He doesn't react.

Not obviously anyway. I know all about that. His lips tighten for a fraction of a second, then relax. So quick, I would've missed it if I blinked, or if I fidgeted or looked away.

"I don't suppose you still have them?"

Now he grimaces. "What's it to you?"

No, then. Another question I already knew the answer to, since I found them all outside the house they were living in. *Her*, with three men. It's absurd.

"I want Kora." I touch the photo, just over her head, and draw our attention back down to it. I love the subtle fear she's displaying. After years, I can recognize it even when she's desperately trying to hide. Even through those bored eyes, there's a girl inside her head screaming. "What do you want?"

He laughs in my face. "Boy, if you want her... you shouldn't be talking to me. I don't own her. Not anymore."

My temperature is rising. It starts in my feet and in my palms. The fiery feeling will travel soon, but it always begins like I've stuck my hands and feet into the flames. Roasted. It moves swiftly, creeping up my throat and toward my jaw.

I don't like to be made a fool. And no one *owns* her except me.

Maybe he recognizes I'm two seconds away from losing it, because he sobers.

"We had a contract," he allows. "And I might've been willing to negotiate with you, but Jace King beat you to the punch."

"Jace King," I repeat. That tattooed beast, the only one I was unable to bring in. He'd be the white whale of my career. Ringleader, I heard, for the other two. Whether that's true is of no consequence. He thinks he has Kora. He may even think he can keep her safe.

"My agreement with him happened before the Titans attacked." He shrugs. "Sorry."

He sure doesn't sound sorry.

The waitress returns with our food and silverware. Between the folds of the napkin is a small baggie of white powder. It has an angel stamped on it. PCP, angel dust. A strong dissociative hallucinogenic.

I tuck it in my breast pocket, back with my wallet. The photos.

I regulate my breathing and slip out of the booth. If he can't help me, if he won't play the game, then there's no point in me staying here. I don't make a habit of wasting my goddamn time. I give him a curt nod, then turn my back on him.

"There is one option..." Cerberus says when I've taken two steps toward the door.

I let a smile flash across my face. He can't see my expression. Can't see the triumph that surges through me. A split second is all I need to hide it again, and then I turn back around. I doubted my instincts for a moment.

But maybe we can work together after all.

CHAPTER 35
KORA

The audio has gone dead. We're not sure if the bug was discovered and destroyed or if it was simply left behind. And that leaves us questioning whether Ben can be trusted or not.

The insurance policy has to do with the subway tunnels. Daniel finding it was a stroke of luck, looking in the right place first, and it came in the way of a sizeable donation from Kronos to the lobbyists who wanted to shut down the subway construction.

How it's involved—I don't know. I didn't even know Sterling Falls *had* subway tunnels. Apparently, the project was alive almost sixteen years ago. It ended abruptly when the city ran out of funding, and partially due to the extreme backlash from several groups inside the city. Kronos included.

Jace motions to Daniel's laptop. The latter turns it around, showing us a map of the city with the subway tunnels superimposed over it. There were several started, but it seems like the main idea was to provide transportation for workers to get to South Falls, then back to downtown, then to the residential areas. There are several that extend into West Falls, the Titans' territory, and more that go south. And all of them overlap near the university.

"Apollo, Artemis—get to the tunnels and see if you can figure out what's going on. If there's something rigged to blow. Stay in contact." Jace braces his hands on the table. "Get Saint and Nyx on the line."

The siblings rise. Apollo stops beside me and touches under my chin, lifting my head. He presses a sweet kiss to the corner of my lips—not nearly enough contact—and then he's gone without another word.

"We're here," Nyx says over the speaker. "There's been some movement, but nothing crazy."

"Guards?" Jace asks.

"Two on patrol on the outside of the house. Kronos and Ben are both still inside. At least four Titans with them. There might be more out back."

"What's the plan?" I ask him.

Jace meets my gaze. "We have to end this. One way or another, Kronos needs to be removed from the Titans. Best-case scenario, we get the sheriff in there and he proves that he's on our side."

I nod my agreement. That was my idea—getting the sheriff to swoop in on our tip, arresting Kronos and whoever else for... well, whatever we can make stick. I've got a message ready to go, pre-recorded and on Daniel's laptop. It'll be sent to Nate, his sister, and Alex Sterling. And hopefully, between the three of them, something can be done.

"Okay, let's go break up a party," I say. "Nyx, we'll be there in ten."

The guys follow me out and to the last car. Apollo and Artemis must've taken the bikes that Apollo and Wolfe rode.

The yellow moon is low in the sky, casting the buildings in a pale light. Daniel stays behind, monitoring our radios and surveillance. Saint should be with him—he still has stitches after all—but he vehemently refused.

There's some animosity between Saint and Kronos. Unfinished business.

I find myself rubbing the hourglass brand on my wrist in the car beside Jace. I dig my nail into the healed scar tissue. We've got to get this right. And hopefully it ends with an arrest.

"Ben is Kronos' son." I glance at him. "Did you see that coming?"

His jaw tics. "No."

We pull up beside Saint and Nyx's car. They've parked on the street a few houses down. Their windows are so tinted, we can't make out that anyone is inside until their window rolls down.

Nyx is driving. Saint has a pale sheen to him, like he's in pain—but he doesn't say anything. I mean, he was literally stabbed only a few days ago. He shouldn't be out of bed, never mind on a stakeout. But he looks forward, ignoring my silent concern.

Jace explains what's happened—that there's some protective measure Kronos has in place, and Artemis and Apollo have gone to see if they can figure out what it is. And then stop it, just in case...

"But we're going ahead as planned. We need to get Ben out of there, too. Kora, Wolfe, and I go in hard and fast from the beach. We'll sweep the house and secure both of them. The only ones who should be left standing at the end are Kronos and Ben. Copy?"

"Copy," Wolfe and I say. The idea of killing Titans doesn't faze me. Not after what they've done to us. But killing Kronos would be asking for trouble. The insurance policy, sure, but also—there's a reason the guys didn't move on him. Someone would just take his place.

Cut the head off, and two more grow back. Although, to be fair, I'm mixing my mythology beasts.

"Nyx, watch the front. Anyone comes out, shoot them."

She grins. "Copy that."

Jace's attention settles on Saint in the passenger seat. "You okay?"

"I'm good." Saint gives him a forced smile.

Well... it's not like we can send him home. I almost wish that Jace will order him to stay in the car—but I don't think he'll listen. And Jace must realize the same thing, because he's silent for a moment. They have a non-verbal conversation.

"Cover Nyx," Jace settles on. "Protect her."

"With my life," Saint replies.

Great. I eye Wolfe, who hands Nyx his long gun. He straightens. We've got a little bit of cover with the darkening sky. I'd imagine Kronos and Ben might be sitting down for that dinner the former mentioned.

"Let's go," Jace says to Wolfe and me.

We use the shadows to approach the house. I am sandwiched between Wolfe and Jace—the latter leading—and we file down the sandy lane between two houses. In the distance, a car engine rumbles. Maybe Nyx getting into a better position, or a passerby. The fine hairs on the back of my neck stand up.

No one bats an eye at us, though. No floodlights come on, no barking dogs. It's silent except for the rushing and crashing of the ocean. Our boots sink into the sand, masking any noise our footsteps would make.

"Testing comms," Daniel says in our ears.

Jace glances back at us. I give him a thumbs-up, and Wolfe mirrors my movement.

"We hear you," Jace responds in a low voice.

"Same," Nyx replies.

"This house is drawing significantly more energy compared to the surrounding houses. Be prepared for surprises." Daniel's voice breaks up a little, a burst of static obscuring his words. "...security system."

We get to the edge of the neighbor's house. It's eerie, being out here like this. Exposed. The full moon is giant over the ocean. Everything is shadows and pale light. I draw my gun. I didn't want one of the rifles, not that they asked.

It's fine.

Ben and I only trained with the handguns he was able to get access to. Which, now that I'm thinking about it, it makes a lot more sense that he *was* able to get his hands on weapons in Isle of Paradise. That place is supposed to be secure, and yet he was granted certain privileges.

I'm an idiot.

Jace hops the wrought-iron fence easily, then drops into a crouch. We wait for a few seconds for an alarm, any sound of distress, but nothing comes. Wolfe kneels and offers his hand. I stow my gun, put one hand on his shoulder and my foot in his cradled hands. He propels me over the fence, Jace grabbing my hips and lowering me on the other side. His thumbs brush my skin where my shirt has ridden up, and a flash of heat shoots through me.

"Thanks." I can't seem to make myself smile. On this side, now, I'm hit with a blast of nerves. It's become so much more real that we're doing this.

One way or another, the Titans can't be allowed to continue.

We're cutting off the head of the snake.

Wolfe lands lightly beside me. I redraw my weapon and take a deep breath.

"Now or never," I whisper.

CHAPTER 36
APOLLO

The tunnels are clear so far. We had to break into one of the closed-down entrances near Sterling Falls University and climb over forgotten lumber and equipment. It's like a ghost town down here. The homeless had broken in and made it their own, time and time again, and the city keeps kicking them out. We pass ragged tents covered in mold, tipped-over coolers, barrels with ash clinging to the bottom.

And the rats. Everywhere I shine my flashlight, the rats are there, moving away. Chattering.

Tem and I both pulled our shirts up over our mouths at one point, passing a decaying body. Forgotten. Undiscovered.

Who knows.

We'll pass it again on the way out.

But right now, we're venturing down the tunnel that leads to West Falls. Well, we do... until the one tunnel splits into four.

"There's not enough time for us to each explore two," Tem murmurs.

Voices travel down here. We learned that the hard way when I called for her, and her name echoed and bounced around us for almost a full minute.

I pull up the map Daniel sent to our phones and zoom in on the four splits. One of them goes closest to Descend, the Titans' bar... and I don't know, I have a hunch about that. If there's any part of West Falls that is one hundred percent Titan controlled, it's that block.

Tem agrees with my logic. She follows me down, but we only get halfway there before discovering an abandoned train car. We're barely out of the neutral zone.

It appears out of the darkness around a corner, and my sister jumps. She makes a face at me before I say anything, and I smirk.

We approach it slowly, going down one side and around. It's completely dark.

Tem pries the door open and climbs the steps. She gasps and drops her light.

It *thunks* down each stair, swinging wildly, until it lands on the tracks at my feet.

"What?" I demand, aiming my light at her horrified face.

Great. Worse than we expected. I join her at the top and shine my light down the aisle.

The train car is rigged with explosives. Barrels with C-4, a plastic explosive, taped to the top. Wires coming out of them all. It's a transportable bomb.

"They could send this right down to the center of Sterling Falls from here," Artemis whispers. "It'd blow the university... the financial district. The whole neutral zone."

"We could dismantle it—"

"Or we could accidentally kill ourselves," she hisses.

"We just need to pull the detonators." I take a step forward.

Something resists against my ankle, and there's a *plink* noise.

A trip wire.

Shit.

I jump forward, toward the barrels. The devices are blinking red.

"This whole thing is gonna blow," she yells. "Get your ass out—"

I rip out the detonators. No clue if it's going to help or just make shit worse, but we're not going to be able to outrun a huge explosion. Maybe a small one, though. I get halfway through the car when Artemis grabs my arm.

She pulls me off the train as it powers to life. The doors slide closed behind us. We sprint down the tracks and around the corner, the glowing light of the train car behind us fading—

Until the explosion.

CHAPTER 37
KORA

I twist the suppressor on my gun and follow Jace into the house. He's done the same with his weapon, and Wolfe behind me. The French doors from the living room were left open, leaving us easy access to get inside.

The space is large, nearly bare. Just a charade of someone living here. High vaulted ceilings, a few pieces of furniture. No decorations. The kitchen on our right seems unused. And there's no sign of people, either. No Titans patrolling, no alarm system announcing our arrival.

The Kevlar strapped to my torso gives me a modicum of security. But I'm feeling a bit like we just stepped into the monster's lair.

In a way, we have.

Voices are traveling from down the hall. We press against the wall, and Jace signals for Wolfe to go first. We clear the rooms as we go, but... the fewer people we see, the more worried I get.

Someone comes out of the shadows. They grab my hair and drag me backward. My scalp burns, and I fall into the Titan. The impact must surprise them, because they let out a huff. They keep pulling until I think my hair might be ripped free.

I kick out, my cry short and quiet. I reach for one of the knifes Wolfe supplied me with and get my fingers around the handle.

Jace whirls around, his gun raised, but it's too late. I stab the guy in the leg and rip the knife out.

He yells.

Shit.

I stab him again and again, until his grip on my hair slackens. I fall, the strands sliding through his fingers, and Jace shoots. It takes him less than a second to get to me, and he pats me all over. Almost frantically.

My hands shake, but I push his away. "I'm fine."

He helps me stand.

"Guys," Wolfe calls. "Get in here."

I wipe off my bloody hand and follow Jace through the doorway. Wolfe is just inside the entrance to the dining room, his gun raised.

Ben and Kronos sit at the table, plates of food in front of them. There are two Titans standing behind Kronos, their stance mirroring Wolfe's. Kronos ignores them. And Wolfe, for that matter. He smiles when he sees us.

Kronos holds out his hands, like he's welcoming us to a feast. "My boys, together at last."

Huh?

Ben, sitting to his right, keeps his gaze glued to his plate.

Kronos eyes him, then us. "Surely your father taught you better than that, Wolfe." He gestures for him to lower the gun.

"I don't suppose you have back up on the other side of those doors?" Jace points to the closed double doors behind the head of the table, where Kronos has once again lowered himself into a chair.

"They won't come in unless they have to," Kronos says. He glances at me. "Ah, the invisible girl. I almost didn't recognize you. But now I do... pity I let you slip through my fingers."

Jace steps in front of me, shielding me from him. Which is good, because I think I'm going to be sick. My stomach rolls. Just being back in the same room as Kronos is making me cold and clammy.

"Enough talk," Jace snaps.

My breath is shallow. I count in my head, flexing my fingers on my gun's grip. Now isn't the time to freak out.

"On the contrary, I think this is an excellent time for *talk*, son."

Wolfe glances at his best friend and raises his eyes.

"Don't call me son," Jace says softly, grabbing one of the chairs and dragging it away from the table.

He motions for me to sit, then does the same to another chair and sinks into it. I sit, trying to hide the fact that my knees were wobbling not a second before. And now it takes true commitment to keep my leg from bouncing.

Wolfe stays standing, on high alert.

"Even when it's the truth?"

Jace stares at Kronos.

My attention is fixated on Ben, who seems... different. Maybe he walked in here with an idea of how things were going to go, and everything got turned on its head. When he does look up, he can't meet any of our eyes.

"My father is a deadbeat," Jace says. "From Emerald Cove. He—"

"Had a very pretty wife." Kronos is positively gleeful. "She liked to wear ribbons in her hair. And she hummed songs under her breath when she thought no one was listening."

I scoff, not believing his bullshit for a second. "You're bluffing."

There's no way.

Kronos doesn't take his eyes off Jace. "Am I?"

"She..." Jace shakes his head. "She wouldn't cheat on my father."

"Unfortunately, your father wasn't known for his loyalty. Is it so hard to imagine that he left her alone one night, and I was there to comfort her? That I gave her something your father failed time and again to do?" He picks up his fork and knife, cutting through the meat on his plate with sure, precise movements. "Or maybe I just saw something pretty and took what I wanted from her."

A chill travels up my spine.

Ben stays quiet.

"You've met Benjamin, I take it. Your half-brother. He's a year younger, which works out... quite interestingly, don't you think?" Kronos tips his head to the side, chewing the meat and analyzing our reactions. "Who will take over when dear old Dad is no longer in the picture?"

I vow not to have a reaction.

To remain stoic.

But this is utter shit. And I can feel the thread Kronos has loosened, the one he'll work at just enough. And then Jace will pull, and the whole tapestry will unravel.

That's how his manipulation works. It's dark and twisted and not altogether logical, but it works. It's kept Kronos in charge of his Titans for years. He's not strong in the physical sense. He doesn't lift a gun when he doesn't have to... except to prove a point. But he controls the environment around us in other ways.

"Tell me why I shouldn't kill you," Jace says.

A bluff. By now, Daniel would've hopefully sent my message to the sheriff and aldermen. Soon, the cops will come bursting in here. We just need more time.

"Ah." Kronos reaches for the full wine glass, taking a sip before slamming it back down. "You're talking about my insurance policy, are you not? The reason you can't kill me." He chuckles. "I'll admit. Before, it was just a matter of knowing your enemy. Now... now it's a little trickier, isn't it? Kill me, and you take over. Or Ben.

"Well, I wonder who they'd follow." He turns to Ben. His son. "You grew up with the Titans. Would they follow you? Would you kill for them, so they'd kill for you?"

Ben lifts one shoulder, then grabs his wine glass. He traces the rim with his finger, drawing out a sweet, single note.

"Would anyone believe that Jace King is actually my son?" Kronos chuckles, almost to himself. "Trust me, son, I've contemplated this for far too long. What I'd say to you when you were finally in front of me and presented with the truth."

"Stop calling me your fucking son." Jace rises. "Give me the reason why we shouldn't end your miserable life."

The door opens, and a Titan slips through. He gives us a wary look but bends and speaks into Kronos' ear.

Kronos bursts to his feet. For the first time, his composure slips. "Get them," he snaps. "And someone get me a car. *Now.*"

The tunnels.

Were Apollo and Artemis successful?

The two Titans who stood behind him suddenly surge toward us. Wolfe raises his gun, and they stop. They exchange a glance.

Kronos spares us another moment. "Until we meet again."

Jace and I watch him go. Part of me wants to rush after him, but we don't. Ben has risen, too, and he holds up one hand as the Titans advance toward us. To my shock, they actually stop.

They listen to him. They leave, even, with just a jerk of Ben's head.

Ben forcefully closes the door behind them and turns to face us again. "Well, now that it's just us... I owe you an apology, Kora."

I tense. "An apology," I repeat. "For what, exactly?"

He shrugs. He seems different, coming around the table and stopping in front of me. "For lying, mostly. I wanted to tell you who I was, but I didn't realize who *you* were either. Not until Nyx brought us back to Sterling Falls and the cards revealed themselves."

"Bullshit," I whisper. "I told you—"

"You and I both know we kept things light on purpose," he replies. "It's okay. I'm glad for our time on the island. You really helped me face my fears."

I reach for him. "This insurance policy Kronos has—"

"That has you worried?" Ben shakes his head. "It'll be okay. He already thinks we're fit to lead. We just need to adjust the plan. We can't kill him. He's our father—"

"My father drank vodka and beat the shit out of me and my mom," Jace says. He steps forward and grabs Ben's wrist. He twists, loosening the latter's hold on my hands and forcing his arm to curl in an unnatural way. "My *father* was a mean alcoholic who thought he was invincible." He slowly marches Ben backward, his grip on Ben's wrist like iron. "That man may think he donated some sperm to my mom, or maybe he fucking forced it on her like an animal. Either way, that doesn't mean I'm going to bow down and call him *daddy*."

Jace releases Ben with a shove, sending him crashing back against the wall.

"Jesus," Ben spits, rubbing his wrist. "You don't have to like it, brother, but it doesn't make it untrue."

Gunfire in the near distance makes all of us drop into crouches. Wolfe comes over and puts his arm over my shoulders, automatically trying to cover me and force me lower, using the table as cover. Shouts break out.

Nyx.

Saint.

I swallow past the lump in my throat and shoot upward, but Ben has already drawn a concealed weapon. He lunges over the table and grabs me, pressing the muzzle to my temple.

"Move and she dies," he promises Wolfe and Jace.

They exchange a glance.

More gunfire rattles toward the front of the house, followed by a crash. And then a scream.

CHAPTER 38
NYX

"What's the best-case scenario?"

I lean down through the open window, flashing Saint a smile. He seems in pain, judging from the paleness of his face. But he hasn't said a word about it, and now he seems to be contemplating my words.

Good. Better to get his mind off things.

Our communication with Wolfe, Jace, and Kora has been sparse. Daniel texted and said his drone had a view of them going inside, but the radios don't work anymore. Jammed, maybe, or some other sort of high tech.

Above my pay grade, honestly.

He also said that the message to the sheriff was sent, so help should be arriving soon.

In theory.

I'm skeptical of just how helpful Nathan Bradshaw will be, when it comes down to the wire. And how fast his response time will be. Which means it's up to us to keep everyone alive.

"Best-case scenario?" Saint asks. "Well, probably... shit, I don't know. We all get home safe. Kronos and Cerberus die, their gangs disbanded. The government loses the corrupt people. Same with the police force. Someone cleans up the city."

"Then we'd be out of a job, don't you think?"

He shrugs one shoulder. "Maybe that's a good thing. I'll spend more time at my tattoo shop, and you..."

Me. "What about me?"

"You can be my muse."

If I was next to him, I'd lean over and kiss him. As it is, I'm outside the car and he's in it. I've got the rifle, and he's got a stab wound.

"What a pair we make." I shake my head. "When you made me jump off that cliff six years ago, I didn't think we'd end up here."

"You didn't see yourself as the stakeout type, huh?" Saint chuckles, then groans in pain.

I lean over again, eyeing him. "Just say the word and we can get Daniel out here to replace you."

"I'm fine," he manages. He snags my free hand through the window and kisses my knuckles. His lips linger on my skin, and I don't miss his shaky exhale.

Movement at the side of the house draws my eye, and I straighten. I take a few steps forward, into the street, and one of the Titans catches sight of me.

They open fire.

I duck and sprint forward, throwing myself against the concrete privacy wall in front of the house. The rest of the fence is wrought iron and completely useless as cover, but this part is supposed to lend some... well, *privacy* to the house occupants.

I steel myself, then lean over and open fire. One, two, three. I manage to hit one of them and take inventory of the rest. They're just... they're pouring out like hornets out of a kicked hive.

But there can't be an infinite number of them. I shoot until my magazine is empty, then reload. I take a deep breath and step out from behind my hiding place. One of the blacked-out SUVs is rolling down the driveway, trying to make a quick getaway.

I glance back at Saint. He's gotten out of the car and is halfway to me when I shake my head. I don't need him to follow me and get hurt. Hell, he's already injured. So I motion for him to stay put and step in front of the car.

I fire at where I think the driver is, even though the tint is so dark, I can't be certain *anyone* is inside.

But instead of picking up speed, the car makes a slow swerve.

I jump out of the way, and it crashes into the concrete privacy wall.

I stare at it, half shocked that I even managed to do that, then back to Saint.

He's almost to me, coming down the privacy wall. Hurrying, but clearly suffering. His hand is pressed over his stitched-up wound, and his eyes go wide.

That's the only warning I get before I feel someone behind me. But it's too late to turn around. Too late to do anything. I glance to my side and see Kronos out of the corner of my eye. He grabs a fistful of my hair, wrenching my head back.

There's a rushing in my ears, and then it happens.

It's just a pinch of pain.

Kronos releases me, and I drop to my knees. The pavement bites into my skin through my pants, but it's the least of my worries. My hands come up automatically, cupping my neck. Hot blood gushes through my fingers, down my front.

You can't die.

Not my voice—Saint's. From ages ago, whispered in the cool night air after a fight. Nursing me back to health, my face feeling like it went head-to-head with a cheese grater. An unspoken fear breathed into life.

That one day, Death will come and take one of us away from the other.

But I didn't expect today, and all at once a tornado of emotions swings through me. Annoyance. Heartbreak. Agony. Relief.

Selfish relief that I don't have to live in a world without Saint Hart.

And terrible guilt that he has to witness this. His gaze burns into me from the top of the driveway, his gun pointed at the ground. That's all I get before my vision blurs.

Dying. The proof is in the blood I'm rapidly losing and the scatter of my thoughts like sand in the wind.

I don't want to think about what kind of life Saint will lead after I go.

I don't want to think about how hard or easily he'll move on.

He's right there, falling down beside me and guiding me to the ground. His hands cover mine, hot against my clammy skin.

I'm so cold. I try to talk, but all that comes out is a gurgle. An infinite metallic taste on my tongue that doesn't go away, no matter how I try to swallow or spit. My fear is a visceral thing, shredding me from the inside out.

How am I going to tell him I love him when I can't speak?

"Shh, shhh," he whispers, voice ragged.

He's crying. Tears fall from his eyes, landing on my chest, my face.

I really am dying. I've never seen him cry before, and that just cements it.

I let go of my torn throat. It's my last act, the last thing I can give to him. I slip my hand out, and his immediately takes my place, pushing hard. Trying to stop my artery from pumping out precious blood. That doesn't matter anymore. My body doesn't even feel like mine.

There are *so many things* I wish I could say to him, and they all press against the back of my bloody teeth. Stuck on my tongue. The last of my breath whistles through my throat.

Instead, I touch my favorite tattoo on his chest. A collection of stars, a little galaxy pushing at the other tattoos. It's right over his heart. He said he got it for me years ago. I hope he knows that it means I'll always be with him.

Through the thick and thin. Through the war, through him finding a new love, kids. Until he takes *his* last breath and meets me in the darkness.

And then...

It's over.

I don't know if my eyes close.

I don't know if the blood stops right away, in time with my heart, or if it'll keep dripping out onto the ground long after I'm gone.

All I know is a sense of fear rips through me—and then it vanishes. It takes everything. The darkness opens up before me, and I don't fight it. There's no more fight left.

CHAPTER 39
SAINT

W hite noise rushes in my ears.

Elora's perfect brown eyes are still staring up at me, but she's not behind them. She's not here anymore. The expression is gone, the slight crinkle in the corners of her eyes. Her lips are slack, parted, blood speckled on them.

Insurmountable grief wells up inside me, that white noise turning into a roar.

Kronos took my love from me, so fast I didn't have time to react. I didn't have time to fucking save her before she was gone.

I lift my hands from her throat and touch my chest. The galaxy tattoo over my heart that she marked. The darkness and the stars that I knew Elora to be.

I'm too hot. My skin is tight.

Every piece of me is on fire.

How the fuck do I exist without her?

I wipe the tears away.

She ruined his only vehicle—which means he might've gone back inside. I look up, look around, and see nothing but bodies. My gun is on the ground a few feet away, dropped in my hurry to get to her.

I check my gun, the magazine, and catch sight of my hands. They're stained red—Elora's blood. *My light*. She's gone—and it leaves only darkness inside me. I close my eyes and take a breath, and all I can smell is her scent. The floral soap she used last, the way her hair hung like a curtain around us when she leaned over me, enclosing us in our own little bubble.

And another scent. Copper. Blood. That's almost over-powering.

My eyes keep burning, my throat works, and I shift my weight. I'm searching for a ledge to stand on without success. Nothing will bring her back—but there is *one* thing that I can do. One thing to make the pain worth it.

The hardest part is to leave her there. I kneel beside her body once more and press my lips to her forehead. I brush her raven-black hair off her face, smoothing it back. It's wrong that it feels so soft, that it slips through my fingers like butter.

"I'm sorry, baby," I whisper. I can barely hear my own words, and my voice is scratchy. All I want to do is scream and scream and scream.

But I can't, so I rise. I follow the path Kronos must've taken, in through a side door, to the hallway that leads back to the opposite side of the house. I flex my fingers on the handle of the gun, my thumb touching on the safety.

I flick it off and pause in the shadows. They're in the dining room. Ben's on the floor in front of Wolfe, a weapon on the table. He wears a sour expression. Kora stands with Jace, facing off against Kronos.

He stands to the side, still with the smug expression. A

trump card that might protect him. Did he think he was safe from me?

I don't give a shit. This whole fucking city can burn to the ground for all I care.

"Saint," someone says.

A woman, but not *my* woman. There's a roaring in my ears, my scream trapped in my skull.

I step out of the shadows and raise my gun.

Kronos looks at me, and he smiles. Maybe he thinks this is an act, that I just want to scare him. The man who held me captive, who tortured me for information, who killed my love. He thinks I'll threaten him but that I won't follow through.

Yesterday, that might've been true.

I've never killed anyone before.

But that doesn't stop me from pulling the trigger now.

The first bullet catches him in the shoulder. He stumbles back, that smug expression finally dropping away. I advance on him. All I can hear is the rasp of the knife—a figment of my imagination—and the wet noise Elora made as she tried to speak.

He stole her voice from us.

I pull the trigger again. I'm yards away, then feet. The second bullet tears through his throat. *Good.*

The third, his face. It opens his cheek, obliterating the bone. He drops, but it's not enough. Not until I'm standing over him and emptying my magazine into his fucking face.

There's screaming somewhere behind us. I kick his life-less body for good measure, until someone grips my arms and drags me off of him.

He's dead. Unmoving, almost unrecognizable.

It's only then that I let out a ragged sob, because the pain hasn't gone away. It doubles, blazing through my body and decimating me from the inside out. I can't breathe, I can't think. I let them take my weight and guide me away.

We make it outside, and I rip free. We're on the beach, Titan bodies littering the sand. I weave, my balance shot, and go to the ocean. I don't stop when the water, still icy from winter, rushes past my ankles. Then mid-calf. Over my knees.

Someone yells for me to stop. To come back.

A wave surges at me, knocking me back, but I keep going until it's deep enough for me to dive beneath the surface. Past the break. The frigid water closes in around my head.

The first time we met—Elora masquerading as Nyx, me as... some younger, more foolish version of myself—we jumped off the cliffs at Olympus. There was a rush, then, that cemented us together. Her hand in mine as we fell. The way the cold water seemed to surge up to meet us.

I kissed her in the water. I didn't know what came over me, just that I had seen her fight, and then I saw her talking to someone else. I recognized her from school, but we never had a reason to connect. Not until that night.

For me? Love at first sight.

Now it's gone. My lungs burn. I resurface and take a ragged breath. There's saltwater on my lips, and the taste of blood. Her blood.

I can't do this. I can't live without her. In all the time we were together, I didn't think she'd go before me. *I* was supposed to sacrifice myself to save her. She's the one who has—*fuck, had*—a promising life ahead of her.

I'm being ripped apart from the inside. Every memory, every happy moment, pounds at my skull until I can't take it anymore. I sink to my knees, going underwater once more. The rolling tide almost knocks me off balance again.

Wouldn't that be lucky? To be swept away... to find my own peace?

You have to fight. That's what Elora would say. I can hear the resolution in her voice even now, the soft way she'd say it. The stern furrow of her brows.

I should've asked her to marry me sooner. I should've taken her out of this city, saved both of us. How much more of this could we have taken?

It's my fault she's dead.

It's then that I open my mouth. Seawater rushes in, but it's too late.

I scream.

And scream.

And scream.

Then everything goes blessedly dark.

CHAPTER 40
JACE

K ronos is dead.

Whether or not he's my father is a question I don't have the answer to—and I'm not up for the task of finding out. Ben screamed when Saint pulled the trigger. Screamed and threw up and then threatened to kill all of us as Saint kicked the shit out of Kronos.

Someone knocked him out.

It may have been Kora—she was closest. I was too busy staring first at Kronos, whose face has been obliterated by the bullet holes that tore through it, then at Saint.

Wolfe pulled him off Kronos and dragged him outside.

There are no more Titans left. With Kronos dead, and the majority of the Titans already caught in our crossfire one way or another, the place is quiet. It's not a good quiet, though. It's the kind of silent that only death carries.

Wolfe, Kora, and Saint are out back... so I go looking for Nyx.

I find her in the driveway. She's just lying there, and my brain doesn't quite comprehend what I'm seeing until I'm next to her. Her throat...

I choke. I fall to my knees beside her and grab her hand. It's still warm but limp. She doesn't squeeze back, her eyes don't suddenly focus on me. Her lips don't curve up in a smile that says, *gotcha*.

Not a prank.

This can't be possible.

An impossible feeling wells up in my chest, holding my lungs hostage. I want to lose my mind. To go back and unload my magazine into Kronos' face, like Saint. But this feeling chokes me.

Of all people, *she* didn't deserve to die. She and Saint had the rest of their lives ahead of them.

Her black Kevlar is soaked with blood. It pools under her, too, like black ink in the moonlight. I want to scream—

And now I understand Saint's reaction.

If this had been Kora...

"Jace? I think the sheriff is coming."

I turn sharply. Kora stands a few feet away, her head turned to the east. The red and blue lights of approaching police cars precede the sirens. But my movement has revealed Nyx, and Kora's gaze lands on her body. The hand I'm still holding.

Kora's hand flies up and covers her mouth, but it doesn't stop the words from pouring out as a low moan. "No, no, no." She stops short of us. "What happened?"

"What do you think happened?" I don't mean the bitterness of my tone.

She sits. Maybe falls, I don't know. She lands hard next to me and wraps her arms around her bent legs. She just stares at Nyx like she doesn't recognize her.

"Kora."

She flinches when I touch her arm.

"Call Apollo," I tell her gently. "We need them to come back..."

She swallows and nods. Her movements are jerky, retrieving the burner phone from her pocket, opening it. Dialing Apollo's number.

It goes to voicemail.

"They could still be in the tunnels," she whispers. "We should..." Her head swings around. "We need to go."

I nod and rise. "Get Wolfe and Saint. Meet me at the car."

We have an unspoken agreement to leave Ben here. He'll wake up next to his dead father—and he can deal with that while we handle our own loss. I hold out my hands and help Kora to her feet, then watch her go around the side of the house. Only once she's gone do I kneel back down and close Nyx's eyes.

Then I pick her up and take her away from this godforsaken place.

CHAPTER 41
KORA

I run down to the beach, where Wolfe is dragging Saint out of the water. Saint doesn't seem fully conscious, and I rush into the surf. The cold water hits my legs and sprays upward, soaking my front. Wolfe is just as drenched, and Saint looks like he went swimming. Even his hair is wet, clinging to his face.

I throw Saint's other arm over my shoulder, and together, Wolfe and I drag him out of the ocean. The sirens are louder now. We have minutes, if that. Wolfe's head lifts, and he understands, too.

At one point, Saint reawakens and falls to his knees. He takes us with him, coughing out water. He spits and hangs his head.

We're quiet for a moment, and I'm at a loss for words. He hasn't said a damn thing, but I can feel his grief like a living, breathing thing.

How do you get over that? How do you even begin to handle it?

I meet Wolfe's gaze over Saint's head.

"Come on," I say, as gently as possible, "we need to get out of here."

We help Saint up again, supporting him all the way to the steps on the side of the house. There, he takes over and shakes us off. He walks ahead of us.

I grab Wolfe's hand and press it to my lips. He gives me a questioning look.

I shake my head, wondering how I'm going to tell him. "Nyx…"

He freezes, reading my expression. "No."

"She—"

He squeezes my hand tighter and pulls me after Saint. We reach the driveway and stop short at the sight of Saint staring down at the place where Nyx died. Her blood is pooled on the pavement.

Wolfe makes a low noise in the back of his throat.

They knew her so much longer than I did. And… I might be in shock. Because her death doesn't feel real. It just seems like something temporary. She's dead now, but tomorrow she'll emerge from her room with Saint, displaying her tattoos and a smile.

"Come on," I urge, guiding him forward. "Jace brought her to the car. We're not leaving her…"

"Of course we're not leaving her," Saint growls. He moves again, his head swinging around like he can find someone else to blame.

But there's no one left.

Horror echoes through me. I press my hand to my chest, trying to stop my heart from pounding against my ribcage.

A pointless endeavor.

We get to the cars. Jace has laid Nyx in the backseat of one. Saint opens the door closer to her head and smooths her hair, then takes care to arrange it across her throat. He puts her hands on her chest, then softly closes her in.

I drop my hand from my chest, the position too similar. My eyes are burning.

This is *Nyx*.

No. This *was* Nyx.

He takes the passenger seat, lowering himself into it with a grunt.

Jace takes the driver's seat.

"Come on," Wolfe says to me, the same words doubling back.

I don't even realize my eyes have filled with tears again until I blink and they drip down my face. The world blurs, and I hastily wipe at them.

I get in the car with Wolfe. Jace drives the other car, making a sharp U-turn and speeding away from this hell-hole. Down the long stretch of road, the cops are approaching. Their lights bounce off the houses, the sirens screaming.

This isn't what I wanted the sheriff to find.

Wolfe starts the car. The headlights bounce against the vehicle we parked behind, blinding us for a moment, and then he reverses. He cuts the same path Jace did, swinging the car around and getting away from the scene of the crime.

I almost expect a few cop cars to peel off and give chase —but they're still a few blocks away. They don't know what they're about to walk into.

So we get away.

We ride in silence for a moment, and I finally glance over at him. He's blinking furiously, his throat working.

"It's okay to be upset," I whisper.

He scoffs. "It's not fucking okay. None of this is okay—least of all my *emotions*."

"Bullshit." I lean across the center console and put my hand on his thigh. "It's just us in here, Wolfe. You can be straight with me."

His hand comes down on top of mine. Instead of leaving it there, or treating it like a comfort, he pries my hand away and drops it back on my lap.

My fingers curl into fists. He's just grieving in a different way. Right? We can't all react to death the same way. It would be irrational to expect everyone to cry.

Maybe that's why I'm not surprised when he pulls up in front of Bow & Arrow and doesn't shut off the car.

"You want to be alone," I guess.

"Nailed it in one." His voice is cold.

I shake my head. "Fine. Then at least go look for Artemis and Apollo. His phone was going straight to voicemail."

Wolfe glances at me, then goes back to facing forward. He nods once, and I get out of the car. It's all I can do. It's all I know what to do.

Everything else is just... a nightmare.

In the club, Antonio meets me at the door. He holds open his arms, and I pause for a moment before letting him hug me. It's surprising, but I grip the shirt at his back and tuck my face into his shoulder. A lump blocks my throat again.

He rubs my back, then releases me. "They're on the third floor. One of the VIP lounges." He slips past me, out into the night.

It's eerie being here at night, with the club completely shut down. No lights, no dancers, no music. The floors are pristine, everything exactly where it should be. I take the stairs to the third floor—up just one level—and down the hall. The sconce lights are on, unlike when the club is open and the halls remain dark, shadowy places.

I find them in a familiar VIP lounge—the one where Marley took me once upon a time.

That feels like a lifetime ago now.

They've set Nyx on one of the tables and covered her with a black tablecloth. Saint sits on the floor near her, staring at his knees.

Jace and Daniel are sitting on bar stools with drinks in front of them.

It seems like we've come to a standstill, and I don't have a fucking solution for it.

Jace rises when he sees me. "Kora."

Saint doesn't react.

Daniel offers me a sad smile. They make room for me between them at the bar, and Daniel reaches over and grabs another glass. Without asking, he pours me a shot of whiskey. I don't ask twice—I just nod my thanks and slam it back.

The smoky flavor is the most overpowering, and I almost choke on it.

"Where is Wolfe?" Daniel asks.

"Went for a drive. I told him to find Artemis and Apollo." My voice sounds... hollow.

"Kora." Jace saying my name is grounding. But then he follows it with, "You need to call the sheriff. He could be at the Titans house, but—"

"*No.*"

I glance over my shoulder at Saint, who hasn't moved—but sounds very firm.

"No?" I question.

"He'll take her away. He can't have her."

"We need to bury her." I get off the stool and go to Saint. I kneel in front of him. "She deserves a proper resting place. Jace is right... I don't think we can do that without the sheriff's help."

He processes it.

I mirror his nod and rise. I dial Nate's number.

"Sheriff Bradshaw," he answers, not at all sounding like I woke him up. His voice is alert and brisk.

I glance at the time at the top of Jace's phone and frown. It's past midnight.

"It's Kora."

I imagine his surprised expression from the way he abruptly clears his throat. "Kora. Are you okay? I got your message and sent cops I trust. Are you safe?"

I blow out a breath. "Yeah... we're okay. You didn't ride to our rescue, then?"

He pauses. "Listen, Kora. I'm going to assume your answer, but I have to ask. Did you have anything to do with the explosion?"

"What?" I put him on speaker. "What explosion?"

He grunts. "I shouldn't be telling you this. One of the abandoned train cars that was put in place to test the subway system exploded in West Falls. It took out a almost a full block of businesses that were above it."

Jace meets my gaze.

Fuck. Apollo and Artemis—

"Was anyone hurt?"

"Not so far," the sheriff replies. "We're searching the rest of the tunnels as we speak."

"Sheriff!" someone calls in the distance. "We got something!"

"Hang on, Kora." The sound of gravel underfoot is all I can hear for a moment, and a low murmur of a conversation that's too muted to pick up. Then everything abruptly stops.

"Please," a familiar voice says. "You have to help my brother—"

The air *whooshes* out of my lungs. How many more hits can we take?

"They took him," Artemis cries. "Please—"

"Kora? You should probably get down here."

Fuck.

THE SHERIFF TELLS us we can pick up Artemis at Sterling Falls University. The police station was recently destroyed by Hell Hounds, so they've moved to SFU for the summer.

Same with the city council—although I don't bother pointing that out. Seems like the school has become a sort of fortress for the government. And to be sure, it's one of the remaining old, Greek-style buildings in the city. A remnant of maybe a simpler time.

Nadine Bradshaw meets us in the hallway outside the rooms the police station is using. They don't have jail cells, I guess, so those they place under arrest have been shipped straight to the county jail outside city limits. But Artemis isn't under arrest—so she's here.

"Ms. Sinclair." Nadine extends her hand to me.

I shake it.

"Nice to see you again. Although I do wish it was under better circumstances." The alderman is dressed in another pantsuit, this time a coral color, with black heels. Her strawberry-blonde hair is pulled back in a twist.

For the middle of the night, she, too, seems well put together.

If we're being completely honest, I'm glad for the distraction. Coming down here, that is. Anything other than focusing on the grief bubbling over at Bow & Arrow.

"And you must be Jace King," Nadine adds, shaking his hand, too. "Pleasure."

He grunts. "Where is she?"

"Artemis Madden? She's just inside. My brother had a few questions for you—"

"We won't be answering any questions," I say quietly. I pull her aside. "Actually, I called your brother because our friend was caught in the crossfire of a Titan shoot-out."

She winces. "I'm so sorry to hear that. Is he...?"

"She died on scene." My voice is surprisingly steady. "But we took her out of there... we couldn't leave her."

"Of course." Nadine pats my hand. "These are strange times—I don't blame you. And I'm so sorry for your loss. Where is she now?"

"Bow & Arrow—the club in North Falls."

She sighs. "I know it. I'll send EMTs in an ambulance to retrieve her. She'll be taken care of from there. I suspect you already know what I'm going to say? That the morgue is full—"

"We don't need her examined. Just to get her death on record so we can give her the funeral she deserves."

Nadine nods. "I'll see what I can do— Ah, Alex."

Alex Sterling stops in front of us. He looks a little less put together than Nadine. Maybe they all keep odd hours, but I sincerely doubt that. He gives me a tight smile, then focuses on his colleague.

"It's all hands on deck," he tells her. "The mayor is requesting intervention on this gang war... *finally*. We're to vote."

"What are your options?" I ask.

He frowns. "Well, we can militarize our police. Or call in the National Guard. Or..."

"Kora," Jace calls.

Alex Sterling glances over his shoulder at Jace, then does a double take. He turns fully, facing the younger man.

They have a stare off. It's a little strange, but then they both seem to snap out of it. Alex turns back to me. "I'm sorry, it's a complicated process. Many different factors go into our options. Please excuse us." He takes Nadine's arm and guides her away from me.

Jace stops beside me as they head toward the elevator. We watch them in silence until they've disappeared inside it.

"That was weird," I whisper to him.

He shrugs. "I don't know why. I've never met him before. I just didn't like how he smiled at you."

Huh. "That was Alex Sterling."

He jerks. "That fucker is a Sterling?"

"Yeah...? What am I missing?"

He sighs and tips his head. Daniel has gone into the offices for the police, so it's just the two of us. And even though it's nearing two o'clock in the morning, and my eyes are burning from crying and exhaustion, curiosity buzzes through me.

"The Sterlings founded the town."

I nod slowly. "I think I knew that."

From a dinner with the sheriff—one that Alex crashed, I believe.

"Did you know that the whole family was wiped out?" He watches my reaction.

Which is... I don't know. My mouth opens and closes, and I shake my head. "I need more detail."

"A hundred years ago, a single family moved into Sterling Falls and claimed it as theirs. They established a government, businesses. It was a fishing town, but there was the reservoir, the beaches... the original Sterlings realized that, with a little cleaning up, it could be a tourist town. Attractive to those looking for beach vacations, whatever." Jace points to a bench, and we both sit.

"The Sterlings procreated, as families do." He sighs. "The government seat, which slowly transformed into an alderman position, was passed down to the eldest son of the eldest son, on and on. There wasn't a problem—not outwardly at least—until fifteen, twenty years ago."

"What happened then?"

"The family was slaughtered. Not just the eldest son— his wife, his daughter. His brother and his wife, his sister. There were only a few left alive, but they had no claim to the inheritance. Or the city."

I can't imagine that. "It was just one person who killed them all?"

"I don't know. It didn't happen all at once, mind you. These murders happened over the course of a year, maybe more. People are fuzzy about the details. They don't like to talk about how something so horrific was allowed to happen over and over."

"That's terrible."

"Alex Sterling was protected at the time. He spent a lot of his time in Emerald Cove as a kid, actually, and the town speculated that it would remain that way. What with the trauma. But to everyone's surprise, he came back and ran for alderman. The rest..."

"Wow." I fiddle with my fingernails, picking at the dirt caught in the beds. "That's intense."

"Yeah. It wouldn't be the first time this city has drenched itself in blood." He nudges me. "This war, the previous one, it's just a cycle that we can't seem to break."

I take his hand and squeeze. I have to believe we're doing this with purpose. That there will be a good outcome at the end, regardless of the sacrifices we have to make. The sacrifices we make over and *over* again.

"Kora?" A soot-covered Artemis runs down the hall. Her clothing is scorched in some places, and her dark hair is a mess of waves. She looks otherwise intact. Behind her, Daniel moves down the hall at a slower pace.

I rise and barely get my arms up in time to receive her.

She throws her arms around my neck and trembles against me. Her lips are at my ear, and she breathes, "He took them."

"What? Who?"

"Parker," she says, her voice wavering. "He held a gun to my head and made Apollo tie himself up. Then Wolfe came—"

Oh god. I untangle myself from her embrace and grip her shoulders. "Where did he take them?"

Jace steps forward. "Who?"

"Parker took Apollo and Wolfe." Ice flashes through me. I back away from them, covering my mouth. First Nyx, now *this*? I don't know how much more I can take.

"Where?" Jace snaps.

When Artemis doesn't answer fast enough, Jace shakes her. Her eyes are wide, and her head bobs back and forth. Tears flood her eyes.

"Jace—let *go*." I shove him off her.

"Guys," Daniel warns.

I shake my head and take Tem's hand. She follows me out the door, to the car. Jace and Daniel follow behind, although Jace feels like he's got the gale of a hurricane inside him. He's pissed—of course he is. I am, too. Furious that we forgot about Parker, that we dismissed him as a threat.

In the car, I say, "He wants me."

"He's not getting you." He slams his hands against the steering wheel. "I'm going to fucking kill him."

"He..." Artemis clears her throat. "He gave me a number for you to call."

She hands me an envelope. I tear it open as Jace pulls out of the school parking lot. We left Saint with Nyx, but I suspect the ambulance and EMTs will be there soon. And I don't know if Daniel told Artemis... which means we have to break the news to her about that, too.

I just want to sleep. For a year.

Instead, I look at the familiar number scrawled on the piece of paper. The familiar handwriting. It snaps me back to when we first met. He was charming back then. He liked to flirt, I knew that from watching him around other girls, but he turned up the charm times ten when he was around me.

When he wanted something, he got it. He wrote down his number and slipped it into my hand. But I didn't call him, although I sure stared at that number enough. I typed it into my phone too many times, tempted to text him, or call, but I never did.

And then, somehow he got my number. He called one day and asked me out, and... that was it. I was history.

I still have Jace's phone. Part of me thinks he doesn't even want it back, since the thing only seems to deliver bad news.

When I dial, I hold my breath. It's just like him to play these sick, twisted games. To make me call my abusive ex-boyfriend. And I have to remember that everything is win-or-lose to him.

"Parker Warton," he answers, like he doesn't know it's me. Like he wasn't expecting a middle-of-the-night phone call.

"It's me." My voice sounds alien, even to myself. Higher pitched.

He pauses. So long that I think he might've hung up. Or maybe he's just waiting to see how long *I* can wait. I dig my nails into my palm hard. An old coping mechanism—one that I had forgotten about until now.

The seconds tick by, and I pull the phone away from my ear to check that we're still connected. The time reaches a minute, then a minute and a half.

Finally, he chuckles. "Kora," he says, like he didn't just keep me waiting. "I'm so glad to hear your voice."

"Get to the point, Parker."

He huffs. "Some things never change, do they? Nevertheless, I think I know why you're calling."

"Because you have something of mine."

"Two somethings," he says. "Yes. I do."

I count to five in my head. My palms are sweating, and I don't know how much more of this I can take. I don't know how anyone could take this. A headache is forming between my eyes, pulsing every time I move.

"Put me on speaker so that boyfriend of yours can listen in."

I do, then mumble that it's done.

"Here's the deal, Jace King," he starts. "I want what you have, and I'm betting you want what I have."

Jace grimaces, meeting my eyes in the rearview mirror. He doesn't say anything, though.

"Tomorrow night. Ten o'clock."

"Where?" Jace asks, tone brisk.

"Olympus."

I shiver. The line goes dead, and I toss it to Daniel. He immediately removes the SIM card and snaps it in half, then tosses it out the window. He drops the now useless phone in the cup holder.

"This is because of that contract you signed," I say. I close my eyes and pinch the bridge of my nose. "This is because whatever deal you struck with Cerberus is still active—and he wants to own me. He'd do anything to get me."

Jace hums his agreement, but then the car slows. He's pulling over, and he gets out of the car in a flash. My door opens, and Jace pulls my hand away from my face. He kisses my forehead, the bridge of my nose. The corner of my lip. "I swear on my life, princess. He won't ever touch you again."

God, how I wish that could be true.

CHAPTER 42
KORA

I wake up to Jace parting my legs and pulling down my underwear. The blankets we found in the basement are tangled under me. He looks up when I run my hands through his hair, and then his mouth descends on me.

I arch as his tongue swipes against my clit. My fingers twist in his hair, directing his attention. He grips my thighs and spreads me farther.

Too many times, I'd been woken by Parker fucking me, pushing my head into the pillow. Using me for his own pleasure. And I thought I'd be traumatized by that forever. I even told Wolfe as much, made him promise not to do anything like that to me.

But this is different. This is for *me*.

He slides two fingers inside me, and I let out a whimper. He nips my inner thigh, then goes back to sucking and licking me. His teeth graze my clit, then he sucks it into his mouth and lavishes it with his tongue.

My orgasm climbs up through me, a blast of hot need. My thighs tense, and I clench around his fingers.

He climbs up my body and thrusts into me without hesitation. I'm wet, but he still stretches me in the most delicious way. His forearms frame my head on either side, and he ducks down to kiss my throat.

"You know I wanted to beat the shit out of Wolfe and Apollo for marking you? When I could do nothing," he says between bites and kisses. "Now I get to do this... *and this*." He goes lower, still thrusting into me in a steady, slow rhythm, while he kisses down to my collarbone, then back up.

He finds the sensitive spot just under my ear, and I gasp.

"I'm sorry for what's going to happen," he whispers. "And I'm so fucking sorry for what's already happened."

My heart pangs. For a second there, I had forgotten about... everything. This whole clusterfuck of a week.

I wrap my arms around his neck. My legs lock around his hips. "We need to make it right, Jace," I whisper. "We need revenge, sure, but... justice. Salvation."

He groans and presses his forehead to mine. His pace quickens, along with his breathing. "You're my fucking salvation," he groans. He stills inside me, coming hard.

We lie like that for a minute, recapturing our breath. His arms snake under me, hugging me tightly to him.

I hug him back.

"I'm afraid," I admit. "Of what we're going to see when we arrive at Olympus... What happened to Apollo and Wolfe. Will Cerberus have punished them for leaving?"

"It'll be okay," he says. "They're strong."

I want to believe him. I do. But there's just that little part of me that reminds me that Parker is a monster—and of all the monsters I've known, he's been the worst.

Because he just hasn't quit trying to chain me to him.

I don't know why this obsession with me has got him in a stranglehold.

"I'm afraid that the only way to stop him is to kill him."

He hugs me tighter. "Princess, if you don't know by now that we'd kill for you... I don't know what to tell you."

I swallow sharply.

Someone knocks on the door. "I need to get Kora ready," Tem yells. "So get decent."

He helps me up off the cushions on the floor. The makeshift bed wasn't terrible, although my muscles are stiff, and I could probably sleep another few hours. I wipe under my eyes and pull my clothes back on, ignoring the splotches of blood from the Titan I stabbed, and the smear where I tried to get Nyx's blood off my hands. I don't even remember touching her, but somehow it got on me... and then everywhere.

I sober at that thought. Fast.

The EMTs were waiting outside in the ambulance when we arrived back at the club last night. We broke the news to Artemis when we got there, and she broke down. She sagged against Saint on the floor as they took Nyx away.

I couldn't handle her grief. Or any of it. So I went to bed after that.

The sun was already high, and exhaustion tugged mercilessly at me. Jace found me a quiet place, one of those private lounges, and pulled the cushions off the bench seats. He made a little makeshift bed and found blankets, then left me alone. Until I woke up to him anyway.

Now, Tem leads me through a side door on the second floor. We go down a long hallway, and she unlocks another door.

It opens into a small apartment.

Saint is asleep on the couch, a blanket covering his lower half. His expression is pained, even unconscious. A combination of physical and mental anguish, I'm sure.

We tiptoe past him, down another narrow hall to the bedroom and bathroom. She gives me a towel and gestures for me to go into the bathroom.

I step through, then turn back around. "You all have a problem separating your personal life from work," I whisper. Antonio has the apartment above the restaurant, Jace, Wolfe, and Apollo have rooms at Olympus. And she has an apartment at her club.

She gives a half-shrug. "What can I say? I don't need more space than this."

I eye her, but she shuts the bathroom door between us. It saves me from asking how she feels, or if she's okay. It saves us from an uncomfortable conversation.

I sigh and set the towel down on the counter.

After a fast shower, in which I try not to think about anything important, I comb out my hair and wrap the towel around myself. My movements are methodical. At this point, I've shut off my brain. I don't have the mental capacity to even fucking cry.

I stare at the fogged over mirror until I'm done.

I meet Tem in her room, and she gives me clothes to wear. A tight black shirt, white high-waisted pants, and a gold chain belt. Gold cuffs on both wrists—maybe that's symbolic, maybe not. Light makeup, nothing more than mascara and a little shimmer on my lids. She curls my red hair, pinning back tendrils that would normally swing forward and into my face.

When she finally rotates me to face the mirror, I start.

No red lips or dark eyeliner.

It's just me.

"I figured you wanted to be as recognizable as possible," she says. "You know. To send a message."

I nod, and butterflies erupt in my chest. "Right."

As opposed to the last time she and I snuck in, when I wore the blonde wig. I take a deep breath and leave her bedroom. Saint is still asleep on the couch, and Artemis gently pulls the blanket up over him before following me out of the apartment.

We find Jace and Daniel in the main room of the club. Jace is dressed in his usual outfit: dark-wash jeans and a form-fitting black t-shirt. He pauses when he sees me, looking me up and down, and visibly swallows.

My cheeks heat.

"You clean up," Daniel offers in my direction.

Tem sighs. "Shut up, Dan."

Jace focuses on Tem. "You're staying here?"

"I figured Saint shouldn't be alone, so... yeah. I've got to make a phone call anyway." She steps up and kisses Jace on the cheek. "Bring back my brother in one piece."

"We will."

Daniel doesn't come with us. In his words: "I'm not really a fight club sort of guy..."

Fair enough.

Jace and I ride down the main road of North Falls, which once seemed to have a bustling nightlife—thanks, in part, I'm sure, to Bow & Arrow's success. Now, however, with the curfew, it's a ghost town.

The only sound is his bike, which roars under us.

We leave the tourist area behind. The road slants upward, and soon we're flying along the cliffs toward Olympus. I take a chance and let go of Jace's waist, throwing my arms wide. The wind whips at me, but I relish the chill in the air. It wakes me up.

I tip my head back and stare at the stars. It's easy to imagine Nyx is up there, looking down on us. The goddess of the night. In a way, I feel like she's flying along right beside us, urging Jace faster.

Is this what she would've wanted?

I hope it is—because this is all we have.

We pass the spot Wolfe went cliff jumping.

Nyx jumped, too.

When this is over, I'll grieve for her properly. We'll put her to rest—because it's the least she deserves.

We arrive at Olympus, and an ache fills me.

Too much has happened here. Too many memories cramming to be the first remembered, first relived.

It's funny how the bad things hold more sway than the good.

But the happy memories are right there, too. Everything that shaped my relationships with the guys. Wolfe as Ares, stealing me away from the violence that made me cringe. Sitting on his lap, his lips at my ear. Him pulling me upstairs and showing me how a man *should* treat a woman.

Staring down Jace in his Hades mask.

Running my finger through the gold paint on Apollo.

The *kiss* in the foyer, the red handprints left on my skin.

Jace parks, the engine fading to silence. We're probably the last to arrive. There are cars haphazardly parked all over the lawn. The crowd inside Olympus is loud, the energy turning my stomach.

I pull off the helmet and rest it on the handle of his bike, watching Jace do the same thing. He flips the seat up and removes a thin white box. He removes the lid and offers me the open box.

A flower mask.

This one covered in charcoal-black and red flowers, with gold dust on some of the petals. I smile up at him and hold it to my face, then turn around and let him tie the ribbons for me.

"Perfect," he whispers, turning me back around. "No one will mistake you... but just in case."

He presents something else: a flower circlet. Except the flowers have been gilded. He sets it down carefully on top of my head, and I raise a hand to gently touch it.

I swallow. "We're sending a message."

"You are," he says evenly. "Because if I don't succeed—"

"Jace—"

He presses his index finger to my lips, silencing me. "Listen. I'm confident, but let's be realistic. *If* he wins, you need to fight for your own freedom."

"You haven't seen them in there." I look away. "They're rabid dogs. Every one of them."

He cups my face, forcing me to meet his gaze. "Not everyone. Not Apollo. Not Wolfe. Not us."

I take a breath again and try to convince myself that we can pull this off.

He picks up his mask and puts it on. It's the original skull mask, with the black metal horns extending from the temples. It still freaks me out, but less so with his familiar blue eyes unchanging behind it. He doesn't automatically transform just because he put the mask on his face.

He's still the guy I know.

And I just need to remember that when he goes head-to-head with Parker.

CHAPTER 43
WOLFE

"Welcome to Olympus," Apollo calls. He strides down the stairs in a plain gold mask, the familiar gold paint streaked across his bare chest. The gold collar around his neck, though... that addition reminds me that this is anything but a normal Friday night. It reminds me that as much as he thought we were free—he's far from it.

My father sits in the throne that lords over the landing. The remnants of the statue he toppled are still on the stairs, pushed to the side but impossible to miss. Ordered to be left there.

A message that this is a new Olympus. A Hell-Hound-controlled Olympus.

We abide by a different set of rules.

I have a dark bruise under my eye from where Parker pistol-whipped me, and more bruises on my ribs from where he kicked the shit out of me. He eventually threw me in the trunk along with Apollo. The two of us stuffed into one trunk... not the most comfortable way to travel.

Imagine our surprise when he popped the trunk and

S. MASSERY

yanked us out, only to be practically kissing the boots of my father.

Yep. Somehow, Parker and my father struck a deal. I can only imagine the parameters. Kora in exchange for us?

Except for Jace, but my father seems to think they're going to deal with him tonight.

I scoffed at that when he first told me. And then he gripped the back of my neck and steered me down the hall. He opened the door and revealed Apollo, looking the worse for wear. That collar... the one he made Apollo wear at one of the fight nights, had a chain looped through it. He was chained to the fucking wall like a dog, with only a bucket and blanket.

My outrage wasn't allowed to explode, because my father just as quickly pulled me out and told me that if I said a single word, I'd be right there with him.

So, I kept my mouth shut.

Now, though, there's a large crowd. Bigger than I've ever seen it with my father in charge of Olympus. And the doors are still open, waiting for... something. I sit on the floor beside his chair, my legs hanging over the ledge that drops down to the landing.

I don't feel like myself. My father handed me a mask to wear. It's dark-gray fur with an elongated snout that extends beyond my nose.

A dog.

Apollo and I are both facing forms of punishment tonight.

"You know the rules," Apollo says to the restless crowd. "Step into the ring and tell us your heart's desire. Fight your challenger. If you win, your wish is granted. If you lose... the cliffs."

It hasn't been put so bluntly before, and I notice my father's noise of annoyance under the jeer of the crowd.

"This is a night of celebration." Cerberus speaks loudly, before Apollo has the chance to continue. "The Titans are gone. Their fearless leader slain. We rule this city."

They scream and cheer. They're Hell Hounds, they're supporters, they're East Falls residents who have lived under Cerberus for so long, they don't know any different. Or maybe they know what it really means—that the war will be over. With no one to attack, our streets will be safer.

"Let's get started." Cerberus slams his fist into the arm of the chair. "First fighter."

The atrium hushes. The crushed-glass-and-sand circle was drawn earlier today, and Apollo is barefoot. It took him most of the evening to pick out the glass last time. I can only imagine what this will do to him.

Especially since he doesn't even fucking know about Nyx. I didn't have the heart to break him—not when we were both bound for the Hell Hounds again. The image that is burned into my head isn't a nice one. It's of her body in the car, Saint hunched over her and trying to cover her torn throat with her fucking hair.

I close my eyes and force her out of my mind.

Kora, too, and the disgusting things Parker told us he was going to do to her when he finally got her back.

He deserves to die.

I sit up at the movement through the crowd.

Parker—easily recognizable, even with the mask—steps into the circle. It's funny how much people think those masks obscure their features. How they think they're anonymous with a piece of fabric wrapped around their head.

Maybe Parker doesn't give a shit about his identity. He

looks up at my father and me, his gaze lingering on my degrading mask. One corner of his lips curls up.

"First fighter," Cerberus calls. "What do you desire?"

"Kora Sinclair," he answers in a loud, sure voice.

I put my foot under me, intending on rebutting it, but my father's hand lands on my shoulder. He shoves me down, hard. Pain ricochets up my spine, and I press my lips together. I manage to keep the sound from escaping—but I'll be *damned* if he just strolls in here and tries to win her.

On the staircase, Apollo turns back to me. He seems equally angry, judging from the harsh lines around his mouth.

Murmuring at the back of the crowd, by the door, draws attention.

The crowd parts.

I even crane my neck, unsure that I truly believe what I'm seeing.

Kora.

Flowers on her mask, red and gray. A gold circlet nestled in her dark red hair. She looks every inch Persephone. Goddess of the underworld. But... light, too. The light that we all need in dark times like this. She walks down the cleared aisle without hesitation and stops just shy of the circle. Her hands stay at her sides, loose. Her gaze doesn't stray from my father.

My blood is fucking boiling that she's practically being strong-armed into being here.

"Kora Sinclair," Cerberus drawls. If he's surprised at her presence, he doesn't show it. "You're the object of this fighter's desire. Perhaps that's what drew you to Olympus?"

Of course she was going to come. After Parker gave Artemis that phone number for them to call, stringing us on the hook like bait to get what he wanted.

She lifts her chin. "I'm no object, Cerberus. I think you know that better than anyone."

"And you have elected a champion for yourself," he says. "I'd ask if you plan on fighting yourself, but we both know your situation."

A contract. Jace mentioned at the safe house in West Falls that Cerberus transferred it to his name, but we all thought it might be destroyed in the firefight.

But my father mentioning this, however vaguely, means it's still active. My gut churns.

"You know who will fight for me," she says quietly, unrattled.

Jace, in all his glory as Hades, strides down the still-cleared aisle. His mask is something to be feared—the skull with metal horns twisting out of it. A relic, at this rate. And sure enough, the space around him widens. There are people here who remember him. Who have seen him fight.

A thrill seems to shiver through the room.

He pauses beside Kora and touches her arm, then steps over the line and into the circle. He tips his head, staring down Parker, and a tendril of hope strikes a chord inside me. The first positive feeling since we found Nyx...

Hades pulls his mask off and tosses it to Kora.

Bare-faced for the first time in Olympus. Ever?

Murmurs break out again, like the crowd has been snapped from their reverence. Hades back in Olympus— surely it's a sign, isn't it? That he's come to reclaim his space in the way Apollo and I couldn't? That must be what they're thinking.

"Challenger," Cerberus says, a false bravado ringing through, "do you have a desire?"

"I do," Jace answers. He says no more before Apollo has

joined them in the ring. He says something low to Jace and Parker, then steps back.

There's no more preamble, no more time for questions.

Parker strikes first.

I lean forward, intent on learning his weaknesses. *Just in case.* He's controlled. Refined, even. Probably using the fighting moves they taught him at the police academy. He struggles to get a hit on Jace. My best friend moves like a viper, faster than I've ever seen him. He darts forward, landing a punch to Parker's throat.

The only time I bet that asshat will let his guard down.

Parker stumbles backward. I can't see his expression from this angle, but I bet he's mad. He doesn't seem like the type to keep his cool.

If the crowd is cheering, screaming, I can't hear it.

My gaze lifts over their heads to Kora, at the edge of the ring. Her thumbs are hooked in her pockets, and there's a bubble around her. No one wants to touch her, not when she arrived looking like Hades' wife straight out of the myth.

The spike of jealousy that shoots through me isn't unexpected. Unpleasant, sure.

Parker hits Jace in the mouth. Blood sprays out of the latter's mouth, and they dance around each other. Something changes in Parker, though. The animal who Kora must know finally breaks free from the carefully controlled mask. Awoken by blood, I think.

He flies at Jace, screeching, and lands two punches before Jace shakes him loose. They separate for only a moment before they're trading blows again. Parker hooks his foot around Jace's leg and yanks, and they both go down. They're rolling around on the floor, grunting and snarling. Their teeth are bared, bloodstained, and they offer no regard for the glass mixed with sand that they pick up on their skin.

Finally, Jace lands on top. He gets in a punch, then two, straight to Parker's face. He keeps hitting him, hitting him...

No one moves to stop him.

He's got a point to prove.

But Parker seems to have another trick up his sleeve. He pulls something from his pocket, and it only takes a split second for me to register the blade.

Without preamble, he stabs Jace in the side.

Jace roars, pitching sideways. Parker climbs to his feet, his grin bloody.

I glance at my father. "Dad—"

"Shut. Up."

On the floor, Kora is equally stricken. Malik has appeared out of nowhere, and he holds her back. Rightly so. Otherwise, any of us would end up in the ring and it would be up to my father to decide the outcome.

Jace lunges for Parker, dodging the knife in his hand. He keeps one hand on his side, staunching the bleeding. Doesn't help much—blood drips down his side, soaking the waistband of his pants.

"Finish it," I yell at Jace.

My father smacks the back of my head.

Kora screams at Jace, too. Malik has to drag her back another step.

Parker goes for Jace again, swinging the knife. He stabs at Jace with a manic expression, and Jace dodges. Barely. My best friend kicks out. His heel connects with Parker's wrist, and the blade goes skittering across the marble floor. It's stopped by the ring of sand.

Jace charges at Parker and gets him around the middle. Kora's ex beats at Jace's back, but it doesn't stop

Jace from taking them both back to the floor. Their fight gets dirtier. It's a subtler shift, unlike when Parker's mask broke apart.

Blood slicks the marble.

They're getting nowhere, and I can't fucking watch anymore. I focus on the wall over their heads.

"Break it up," my father orders.

Fuck you, Dad.

The plan backfired. Whatever their plan was.

Apollo is motionless, too, on the second to last step. His back is tense, muscles clenched, but he, like me, doesn't react.

Eventually, Kora says something. Her lips move, but it's lost in the resounding percussion of the crowd. They press up close to the circle, their bloodlust awakened.

She says it again, and I think I catch the words she's mouthing. *Someone stop them.*

It's Malik that finally crosses the line and drags Jace off of Parker. Blood is seeping out of Parker's nose and mouth. His eyes are swollen almost all the way closed. Jace doesn't look much better, with a split lip and eyebrow, and the stab wound...

Now Apollo, Saint, and Jace all belong to some sort of posse.

Injured Torsos Anonymous.

I shake my head roughly and hop down onto the landing.

Apollo steps over the line and stops in front of Jace, who is still held up by Malik. He takes the mask from Kora and puts it back on Jace's face, letting him tie it. Then he raises Hades' hand in the air.

Silently declaring a winner.

He was on top, after all.

And Parker is pushing himself off the floor on his hands and knees—but he doesn't make it very far.

Kora has the knife in her hand. She doesn't hesitate to stride across the circle and slam her knee into Parker's spine. He flattens to the floor.

I silently cheer for her and trot down the steps, stopping just shy of the sand.

She grips his head by his hair and yanks it up, so his throat is exposed, and holds the blade there.

The crowd goes quiet.

Cerberus rises. "Murder, Kora?"

"Do you know what he's done to me?" She slams his face down, and he groans.

His hands slip on the wet marble, trying to gain purchase and utterly failing. I'd be proud if I wasn't worried.

I can't let her do this.

She's not a murderer.

This is grief and anger and a culmination of the last seven, eight months of her life now pressing down on her. I step over the sand line and crouch beside her. It's like there's not a full room of people staring at us, waiting to find out what Kora will do.

It's just us and the ragged breathing of the man who abused her.

"Kora," I whisper, touching her wrist.

She flinches, and the knife in her grip cuts into Parker's throat. Just a shallow nick.

I slide my hand further down, until I'm holding the knife, too. The last time I was this close to him, I told him that if he came for Kora, he'd never walk out of this city.

I take my promises seriously.

"Let me do it," I whisper to her.

Her skin is hot to the touch. The mask suits her. Lends

her that vulnerability that I fell in love with almost as soon as I saw her.

She releases his hair. Her hand loosens from the knife, slipping out from under mine. Leaving me holding the small hunting knife Parker snuck into Olympus.

Apollo puts her back on her feet, and I use my foot to roll Parker onto his back. His eyes roll, wild and bloodshot. I lean over him and smile.

"You remember the promise I made to you?"

He squirms, trying to crawl backwards away from me.

"You're not walking out of Sterling Falls," I say. I glance back at Jace. Kora. Apollo.

I don't want to kid myself that I'm doing this just for them, or for her. I'm doing this for me, too. Because I don't have any other fucking outlet.

I smash my foot down on his knee. The joint pops, and he screams. The sound echoes in this chamber, even with all the people around. Kora gasps, her hand at her mouth, but she doesn't seem upset beyond that.

It makes me wonder if Parker ever hurt her like that. Stepped on her until her bones threatened to crack beneath his weight.

Disgusting piece of scum.

Without a word, I grab his arm and begin my march to the edge of the cliffs. Malik takes his other arm, and together we drag him toward the door.

Behind us, my father asks Jace, "What do you want?"

There's a pause. Then, "Wolfe and Apollo, free from your service."

My abdomen tightens. I hesitate, my steps slowing. Malik eyes me, but I keep my expression behind the dog mask cold as ice. I glance over my shoulder.

My father sits back on his chair. He tilts his head, no

doubt thinking about how to get out of it. There's no way he'd give up both of us without protest.

True to form, he seems to reach a solution. "One will have to do."

I close my eyes, wondering how the fuck Jace is going to pick between us. But... he can't pick me. I need him to save Apollo.

For me. For his sister. For Kora.

They're all suffering without Nyx, and I'm no good to them.

I try to convey that, even though the bastard doesn't so much as glance at me.

"Apollo," Jace says.

My heart skips, and dread flushes through me. I try to convince myself that this is what's best. That this is the same conclusion I had come to just moments ago.

Can't say it doesn't hurt, though.

Malik and I exchange a glance, and then we keep moving. Through the door and out into the cool night. Doesn't matter—my father's words drift out on the wind behind us.

"Done," he agrees. "Let's get on with our night."

CHAPTER 44
KORA

Cerberus eyes the crowd. We're all restless. The scent of blood is sharp in the room, distinctly copper. I can almost taste it. It's invaded my mouth, my lungs. Jace kneels outside the circle, his job complete.

Apollo is free.

And Wolfe... *isn't*.

But there's got to be something I can do—and I land on the decision mere moments after Wolfe and Malik return to the atrium without Parker.

I wish I had followed them out to see my ex topple over the cliff.

For a moment, I thought I was going to kill him—and in the same manner Nyx was killed, no less. I think the action, drawing the blade across his throat, would've scarred me far worse than actually killing him.

Wolfe, in a demeaning mask that his father no doubt chose, climbs the steps and sits just below the landing. Overlooking the crowd, but very distinctly apart. They all eye him in a new light. The crowd had to know he was vicious. It's built into his very DNA. But now they've witnessed his savagery with their own eyes, and they're afraid.

All the more reason for me to do what I must.

"Next fighters," Cerberus calls.

Now or never. I take a deep breath and step into the circle.

Jace and Apollo both call for me at the same time, and I imagine they reach for me, too. Grasping at thin air. I thought I might fight—but I didn't know until I found the motivation.

The crowd breaks out into murmurs.

Cerberus lasers in on me. "You do know, Ms. Sinclair, that some lines can't be uncrossed? And this is one of them."

I smile tightly. "I'm well aware of your rules."

He shakes his head. "I'm just trying to protect you, girl."

I figured that, too.

"Fine," he says after a moment. "A favor, I presume?"

"Yes." I don't elaborate—and I don't think I need to anyway.

Wolfe is watching me with a blank expression.

I raise my arms. "What, you don't think I should ask you for a favor?"

"I think you're going to ask for something I refuse to grant," Cerberus says. "If you think I'd willingly let my only heir go, after finally getting him back?"

He's going to inherit the Hell Hounds. I should've known that. Should've realized it. Like Ben or Jace would've taken over the Titans, it's something a father passes down to his son.

My stomach somersaults. "Fine," I grit out. Change of plans... "I'll ask for something other than him, if that suits you."

"It does," Cerberus says. He looks out around the room. "Well? Any challengers?"

A man moves through the crowd, nudging people out of the way. He steps in, and my lungs seize.

He's giant.

I mean... I should've expected someone like this. Someone who would take advantage of *me*, like they can easily win and expect a free favor from Cerberus.

Wolfe rises. He strides down the steps and circles the man closely. The fighter's shoulders bunch when Wolfe is directly behind him. If I didn't know better, I'd think Wolfe looks truly deranged in the dog mask.

And then he stops in front of me.

"Quick, sure movements," he whispers, his eyes pained. He goes right back to being the version of himself the crowd wants. A psycho. The one who broke Parker's leg, who dragged him out by his wrist. He circles me, too, trailing a finger across my shoulders, from one side to the other.

Wolfe leaves the circle. He returns to his stair below the landing.

No preamble. No one yells start.

I picture myself in the library basement with Ben, learning how to spar. I blink and I'm in the self-defense class, going over their basics. Then with Jace, grappling in their basement gym.

After a certain point, I've got to trust that I can do this. That I'm more determined than this man, that I'm more courageous, that I'm more insane.

He steps forward, but I'm already in motion. I let out a scream as I go at him, and the noise seems to get under his skin.

He might've been taught to never hit a woman.

Or maybe, like Parker, he prefers to do it behind closed doors.

Either way, the little hesitation gives me the first opportunity to strike, and I do. I hit him where it counts. Throat, groin. Two strikes, and I'm out, backing away as fast as I approached. He hunches, grunting, and I attack again.

He anticipates it this time, and he has a longer reach than I do. His open palm catches me across the mouth and sends me reeling.

I land on my hands and knees. The copper taste is more pronounced. My blood, now, the inside of my cheek cut by my teeth.

Apollo is right there, begging me to get up.

I spit blood and shove upward, then dodge to the side as the big man comes for me again. I spend a few precious minutes of energy simply avoiding him. He's getting tired, too, of trying to catch me. My lip and cheek are throbbing, but I push that aside.

In and out.

Quick. Sure. Movements.

I repeat that like a mantra.

And then he slips. Just the smallest wobble, his foot sliding in Jace's blood. I dart forward, taking advantage I get in another shot to his groin, ducking his punch, and anticipate him doubling over. I whip my knee up and crack him in the nose. Blood gushes out, and he wheezes.

The giant goes down to his knee, and I punch him as hard as I can in the nose again. Throat. Nose, one final time. It's my apology to Wolfe. To Nyx. I hit this fighter and I wish that the pain lancing up my arm will absolve me of the guilt, but it doesn't. So I punch him again, harder, while his gaze unfocuses. He's not seeing me anymore.

There's a *crack*, maybe it breaking, and his eyes roll back.

He falls with a mighty crash, landing on his side.

His head bounces off the marble.

I'm breathing heavily when I straighten, and I wipe the blood from my lip.

Silence?

No—I just can't seem to hear anything. My ears are ringing, the adrenaline making white spots flash across my vision. But after a few deep breaths, my ears tune back in to the deafening noise.

Cerberus strokes his goatee. Wolfe has tossed his mask, and he rushes into the circle. He lifts me and spins me around, then plants a kiss on my lips.

I lean into him, cupping the back of his head.

"Goddamn, that was beautiful," he says. "You okay?"

My feet come back to the floor, and he raises my hand in the air. How many times have I seen them do that to the winners? But this time it's *me*, and it's surreal.

It's pure luck, too.

I can't help but imagine how Nyx would react. She'd be proud, I think. But in a quiet way. We'd celebrate later, in private. A lump forms in my throat instantaneously.

"Your favor, girl." Cerberus draws the attention back to him. "Wolfe, come here."

Wolfe slowly releases me after one last hand squeeze. He climbs the staircase up to the landing, then the next level. He disappears from sight for a moment, then reemerges next to his father. He stands back, half hidden by the shadows.

Cerberus focuses on me.

"Anything except your son," I remind him. My heart is beating out of my chest. Somehow, I'm more nervous to ask the favor than I was to fight.

He nods, gesturing for me to continue.

"I want Olympus." My voice rings out across the atrium, strong and steady. Better than I could've hoped. There's no mistaking what I said.

Behind his father, Wolfe smiles. His teeth flash in the low light.

Cerberus goes blank for a second. "Olympus," he repeats.

"I want you and all your Hell Hounds to get the *fuck* out of Olympus," I reply. I point to the giant man on the floor. "You said anything except your son. I want this."

He sighs, rubbing his hand down his face. Finally, he stands. He comes around, down the stairs, and stops in front of me. He's just a little taller than me. He carries that dangerous vibe that's always made me wary of him. Like he's willing to do anything... as long as he can see a way for him to be victorious.

And that's what we're doing now, facing off against each other. Calculating our odds.

He exhales, smiling slightly. "You want this place? It's yours. It's only right, after all."

I tilt my head. "Why's that?"

He shakes his head, and I sense he's about to take immense joy from what he's about to tell me. My brows furrow, because I can't imagine *what* he has to say.

"Jace hasn't told you? You're the missing Sterling."

White noise buzzes in my ears. I'm... confused.

"You're wrong," I say. "Jace... Jace said they were wiped out."

He steps closer, and his gaze goes behind me. "You think Jace, your *husband*, would tell you that you're the heir to this whole damn place? When he can control it through you? No, I don't think so. But I'll be nice and give you this one last thing, free of charge." He pauses and leans in even closer.

His breath touches my cheek, but it still isn't enough for him. He pulls me toward him, until his lips are at my ear. "Who is Korinne Sterling?"

He releases me.

The name is like an echo of a dream I had long forgotten.

I look down at the black stone that hangs at the end of the necklace.

The one... I don't remember my parents giving to me. I thought they had, because it's always been with me. But what if I've had it longer than that? I lift it out from under the collar of my shirt and flip it over, reading the inscription upside down.

To KS, with love.

From my parents? My... birth parents. The Sterlings. The ones who were murdered because of their name.

Cerberus is making his way toward the door. The crowd is dispersing. I glance from Wolfe, still upstairs, to Apollo and Jace. Jace is on the floor. Apollo has a bloody ball of fabric pressed to Jace's side. There's a lot of blood, but he's risen up on his forearms. His gaze is trained on me. His expression curiously blank.

Like he knows that I know.

But I don't know everything, because—

"Jace is my *husband*?"

TO BE CONTINUED

Thank you for reading!!! So sorry about the little cliff I left you on... *Queen*, the conclusion to the Sterling Falls series, will be coming soon.
http://mybook.to/queensf

ACKNOWLEDGMENTS

Thank you so much for reading! I hope you had some tissues handy (if you're a crier). Don't worry—I'll make it up to you in Queen. Pinky promise.

A big shout out/thank you to my team. Early readers with invaluable advice, and listening to me work through the plot — Rebecca, Erica R., and Ari, and author extraordinaire Jolie Vines. I appreciate you all so, so much!

To my editors, Emmy Ellis at Studio ENP and Paige Sayer Proofreading, and my wonderful cover designing team, Qamber Designs - thank you for helping me make the best book possible.

Thank you, thank you, thank you!

ALSO BY S. MASSERY

ABOUT THE AUTHOR

S. Massery is a dark romance author who loves injecting a good dose of suspense into her stories. She lives in Western Massachusetts with her dog, Alice.

Before adventuring into the world of writing, she went to college in Boston and held a wide variety of jobs—including working on a dude ranch in Wyoming (a personal high-light). She has a love affair with coffee and chocolate. When S. Massery isn't writing, she can be found devouring books, playing outside with her dog, or trying to make people smile.

Join her newsletter to stay up to date on new releases: http://smassery.com/newsletter

Made in United States
Troutdale, OR
01/10/2024

16870399R00235